SINS OF THE PAST

THE FORGIVENESS TRILOGY

C.A. MCKENNA

RAVEN TALE
PUBLISHING

Copyright © 2023 by C.A. McKenna

Published by Raven Tale Publishing

All rights reserved.

This book may not be duplicated in any way without the express written consent of the publisher, except in the form of brief excerpts or quotations for the purposes of review.

The information contained herein is for the personal use of the reader and may not be incorporated in any commercial programs or other books, databases, or any kind of software without written consent of the publisher or author. Making copies of this book or any portion of it, for any purpose is a violation of United States copyright laws.

This is a work of fiction. Names, characters, places, and incidents either are the product of the author's imagination or are used fictitiously. Any resemblance to actual persons, living or dead, events, or locales is entirely coincidental.

ISBN: 9798870187037

❀ Created with Vellum

For my Mum, Yvonne.
Thank you for always believing in me.

1

"You're going to break your bloody neck you know!"

"Is this really necessary? Can't you test your theory in a safer environment?"

Kaleb stood at the edge of the world. Before him stretched the College grounds, their many buildings sprawled in what seemed a random pattern. The College was one of the oldest institutions in Astril City, with the oldest buildings' architecture reminiscent of old Thalia, one of the many ancient cities that the sprawling metropolis was built upon. This meant grand, multi-story buildings of white marble and lots of tall columns. Being an institution as old as it was, the other buildings served as testament to the changing styles over the last few hundred years, creating a very eclectic collection overall.

Directly below was the parkland that the College owned, and it was among the most extensive spans of outdoor space to be found in the city. There were, of course, public parks, and some of them were huge, but the College retained a truly staggering example of green space. It was popular among the students and staff of the College, providing spaces for research, relaxation, outdoor study, and the like. With magi-lift rail connections, the expansive space could remain easily accessible between lessons for students that needed it.

Standing above it all, though, the wind in his chestnut hair and billowing through his loose-fitting T-shirt, which hung around his slender frame, Kaleb fought down a shiver as the air currents brushed against the caramel-coloured skin of his bare arms and just took it all in, feeling the eddies swell around him. Though he had experience in all schools of magic, wind magic was what he was drawn to. It just . . . made sense to him.

And even here, on this hilltop, standing at the edge of the small bluff, it felt as though he had the entire world spread before him. It didn't matter that the drop was only about fifteen meters. It was high enough. It was the general elevation of this location, and the strong winds present today, that made it the perfect spot and time to put his theory to the test.

His best friends, however, disagreed.

Melissa and Kaleb had been friends since they were very young. It was Melissa and her family that had been there for him when he'd lost his parents and older brother, and he'd spent nearly every holiday at theirs ever since, even after moving into the College dorms. Kaleb would do anything for Melissa. Anything, except listen to reason when he had one of his wild ideas. There was a mixture of disapproval and fear swimming across her green eyes, as her dyed purple hair blew about her face.

Her girlfriend, Belinda, he had known for less time, but he had to admit, Melissa had good taste in people. She was dark-skinned, with dark hair, but her eyes were the most electric blue. She also stood a several inches taller than Kaleb, and the expression she wore was thunderous. Belinda had a *strong* protective streak about her and was fiercely protective of her girlfriend, and that extended to the man who had grown up as basically her brother.

Neither of them saw the sense in what he was going to try.

"Look, ladies—"

"Don't you 'look ladies' us!" Belinda's voice cracked with anger.

"Sorry! You know I don't mean it like that, but seriously, this is safe!" Kaleb assured them and summoned wind around his feet, lifting him slightly off the ground to demonstrate his point. "I have long mastered light levitation, and though different, the theory is sound. If I shape the wind correctly around me, and force the air pressure below me, it will create a lower air pressure above, and force the air to accelerate down behind me. On a windy day like today, I can just glide, I don't even need to worry about acceleration outside of the effects of gravity."

Through his micro-lecture, they'd stared at him stony faced, but then Melissa relented. "Okay, fine. So, say you're a genius . . ."

"Thank you."

"Shut up, just, *for instance*, say you're right, why hasn't anyone else attempted this before? Why aren't we all flying around without the aid of airships, jets, and air cars? *Surely* someone would have tried this by now?"

"Well, others have tried . . ." Kaleb admitted.

"And?" Melissa pushed.

"Well, no one has ever been successful . . ."

"*See!*" Melissa exclaimed.

"BUT! But!" Kaleb moved his arms in a calming gesture. "The last person to try did so over three hundred years ago, and our understanding of flight and aerodynamics was vastly different! With the added knowledge I have now—"

"But nothing. If this theory is so sound, let me try it too," Melissa said, stepping forward.

Belinda lightly touched her shoulder. "I don't think that's a good idea either, Hun."

Melissa shrugged Belinda's hand off, half turning back to

her. "No, Hun, if he's so confident . . ." She looked back at Kaleb, pointing a finger at him. ". . . if this is *so safe*, then it should be safe for me to attempt it too!" Anger was clearly building up in her as she stalked towards Kaleb.

"Um . . . well . . . Mel, the thing is . . ." Kaleb stammered, struggling to find the words.

"No, don't you 'Um, well, Mel' me! If it's not safe enough for me to do it, it's damn well not safe enough for you!"

Kaleb let the air dissipate from around him, his feet returning to the ground. He *was* confident that it was safe enough for him to do it. He had studied aerodynamic principles extensively; he was, quite frankly, prodigious with wind magic, and he had run tests on inanimate objects.

What he wasn't confident in was Mel's ability to pick it up on the spot without breaking her neck in the attempt. He couldn't let her do that to herself.

He suddenly had a strong sinking feeling in his stomach, flashing on an image of Mel, broken and twisted at the base of the bluff because of his own arrogance. Understanding hit him like a brick to the face. This was how they were feeling about him right now. They were both visualizing his body, in that same broken and twisted manner. Was he being selfish? He didn't think so, but he couldn't put his friends through that stress. There would be other windy days. He could test this out another time, perhaps factor in safety measures, like crash mats. Where would he get crash mats? That wasn't important right now.

"Okay . . . fine." He sighed, slowly walking back towards them. He could see a tension lift from them both, though Mel's eyes were still fire. "I'm being stupid, I clearly haven't fully thought this through. Let's head back to the student halls." He held a hand towards Mel.

Doubt crept across Mel's face as she narrowed her eyes. She was clearly thinking he was up to something, or that she had won too easily. It wouldn't be the first time that he'd snuck off after agreeing he wouldn't do something.

"No, look, I'm serious, and I'm sorry. I'll park this idea." He looked her straight in the eyes, gesturing sincerely with his outstretched hand. "If I'm not willing to let you try, it's clearly too dangerous."

She took a couple of deep breaths, and as Belinda stepped up to her other side to take her hand, the anger seemed to wash away with relief. She took Kaleb's hand, and they headed back towards the main campus.

As they started back down the hill, Melissa smiled. "Yes, you are stupid. But you're our stupid."

"THOUGH RECORDS from the time are few, with most believed to have been destroyed in the cataclysm that brought the desert into existence, it is believed that Mages at the time were experimenting with spells that would cause destruction at unprecedented scales. Scholars believe it was their research into these spells that may have triggered the cataclysm that destroyed the civilization known as Akonia. So, can anyone in the class tell me what attributes about the Akonian Desert make it unique?"

Professor Hayley Glennon stood at the front of the class. She was a tall, dark-skinned woman, standing about six feet and towering over many of her students. She was the professor for the study of artefacts and events of magically historical significance at the Mage's College, though what that really boiled down to most of the time was a history teacher. As expected, a fair number of students raised their hands to answer.

She gestured towards a blonde-haired boy named Lexi to answer.

"It's not naturally formed, unlike the arctic deserts of the North. There is no reason an arid desert should have formed where it did."

"Yes, though as I just mentioned the cataclysm and how it's believed to have formed the desert, I am looking for other examples. What else?"

It was, in fact, the only known desert of its kind. Some believed that there were other lands beyond the Great Ridge which might have similar deserts. The arid conditions of some of the southern isles indicated that any mainland areas that shared a similar latitude might form great areas of dry land. The idea that there was anything beyond the Great Ridge that surrounded their continent was one that sparked a lot of debate, but technology had yet to reach a point where they could even traverse it.

She gestured to another raised hand. This time it was Melissa, her purple hair tied back in a ponytail. "Magic doesn't exist in the desert, Professor."

"Yes, good, that's right. Does anyone know why?"

The hands that were in the air fell to their desks. She wasn't surprised. It was a heavily debated topic, as there was little anyone could do to prove theories. With magic not working in the region, even the machinations of the Engineers' Guild struggled to find out anything of worth. Mages largely refused to visit the region. It would kill any that were old beyond normal life spans, and made most others feel sick if there for any length of time.

"The most popular theory is that the cataclysmic event that happened thousands of years ago was strong enough to sever the connections of magic in the region. It is a fact that there are centers of magic, convergence points, where magic flows to, and from, like a beating heart. Our closest example of this is Heaven's Peak on the northern shore of Lake Dawn. So, this theory posits that the mountain at the centre of the Akonian Desert was such a convergence point. With all its connections cut, the land around it died, like a body starved of blood."

As she let that last hang in the air a moment, her students pondering the analogy, the bell rang to indicate the end of the lesson, and her students started to pack their things, in a hurry to get to lunch.

"Good work today, all. For next lesson, I would like you all to write a short piece on whether you agree with this theory about the Akonian Desert and why, and if not, what your own theories might be. Oh, and Kaleb, please stay behind a moment."

There was a light murmur among the students at that. It was no secret that Kaleb was her favourite student. Though teachers shouldn't show favouritism, Kaleb really was something special, and she saw a lot of herself in the kid: orphaned when fairly young, showing signs of being a genius in their field of magic, insatiably curious.

Kaleb waited until everyone had left, his friends leaving last, before approaching the front of the class.

"Yes, Professor?"

Kaleb didn't sound worried at being left behind. Instead, there was that curious edge to his voice that seemed excited for whatever it was she had planned for him. There was no way he could anticipate what she had in mind this time, though.

"Thank you, Kaleb. I appreciate you giving up some of your lunch to speak with me."

"Of course, Professor."

"Yes, so, anyway, the College has approved funding for an expedition, which I will be leading. As such, I will be gone for an extended period. We hope for this to land largely during the summer break, but there is also a good chance that I will be away during term time as well."

Kaleb's expression soured ever so slightly at the idea that Hayley wouldn't be around for some of their lessons. She knew that he loved her lessons, absorbing all the lessons from the past so he could build upon ideas and improve them with his own spin.

"The expedition will be to the Undercity. We believe we have located the site of the ancient Mages' Guild, and we want to be the first to catalogue what's there, securing any dangerous artefacts."

There it was, that spark in Kaleb's eyes, that hunger to know what was there, to find out what history had been hiding from them for so long. Given the chance, Kaleb would consume all knowledge on magic that he could. He had a long way to go, but for his age, he was already well ahead.

"So that leads me to my reason for asking you to stay behind today. You would have found out about the expedition eventually through the normal means, but by then, it would be too late. So let me cut to the chase. I want you to come with me, Kaleb, and serve as my assistant."

"What? Oh, my God!"

"No. Way. That's amazing!"

Kaleb's jaw was slack, even through the outbursts from the corridor. Rolling her eyes, Hayley called at her classroom door, "Melissa, Belinda, why was I foolish enough to think you'd give a professor privacy when speaking to another student?"

The pair sheepishly entered the room, but their meekness was overshadowed by their excitement for Kaleb, as they started to squeal with happiness, running over to hug the stunned boy.

"But . . . I . . ." Kaleb was struggling to organize his thoughts, but he eventually managed to form a sentence. "Students aren't allowed on expeditions, Professor. How?"

"Yes, it's policy that students can't join expeditions, but it's not unheard of. We have the dean's express permission, and we'll take every precaution. I think this will be an invaluable experience for you. Your passion for history, and your appetite for taking on old theories to try and prove them wrong, is refreshing, and needed if the College is going to remain relevant in future years. This expedition needs you."

Kaleb managed to untangle himself from his friends, and overwhelmed, took a seat at the front of the class, before looking up with a massive grin.

"Thank you, Professor. It'd be an honour to join you!"

2

Portable flood lights had been set up around the excavation site, creating pools of unnatural light in the otherwise pitch-black darkness of the Undercity. Although the lamps appeared Mundane, or Non-magical, the lack of wires connecting to any external power sources gave a hint to the lamps' true nature: imbued with the power of earth and wind, magic stones embedded in the devices would discharge at a rate far slower than any equivalent-sized batteries. That made these Arcane Tech, or A-Tech, devices perfect for such expeditions, and they allowed the Mages to focus their attention and magic on more critical tasks.

To Kaleb, though, they made up some of the everyday items of a Mage excavation team and didn't provide any of the marvel that such things had done when he was a young student. They might as well have been Mundane, non-magical, tools. No, what held his attention now lay just a few feet in front of him.

The Grand Library of the ancient Mages' Guild maintained a surreal level of grandeur despite the deep layer of dust and rubble covering the area. Thousands of shelves lined with a blend of stone and woodwork stretched into the shadows, intricately carved with the likenesses of great wizards from a lost age. Kaleb was in what they guessed was the study of the Master Librarian, a room that needed to be accessed via scaffolding due to the entire complex having collapsed onto its side long ago.

"Professor, I think I've found something!" he called up to the main room above him. As Professor Glennon's lead assistant on the excavation, he was tasked with cataloguing the contents of this room. The professor was overseeing a myriad of other tasks throughout the site and had several assistants doing much the same. With the sheer volume of information that potentially lay in these walls, it would take decades to go through, and they were largely concerned with getting it out without damaging the ancient works.

The Mages' Guild of Nasadia had served as the precursor to the Mage's College that they now all served, though the Mages' Guild of old had held far more power in the world of its time. Mages were often appointed as advisors to the monarch, influencing the kingdom, and many other members of the guild had collected the knowledge that surrounded the excavation team, which accounted for one of the largest single collections of knowledge in the ancient world. Unlike the numerous tomes scattered around him, though, the artefact in front of Kaleb looked neither old nor dust-covered, but instead shone with an ethereal light of its own. The light emitted from a set of glyphs covering an immaculate glass case, and inside . . .

"If this is another Encyclopaedia Arcana, Kaleb, I'm going to —" Professor Hayley Glennon cut herself short as she caught a glimpse of what Kaleb was looking at over his shoulder. "It can't be . . ." She moved Kaleb out of the way with a distracted shove, eyes fixed on the glass case and its contents, which Kaleb had uncovered. Covered in black-stained leather, etched with symbols that Kaleb did not recognise, was a journal. His mentor was enthralled, and she couldn't seem to decide what to look at first, the book or the case it was trapped in, covered in those glowing runes.

"The case alone is a marvel . . . for magic to have lasted as long as this, and still be active! They really must have wanted this thing kept safe . . ." The look on the professor's face told Kaleb that she was scouring her mental library for reference of what was before her. With her incredible memory, she could recall nearly anything that she had read in the past.

"But what is it, Professor?" asked Kaleb. He had been studying at the college since the age of five and had been acting as Professor Glennon's assistant for the last year. Though not uncommon to see her react in this way, she seemed different this time. Though most of what they dug up was interesting enough, this marked the first time they had found an active enchantment that had to be more than five hundred years old, at least.

"If I'm not mistaken, and I don't think I am, this is the Shadow Journal. At least, that's its common name among scholars. Its true name is Fom'yelet. It is rumoured that it contains the writings of an ancient follower of the cult of Mystral. I didn't in my wildest dreams think that it would be sitting under our feet this entire time. The writings on it that still exist speak of it being lost at sea long ago . . ." She traced her fingers over the glyphs on the case, and their glow intensified. Pulling her hand back, she smiled, though it looked as if the contact had stung.

"Are you all right, Professor?" Kaleb asked, worried, but Hayley's eyes shone with excitement.

"Sneaky devil . . . though brilliant . . . the glyphs, they drain the magic from whoever makes contact with the box. It's what has kept the magic alive for so long. It's probably been feeding off any poor creature that happens upon it over the ages. I suspect that if I had placed more than a finger on it, I'd be dead. As it is, I'm not going to be casting any magic for a while." She sounded so casual in this, as if losing the ability to use magic happened every day. "As such, I'll need you to see to the transport of the book and case . . ." A wave of dizziness suddenly came over the professor, and she abruptly sat on a pile of rubble. "Oh, my . . ." Despite her current condition, the wild grin never left her face.

Kaleb moved to help, but Hayley waved him off, and he looked between the case and his professor like a lost pup, adding to Hayley's amusement. "It's fine. It must have taken more from me than I realised," she said to try and ease his concern. He nodded warily and turned his attention to the case.

"How are we going to move it, if it's likely to kill anyone that touches it?" Nearly all the gear they had with them contained some kind of magical charge, or directly took their power from imbued stones. This gave them a lot of freedom with their mobility in such a hostile environment, but in this case, the glyphs would render anything they used useless on contact.

"Get me the Rune-Link. I get the feeling we're going to need to call in the bigger guns."

Dean Robert Turner sat at his desk, perusing a communication that had just come through on his terminal. It was from Professor Glennon, stating that the extraction was complete, and they were now enroute back to the college.

The extraction, of course, was of the fabled Fom'yelet and the case that protected it. An extraction whose cost had stretched the College's funding to its limit, marking it as one of the most expensive ventures they had undertaken in modern times.

The mere act of setting up an extraction route had been a

full-scale operation, resulting in the most complete network of roads that the Undercity had seen since its fall so long ago. Exhibitions thus far had mostly been conducted using magical transportation, or with the assistance of Kalek contractors. Not only were the bug-like race great at excavating, they could carry huge loads. As it turned out, though, both would prove useless in this endeavour, requiring the case to be transported using Mundane means, and that meant hiring engineers.

Carrying out their craft with an artistic flare, members of the Engineers' Guild made their work look like magic to outsiders. They incorporated a deep understanding of architecture, science, and computing, combined with their extensive knowledge of everything engineering. Though their work now branched a lot from their namesake, their roots were deeply embedded in the ancient guild, and so the name had stuck. Jealously guarding their secrets from outsiders, they remained in high demand, and as such, powerful.

This fact alone made them unbearable to be around, but the undertaking with the excavation had meant Robert was having daily meetings with the Guild's grand master, Timothy Jenner, as he had chosen to oversee this endeavour personally. It had taken a lot of sweet talking, and a fair amount of financial promise, to stop Timothy from getting the press in at the start of the operation. The engineers would claim most of the credit and all the limelight, but Robert's main concern right then entirely involved getting the artefact safely quarantined for study. Adding the press would complicate matters.

Robert reached for his cup of coffee at the same instant his door chimed. Groaning, he placed the cup back down and said, "Enter," successfully managing to keep the annoyance out of his voice. He wasn't expecting anyone, but it came as no surprise to see Timothy framed by the doorway as the metal barrier slid into the wall. "Tim, what a nice surprise. How's Ryan? Please, take a seat."

Timothy stomped across the office in his large black boots, and with a large grin, he stood looming over the dean's desk. At over six feet tall, loom he did, and he would use his intimidating height and build in this manner whenever he wanted something.

Timothy Jenner rarely took a seat.

"Robert! Ryan's fine, complains I work too much, yadda yadda, and he's right, of course! Bless him!"

It was a surprise that Tim's husband put up with just how much he worked, honestly, but Robert was glad that he'd found someone after the accident that took his wife and kid. Tragic, and it would have been more so had Ryan not dragged Tim out of the pit of despair he'd spiralled into. Robert made a mental note to invite the two of them out to dinner sometime. As overbearing as Tim could be with work and the Guild, it was important to take a break from it all, and they *were* friends, after all.

Tim now jabbed a finger at Robert, not in a threatening way, but in a 'The next words out of my mouth broker no argument' sort of way in which Tim was used to doing business.

"I want to be there when they bring it in." Cutting to the chase as usual. He was a man who didn't do pleasantries for long if it could be helped and always got straight to the point, ensuring that his motives shone clear as crystal. It meant that you always knew where you stood with Tim, something Robert admired. But the man was like a cliff against the wind; changing his mind was hard, and sometimes took a very long time.

"Look, Tim, the operation is going to be delicate as it is." The College had a reputation to uphold, and so did Robert. They had set their terms around the extraction and delivery of the artefact, and in those terms, press was expressly forbidden. But Tim always tried to keep someone from the press around when he was involved.

"Precisely why I should be there! Who better to oversee the work of engineers than I? There is literally no one else more qualified, and as you say, it's a very delicate operation. We have a reputation to uphold as well!"

Stop reading my mind, Robert thought. Timothy knew he was right, which didn't make the insufferable grin he wore make Robert want to punch him any less.

Closing his eyes and taking a deep breath, the dean stood. Though not holding the same imposing stature as Timothy Jenner, he held a presence that only the master of the highest school for magic could achieve. "Fine, but no press, Tim. I mean it. This can't go wrong."

Looking hurt, Tim spread his hands. "No press, I promise. Just a few cameras, like during the excavation."

Robert knew Tim was testing the waters to see how far he could push it. The cameras would technically not be press, but they were still against the terms that had been set out.

"No. We can't have some amateur hack with a camera vying to get a close-up when we're moving something that could potentially kill everyone in the room!" Friend or no, Robert felt his pulse rising at Tim's stubbornness. Why couldn't the man understand how important a discovery this was? Why couldn't he be content with the extortionate fee the Guild had slapped the College with and keep his nose out? "You have to understand how dangerous this is, right? You've already lost a man to the artefact during its transit. Would you willingly put that risk on others?"

At this, Tim did take a seat. Robert stared down at the engineer. He may be a pain in the dean's side, but Tim cared deeply about those that worked for him, and Robert knew he'd been cruel to push *that* button.

"That . . . that was unfortunate. We took every precaution, but reports say he just . . ."

Robert had read those reports. The young engineer had acted as though possessed, according to those nearby during the incident. His screams reportedly echoed through the entire Undercity, as he was reduced to a skeletal husk. Robert barely supressed a shudder.

"I'm sorry, Tim, that was unkind. One camera. *One*. With one operator, that's it. Deal?" Robert extended his hand to the grand master. Standing to accept it, Tim grasped his hand tightly and shook, a single tear escaping down the engineer's cheek.

"Deal."

Two months this had been in the works, and Hayley stood at the rear of the main loading bay of the Calvador Williams Building. It was one of the oldest buildings on site, named for one of the founding deans of the College and used mainly for research and experimentation, perfect for the package they were receiving. She watched as the trucks backed up slowly with their Mundane engines and their reliance on large rubber wheels. Most A-Tech transports hovered, smooth and very quick. But magic had been intentionally kept out of this situation, to the point that all vehicles and mechanisms that rely on magic had been removed from the area. That had taken the better part of a week, and highlighted the fact that maybe the College relied a little too heavily on magic.

Hayley had permitted Kaleb to be present. Considering that he'd discovered the artefact, it only seemed fair. As a student, he wouldn't get full credit, as that would mostly go to her for leading the expedition, but she would make sure he got his due. All other students had been kept away from the area, and the only other Mage permitted in the loading bay was the dean himself. Shadowing the dean closely was the insufferable grand master of the Engineers, and she frowned to see a video camera operator trying to get the best angle on the action. The Engineers' Guild had made this all possible, but why they needed footage of every little moment eluded her. With a smirk, she noticed that even the smarmy Timothy Jenner was starting to get agitated.

She knew, as with everything the Engineers' Guild did, they would take the lion's share of the credit for the extraction, and the College would get a passing mention. Sure, the percentage of the profits the college would be due ensured that they could remain operating more easily over the coming years, but money failed to excite Hayley. Leave that for the accountants. It was the opportunities that the case and the tome it housed presented. The Fom'yelet could prove to fill a gap in their histories thought all but lost.

Few writings about the Dark Lords had survived the fall of the three nations. Nasadia had taken the hardest hit, which, considering they had kept the most extensive records, was a tragedy. So, to find this, the Fom'yelet, *the* Shadow Journal—it was career-defining.

There was a strange tug on Hayley's sense that she tried to convince herself was the drive of curiosity, that the draw to the power within the case was merely representing a desire to gain knowledge and to share the secrets locked within. She was having a hard time convincing herself of the lie, though, because anyone with a hint of magical talent had . . . felt . . . the draw of the Shadow Journal. Dull at first but growing increasingly . . . irresistible. As that one young lad had found out to his folly during the extraction. If he had chosen, he could have been a Mage with the talent he had, but alas, his choice eventually proved fatal.

The professor had strong suspicions that the lure of the tome, and the glyphs on the case, held a connection stronger than coincidence. The fact that Kaleb had not succumbed to the same urge was a miracle, but after that first incident, they'd endeavoured to keep all Mages working in the area at a safe distance while arranging transport. The fact that one engineer made it through their screening left a sour taste in everyone's mouth. She should make a point to find out the lad's name.

It also meant that strict time limits were to be put on place on the study of the artefact. No Mage was to be left alone with it, and study was to be conducted in thirty-minute blocks, with no Mage to return in the same day. It meant that study might be slow and cumbersome, but safety was paramount.

The loading ramp to the transport trailer was lowered, and all other thoughts left her mind, as it was the first time since the excavation began that she had seen the artefact with her own eyes. The temptation to meddle with it while in transit would have been the end of her, and so she and all other Mages on the expedition had returned as soon as the engineers had things in hand. As such, the Mages had busied themselves creating a safe room to enable them to study it, which would reduce the risk of accidents.

"That's it, lads, stick to the sides, let the camera get a nice view." Now that the artefact could be seen, Timothy started to strongarm the operation to best position everything to show how great the Engineers' Guild was. She couldn't blame him really, but he executed it all with such an air of smugness that grated on her nerves.

From then, the operation to move the artefact would be handled by a select group of engineers as it made its way to the specially designated room. There would be a rotating schedule of carefully selected Mages that were allowed to study the Fom'yelet, and first in line . . .

Dean Turner passed Hayley in pursuit of the Mundane trolley set up to move the artefact. "Come along, Professor Glennon. It's time to see if we can't crack this nut."

3

The specially constructed room for hosting the artefact could be found in the lowest of the sub-basements of the Calvador Williams Building. It had been set up with a standard elevator shaft to and from the surface, all completely void of magic in any way, itself a task that had taken up a lot of the time from the start of the extraction process.

Lining the walls of the room was unrefined Jin Ore. When electricity was run through the ore in this form, it had the unique property of producing a dampening field, which prevented the use of magic or items reliant on magic within the range of the field. The application of the ore to the walls gave the room a very smoothed-out, cave-like appearance, which did nothing to help with the feeling of being in a tomb when they were so far underground.

If it wasn't for the Astril government agreeing to fund the research on this project, their budget would never have stretched to line a room this size with Jin Ore. Having been extensively mined for both its magical dampening properties in its raw form and for being one of the strongest and most magically receptive materials once refined, making it invaluable in A-

Tech production, it was the most expensive resource in the Alliance. It didn't help that the cat-like Tren'Jin, for whom the ore was named, were the only beings able to work with the ore, for reasons that had eluded every Mage that had ever studied it. The fact that the government was willing to fund such an expense, though, was always worrying. Politicians never funded anything without ulterior motives.

The Fom'yelet and its case had been positioned on a pedestal in the centre of the room, lit by a set of spotlights in the ceiling. Enough space had been left between the walls and the case so that the case itself wasn't affected by the ore's dampening effect once powered. The range of the dampening field was well documented, so they knew they would be able to safely study the book at the pedestal without its or their magic being affected. There was an assumption that the ore would render the glyphs inert, which they wanted to avoid until they had been well studied and recorded.

Hayley and Robert made their way through the cavernous room to just in front of the pedestal. A table had been set up at the side with some instruments that could prove useful, including some notebooks and pens. When working with the unknown, Mages always preferred physical copies of their notes. Hayley turned to Robert, the government's possible interests on her mind. "So, why is the government willing to sink so much money into this project? Surely, it only has application as an important piece of history for them. I get the Engineers' Guild, a chance to show off to investors is always a win, but the government?"

"Because they believe there may be a spell that can be weaponized. Failing that, they want our research on the glyphs. Some crazy idea about enchanting projectiles and being super effective against the Carnah'lor." Robert waved his hand dismissively, eyes focused solely on the book beyond the glyphs.

"That's horrible! We're at peace with them. Why would—"

Robert cut her off. "Because we're not at 'peace.' We're merely in a ceasefire. We've been at war with them for as long as we've known they existed. Why? We don't even remember anymore! So, the only thing that matters is that we're better at fighting than they are when we eventually go back to war." Robert was very matter of fact in his response, cold, clinical, though Hayley knew him well enough to have sensed the spark of heat in the midst of it all. She knew he wasn't chiding her, and he was, of course, right, as much as they both might hate it. Robert had lived through the last war, young man though he was then. Hayley had been born during the ceasefire, and she was well aware that she had little concept of the horrors Robert had faced in his past.

STEPPING up next to the dean, Hayley placed a hand on his shoulder and gave a comforting squeeze. He reciprocated, placing his hand on hers and giving a light squeeze back, and some of the tension in him seemed to relax a little. It was not a gesture that they would casually show among the students or faculty, but here, with no one else around, well, Robert had been like a father to her, and they cared deeply for each other. If they could help it, they would guide the research into projects that would help the citizens of the Alliance, but the government Mages could take the most innocent research and turn it into a tool of destruction. So, if they didn't do the initial work, it would be done by those with nefarious purposes from the offset, and at least this way, some good might come of it first.

She looked down at the case enclosing the Fom'yelet and shivered with anticipation and concern at the same time. That tug wasn't all from the book. She hungered to know its secrets and had ever since the case had nearly killed her during the expedition. She moved over to the table of instruments to survey them. They had planned to start by introducing powered Jin Ore slowly, to leach at the power of the glyphs and study the reaction without bringing the ore into contact with them. There was also a camera on the table, and Hayley set about getting it turned on, so they could take some images of the glyphs as they were before they started work.

"Oops..."

Hayley's eyes widened with shock as a loud smashing of glass reverberated around the room, its source behind her. She turned to see that the dean had dropped a large chunk of powered Jin Ore onto the case, shattering the glass and destroying the glyphs that they had intended to study. In that same moment, she heard a sharp intake of breath from behind her but was too focused on what had just happened. "Robert! What have you done? That case was older than we know, and the glyphs! What about the government? *Why* would you do that? I just can't—" She broke off as she remembered that someone else in the room had gasped.

Turning, she saw her student standing near the elevator. "*Kaleb*!? What...?" But she just shook her head. She wanted to feel disappointment, or even anger, but she had to admit to a feeling of pride at the boy's curiosity, and could she really blame him? She would have absolutely done the same in his position. "Get in here. Don't touch *anything*, and stay quiet, okay? And don't think that you're not in trouble for this. We'll talk later!" He nodded and joined them as she turned back to the shattered cabinet. "Robert..."

He shrugged. "My hands 'slipped.' Guess I'm getting old, though worked a treat on dispelling the glyphs." He began reaching in towards the book.

"STOP! Robert!"

He jerked back, fear etching his face. "What? What is it?"

"This is the first time that book has been exposed to open air in centuries! You're going to just touch it with your bare hands? What effects do you think that will have on the pages?! We also have no idea if there is an enchantment on it, or what made it so dangerous that someone felt they needed to seal it in a case with glyphs that literally *kill* anything that touched it! Not to mention we have *no idea* what effect the Jin Ore may have had on the book! I . . . I'm at a loss for words!" Hayley scolded her boss, looking terrified and livid at the same time.

The dean breathed a sigh of relief.

"Loss for words, indeed! You had me worried for a minute." His eyes seemed unfocused when they looked at her, as if they were struggling not to tear themselves back to the book. "I've been at this since before you were born. I think I know what I'm doing, young lady."

"Well, yes, but . . . young lady?!" Hayley was struggling to fight against the shock of the situation. Robert hadn't called her young lady . . . ever!

"And as for the Jin Ore, there seems to be no reaction to its contact with the book, but just in case . . ." He reached into the case and took the electrified piece out, cutting the charge. As he did, the book's cover flung open, and the pages started turning rapidly until it lay open at a hollowed-out section. Within the hollow lay an amulet.

Robert's eyes were now glued to the book, a light seeming to ignite in them, complete focus on the prize that lay before them. "This . . . it's so old . . . it clearly predates the journal . . . and look here, writing etched into it . . ."

"Robert, that's enough, really. This has gone too far al—" The sound of metal sliding against metal cut Hayley's words short, though, and she turned again with wide eyes, Kaleb pale at her side. "The doors! Robert, there's something wrong here, we need to leave! NOW!"

"Yes, yes . . . leave then, but first . . ."

Before the dean finished, he had wrapped his fingers around the amulet. At first, nothing seemed to happen, but then his eyes rolled back in his head as he opened his mouth, chanting in what sounded like ancient Akonian, but different somehow. His body lifted into the air, smoke emitting from his hand where he held the amulet, the smell of burning flesh filling the room.

And then he screamed.

Hayley's blood ran cold as the sound pierced through her soul. Light spilled out from the centre of the amulet, as Robert's skin began to wrinkle, and his hair lost what colour it had. His screams grew louder, before becoming hoarse and then fading altogether. Another figure began to materialize as Robert's life ebbed away.

"ROBERT! NO!" Hayley had no idea what to do. The Jin Ore in the room prevented her from . . . *no, wait* . . . that's when she noticed it: she could still feel magic. In the second it took her to realise that the walls had been turned off, she turned to the steel door, channelling the streams of magic all around her into her hand. Raising her palm, she screamed, "*Nato!*" unleashing a torrent of fire which slammed into the barrier keeping them here.

"Pro- Professor?" Kaleb managed weakly, tears streaking down his face. There was another voice in the room now, a guttural roar of a beast seeking freedom. Hayley didn't have time to offer him comfort right now. She knew they needed to get out, and Kaleb didn't have the magical strength to pull this off, and they didn't have the time to form a circle, for what good it might do.

"We don't have ti . . ." She trailed off as suddenly her voice sounded far too loud. The screaming had stopped, and the only sounds came from the torrent of fire and Kaleb's sobbing. "Robert . . . are you—?" Glancing back, her eyes went wide. She nearly let her spell drop as she struggled to process what she was seeing.

Where Dean Robert Turner had stood now lay a pile of bones and ash. In front of the dean's remains, holding the amulet still spilling light from its centre, stood a vision previously confined to story books and legend. A figure that they had read about many times in their studies of the Guardians of the Realms.

She knew instantly who stood before them.

The Dark Lord, Mystral.

Master Engineer Timothy Jenner stared at the monitor in front of him. He had set up a surveillance feed of the artefact room, under the pretence of recording the experiments for later review. Only, he hadn't let anyone in the College know this. It was only the Guild that knew they were setting this up, and in actuality, it had been to ensure the plan went off as instructed.

They couldn't have anticipated that the extraction would take as long as two months and spending that much time near the artefact had taken a toll on his mind, body and soul. In the beginning, he'd wanted to ensure that such an important discovery was properly handled, and Tim had always had issues taking a step back from operations of this scale, so he had insisted that he had to be there during the extraction process.

The voice hadn't started talking to him straight away. No, it had waited until a couple of weeks in, until that tug on his senses had started to reach a fever pitch. *"You miss . . . them, don't you?"* At first, he thought he was just overworked, that he was putting himself under too much stress. *"You would do anything to*

bring them back . . . I can give them back to you, you know . . .
Timothy . . ."

As time went on, try as he might, it became impossible to ignore. Everything the voice said, he had longed for, the empty aching hole in his centre that not even his new love could fill. He wanted what the voice promised more than anything: to hold his daughter again. It dug into him, like a knife to the gut, letting all his deepest regrets, all his greatest desires, spill out of him like entrails of longing. It was such that he was afraid someone might notice, might see the gaping wound in his soul that this voice was prying open relentlessly. What it offered was absurd, impossible, beyond any understanding of magic or otherwise that anyone had ever studied. Then why did he believe it?

The pain of resisting the voice lessened as his resolve frayed. He *would* do anything to see them again. He managed to block its influence for another week before he started to weep every time it spoke to him. It had its ethereal grip tight around him, and he did not have the will power to resist. He no longer wanted to.

The voice had broken him.

Even now, thinking back on that night was almost too much to bear . . .

"Can you really do it?" Timothy whispered into the dark. "Can you really bring them back?" He knew the answer before it came, but what happened next, he had not expected. "Those who have faith . . . will be greatly rewarded . . ." the voice said like liquid honey, honey tainted with shadow. As it trailed off, the apparitions materialized in front of the Engineer.

"Timothy, it's so cold . . . please help us . . ."

"Please, Daddy, I'm scared. It's so dark here . . ."

He fell to his knees in the darkness of his tent as he stared up at the visages of his wife and daughter that stood before him, translucent with a faint glow. He knew that these could only be the souls of those he loved most in the world. It had been seven years since he had seen them, seven years since the accident that had claimed their lives.

As he reached out to them, they faded, leaving the tent once more in complete darkness. "No . . . please . . . come back," he said weakly, sobbing with a grief he had thought long since healed, but it was now like a fresh wound, raw and unbearable. "Tell me what you need of me, and I'll do it . . ." And though the voice had no presence, he could swear he felt it smile.

His thoughts snapped back. That was how he had found himself organizing the murder of a young engineer. Timothy had no real magical talent himself, but the voice assured him that this boy did. It craved the energy, demanded it, and so Timothy arranged for the engineer to be on shift more with the transport.

Would the voice whisper to him too? Would it speak of lost loved ones and how It could bring them back? Maybe it made other dark promises. Those promises would never come to fruition, though, and Timothy thanked the Guardians he was no magic user, for he didn't doubt for a second that the voice would have taken him instead if he had reserves worth taking.

His dark master had instructed him on how to lay the trap for the boy. It had to look like it was the case and its deadly glyphs that had done the deed when in fact it was Timothy. The voice had shown him in his mind the runes of a magic circle that would destroy itself when it destroyed the boy. Had whispered in his ear the word that would seal the engineer's fate.

Bile rose in his throat just remembering what he'd done, and the worst thing? It had been for naught! Though he had done everything as instructed, the glyphs were too powerful to allow the magic energy to be absorbed by the prisoner inside. They had taken the energy intended for that dark voice and converted it into mana to strengthen the wards. A new trap would need to be set, and the aching emptiness in Timothy's soul still yearned to be filled. So, he returned to the College ahead of the expedition to make the necessary arrangements.

And now, here he was, staring down at the monitor showcasing the voice's masterpiece. A blind hatred threatened to boil over in him, but not for the voice; it was hatred at himself. It needed a Mage of great power to release it from the prison that it had been caught in so long ago. Who better fit that description than the Arch-Mage and dean of the Mage's College, one of his best friends, Robert Turner.

"Kaleb!? What are you doing there!?" Timothy's attention refocused on the present as Hayley's voice rose from the monitor's speaker. Damn it, how had Kaleb managed to sneak down there? There was nothing he could do for him now, though. It was too late, and after all, he had brought this upon himself. Timothy threw the switch to seal the chamber.

Panic started to set in on Hayley and Kaleb. He could see it in their eyes. Like a haze lifting, realization of what he had done came crashing down on him. What was he doing? This wasn't him; he had to do something! But he sat there frozen, witnessing the horror unveiling in front of his eyes. The amulet that had been hidden inside the Fom'yelet was now clutched in the dean's hands as he began chanting, and then screaming—a scream that Timothy knew would haunt him for the remainder of his life.

He couldn't bring himself to believe what was happening on the screen before his eyes. He knew he was releasing a force unknown to this world, but his mind couldn't comprehend it. As Robert fell to dust and the demonic figure stood in his place, turning its hungry gaze to Hayley, he found tears streaming down his face.

Turning the monitor off, Timothy muttered, "I'm sorry . . ."

THE ELECTRIC LIGHTS in the room flickered out as the figure before them extended to its full height. The flames emitting from Hayley's palm cast the wraith-like figure in an eerie light. The events unfolding had pushed Hayley's sanity to the edge of reason, but she needed to hold it together: Kaleb's life depended on it.

The demonic figure stood a clear eight feet tall and had black scraps of material hanging off its long limbs. Its lower face was covered by a bandana, and its head cowled, showing only two glowing orbs where eyes should be. The skeletal form looked as though it wasn't quite proportioned correctly to carry a being of its size—the limbs too long, the body too thin—but nevertheless, it extruded a power that was undeniable.

Banging started from the other side of the metal door, and voices could be vaguely heard. The Torrent of fire was starting to work, the metal of the doors glowing white hot, its form starting to waver. She could do this! Hopefully, whoever was on the other side would realise they should clear a path. If not, Hayley shuddered to think of the pain she'd inflict on them while trying to escape.

"A . . . noth . . . er . . ." The voice from the demonic apparition scraped out of the creature's dry throat like nails dragged across a blackboard. Kaleb's sobbing intensified, and to her surprise, Hayley felt tears streaming down her own cheeks as she tried to intensify the spell that was their only hope.

Then it occurred to her: there was another way.

Coughing, its voice less strained this time, Mystral spoke again, "Another . . . soul . . . Another soul . . . is needed." Kaleb screamed, and Hayley spun, barely holding the spell in place, to see what ill fate had befallen her protégé. His screams, however, had nothing to do with his own wellbeing, and instead, as it became all too clear, his screams were for her.

Mystral had a hand raised towards Hayley; tendrils of shadow languorously stretched forth across the gap between them. Releasing the fire spell, she quickly reached into her pocket for the collection of stones in there and gripped them in her fist. Why hadn't she remembered she had these on her? At least she had remembered in time to help at least one of them. The dark fingers began wrapping themselves around her body, and Kaleb's screams intensified as he reached a hand for his mentor. There was nothing he could do for her now, though.

"It'll be okay. Kaleb . . . I'm sorry . . ."

She threw the stones into the air, channelling through them as she shouted, "Yteld'guty Galrei!" They began glowing, then spinning around each other as they formed an opening in the air. The circle expanded to obscure Kaleb from view. As they spun through the air, the opening overlapped where he was, and then the stones, the window in the air, and Kaleb disappeared.

It was the last thing Hayley saw before the tendrils enveloped her entirely, and she couldn't help but smile as her world was replaced with darkness, and then she was gone.

4

The Journey back from Astril City proved, as usual, to be uneventful. Travelling in the back of a Hopper 2000 Executive Transport, the Carnah'lor Ambassador Algo always found himself grateful that his people had sent one of their vehicles to pick him up from the embassy in Astril City. The large, well cushioned seats of his private ship were designed to easily hold the large lagomorphic form of the Carnah'lor, unlike most of the available seating in the Alliance. While he scanned the report he'd been preparing, Algo felt his body, if not his mind, relax for the first time since he'd been last home.

The Hopper glided smoothly through the air along the magical currents. It allowed them to sail over the mountain ranges and plains separating the nations with little turbulence. This option was considerably faster than any land route, and in his opinion, much safer than any choice offered by the Alliance.

The Alliance had their own vehicles, of course, but they favoured the Mundane for longer journeys such as this, filling them with explosive liquids and gases, and hurtling them through the air on nothing but well wishes. Who in their right mind would put their faith in such barbaric contraptions?

One of the Mage's College's airships might have been better, but with their large lumbering form, with blimps suspending large, navel type hulls, they were better suited as museum pieces. It's a wonder that their entire nation hadn't been crushed in the last war. Sure, they had smaller equivalents of Rune Ships that zipped about their city, but they were incapable of sustained magical flight over long distances.

Algo let his gaze wander to the seat on the opposite side of his table, where sat his assistant, Taleno. Despite the grey fur, slightly drooping ears, and aged face, Taleno was actually younger than Algo. Even so, the ambassador couldn't help but find the aide distinguished and handsome, which honestly was a problem, but Taleno was too good at his job to re-assign him, and Algo was too professional to ever abuse his power by acting on his feelings. He sighed. The man needed a break, though, and Algo would have to make sure the man took some family time soon.

"They are hiding something, Taleno. But I can't put my finger on it," Algo said as he returned to his report.

"Not to speak out of line sir, but you nearly always suspect them of hiding *something*. When we get back, I will need to set up the logistics for the exchange program you arranged. Having some of our respective citizens living in each other's nations is going to be good for everyone involved, I think." Taleno had not even looked up from his Data Slate, a tablet-like device run entirely by magic, like all Carnah'lor tech. He was probably already sending instructions to his own subordinates back home.

"Yes, you're right. Unlike the Alliance, I want this peace to be a lasting one. As much as I hate their culture permeating into ours, it *will* help hold off another conflict." Algo strongly believed that cultural misunderstandings had led to the vast majority of hostility between the nations, but deeply embedded prejudices made it difficult for him to trust the Alliance's motives.

In the first two wars, it was recorded that the Humans and their alliance had started the conflict. The last war, though started by the Carnah'lor, was the fault of a paranoid leader, one that had to be replaced so that peace talks could begin.

It was part of these peace talks that led to Algo's appointment on the Council of Seven. A council that had traditionally comprised of two Humans, two Phasmia, and two Tren'jin, with the seventh seat rotating between the races once every seven years to ensure balance. It was a corrupt system that ignored the Krayth and the Kalek, who called the Alliance home, and was a sticking point for Algo. The council needed to expand. If they were all going to be truly equal, the other races needed representation as well. He understood some Telum also considered the Alliance home, but most of their nations sat independent of Jubo and the Alliance.

"That aside, the Council were too eager to authorize funding on that Undercity expedition, but less than forthcoming on the reasons. It's a tremendous expenditure over what just appears to be a book. They are conspiring on this behind our backs, and reporting practiced lies or half-truths when in council with us!" Algo gestured passionately in the air, despite the fact Taleno had still not looked up from his work.

"They do not trust us, sir, because we do not trust them. Though their behaviour over the expedition has been unusually circumspect. I have no doubt that this will be in your report, though. Speaking of the Cultural Exchange, we should start looking into provisions to have access centres that connect to the Alliance Network. Our nations are practically isolated from each other, but if we could connect them through technology, it would go a long way to alleviating that."

Algo sighed. Some of the younger Carnah'lor had managed

to procure what the humans call televisions. They acted much like Carnah'lor Data Slates, but only feeding input one way. They were used through the Alliance to transmit government broadcasts and what passed for entertainment among their races. Lots of explosions and noise, lacking the subtlety of their own performing arts. The live broadcasts couldn't reach as far as Jubo at the moment, but there were physical recordings that could be used with them to view historic content. The kids ate it up.

Before he could respond, though, a light flashed overhead to warn that they would be landing soon. "We will talk about the matter later, after I have finished giving my report. If you haven't retired by then, we should meet for dinner."

Taleno smiled, not without a hint of resignation leaking into those tired features. "Dinner it is then, sir. I'll be in my office when you are ready."

He needed to order the man to take a break . . . perhaps he'd give him tomorrow off. He filed the thought for later, though, as the transport alighted on the landing pad of the First Tree. Standing over a kilometre in height, it dwarfed all other trees in the Carnah'lor forest city. To them, the forest was called Jubo, an ancient name that meant home, belonging, family, all in one. The Humans, though, they name everything as if they owned it. The thought of the name they had given their home made him shudder.

Titanwood.

As the landing ramp lowered, the air of his home flooded the cabin. Filling his lungs deep with its clean and crisp texture, he closed his eyes and sighed with relief. Spending a month inhaling the foul smog that passed for air in the Alliance capital was almost more than he could bear. It was good to be home.

Upon opening his eyes, he spotted his sister, Allai, waiting for him at the base of the ramp. Unlike Algo, who stood a clear nine feet, and had dark black fur to the tip of his erect, rabbit-like ears and crimson eyes, his sister barely topped seven, with fur white as the first snows. Her green eyes locked with his, and a smile broke across her deceivingly gentle features. He couldn't help but smile back.

"Allai, it pleases me to see you again. But at this time of day, are you not in neglect of your duties to Galrei?"

The smile never left her lips as she responded, "One should not assume so much with so little information," she said in a mockingly deep voice. "Your own words, brother! Galrei has sent me personally to escort you back to the Chamber of Dreams." Allai was one of Galrei's personal guards, and as Galrei was leader of all the Carnah'lor in Jubo, there were few higher honours to be had.

Together, they stepped off the platform and entered the massive structure that was the First Tree. Algo reflected on how, long ago, the Carnah'lor and the forest had learnt to live as one, using a magic known as tree song to shape the inner hollows to suit the needs of their symbiotic partners. The Yatesh Tribe were the first to master this ability, and as such, were still the best. Nearly all habitation expansions in Jubo went through them. There were Carnah'lor nations that didn't live in the same way, but they were all allied. The Kharb Carnah'lor were focused on an ancient pledge to restore a destroyed land, believed to be the fault of their ancestors. They defended the south against the monstrosities beyond the Y'axot River. They had few trees in their barren nation and had learned stone shaping as a means of forming dwellings. Then there were the Enlior Catnah'lor, who maintained a strange balance between clearing trees and using them for construction, but ensuring new trees were grown to replace every felled one.

Before the Yatesh tribe had mastered their tree song, though, the first settlers had built onto the trees, utilizing felled trees in the same manner the Kharb and Enlior did. These ancient structures made up the oldest and highest locations of the Carnah'lor, maintained for the history they represented. The rest of their home was networked inside the gigantic trees, branches entwining to form natural tunnels that connected them all.

As they passed the functional halls and chambers of the loading area, the corridors became more ornate in their design. Vines, flowers, and branches flowed together on the walls to form living tapestries vivid in colour, while abstract in detail. They depicted scenes throughout the history of their people, taken from the memories of those that lived in the great forest, constantly shifting in their hauntingly beautiful reflection of the past.

Algo's attention wasn't focused on the walls today, though, but on the large archway that led to Chamber of Dreams, the closest the Carnah'lor had to a throne room. There were no large ornate doors like the Humans were so fond of. Indeed, there was no barrier of any kind preventing anyone from entering the Chamber. It was not the Carnah'lor way to restrict movement in this way, and all were welcome in this place.

Stepping over the threshold, it was hard not to be filled with awe and wonder every time. Looking up, you might expect a large, vaulted ceiling, or perhaps an intricate formation of vines and branches to support the lofty space. Instead, everything from the edges of the floor up depicted the open sky above their forest home. As it was approaching dusk, the space above and around them was filled with hues of orange around the horizon of the room, bleeding into light then deep blues as your gaze wandered higher. Around the perimeter, the illusion was broken in places by arches of light that led to other parts of the First Tree, but the feeling was no less humbling.

Through the air floated orbs of light, moving lazily around the room, emitting a soft luminescence on all. These could be moved, focused, or turned off entirely at the will of the Carnah'lor around them, depending on need. But they all came on automatically at dusk unless commanded otherwise. There were others in the vast room, on circles of cushions, or standing against the wall. Many came here for the tranquillity, but much of the inner workings of Jubo were discussed in this chamber, and much of those machinations would be happening at every moment of every day. As such, there were many present in the Chamber of Dreams as Algo and his retinue of Allai and Taleno arrived. At the centre of it all sat Galrei, the leader of all the Carnah'lor. Through her strength and grace, they lived in a time of peace. She rose from her position on the floor and smiled as they approached.

"Ah, Algo, my most trus—" Galrei began, but before she could finish, the air split behind Algo, and the air filled with screams. Human screams.

Turning to meet whatever threat this might be, Algo found himself looking through a portal that had formed, locking eyes with a Human female being pulled backwards, and then something . . . something else behind her. What was that? Not Human . . .

Then the screaming stopped, the gateway vanishing, and before them stood a caramel-skinned Human for what must have been less than a second before both he and the transportation runes hit the ground.

5

As the howling wind of the amulet faded, silence settled on the chamber, and he let the relic that had contained him fall to the floor with a heavy thud. Had he lungs, Mystral would have inhaled deeply then. How long had he been confined this time? Too long, no doubt. That darn case had kept anyone from interfering with the amulet, and there had been silence for . . . so long. What had happened to the world since he had been gone?

What he had gleaned from his accomplice while in transport had been little. The world through his eyes had not made sense, and everything seemed so much larger and colder. This didn't bother Mystral too much. Gensa wasn't his realm to begin with, but he would change that in due course. It would be harder this time round without his brothers. The last time he had been truly free, a number of them had perished, some by his own hands. But Nezbir had always been loyal.

Where the female had been attempting to escape, the doors to the room finally gave way, making space for some Human guards to came careening in, some strange tubes in their hands pointing at him. Mystral pointed at the air between them in an almost casually lazy gesture and created a localized gravity field equivalent of a small star for a fraction of a second. This had the immediate effect of causing the two guards to be reduced to pulp as their bodies rushed towards this tiny centre of gravity.

The room shook slightly under the strain of it. Regardless of how briefly it had existed, or how small the field had been, the world had not liked it, and it would not do to go burying himself after finally gaining freedom. The spinning Mystral experienced, however, had nothing to do with the world protesting, but instead the use of magic itself. His strength had not recovered, and it would take some time. The Mage he had drained had been strong by today's standards, but nothing compared to those of old, and a mere fraction of his own former prowess.

Mystral, therefore, needed assistance, but he needed to first divine where he was in the world. He stepped past the pool of blood and matter that had been the guards and into the hall leading to what looked like a metal cupboard. Looking up and down the corridor, this would seem to be the only point of access, so it must be a lift of some description. Crouching, he entered and took in the tiny room. There were buttons on the inside, and a pad. Experimentally pressing the buttons seemed to do nothing, and he could not see what the pad could be used for.

Frustrated, Mystral tore the ceiling from the room, a snapping of heavy cables resounding up the shaft that now lay bare above him. Leaping onto what remained of the carriage's roof, he began to climb at unnatural speeds. Before long, he cleared the vertical tunnel and emerged into a large room surrounded with metal and stone surfaces. The architects of this place lacked any flair, it would seem; everything was functional only.

There were another two guards that seemed to be awaiting his arrival, and started to make noises with those tubes they seemed keen on holding. Small pangs of pain flourished over Mystral's body as the projectiles hit him. So, they were weapons, and the fact he could feel their influence served to emphasis his weakened state. Reaching the guards in a single step, he placed a hand on each of their heads, screams erupting from them as he drained their life-force.

With the morsels out of the way, he quickly found a route leading outside. Mystral encountered few others on his exit; none of the others were guards. It seemed they were either underestimating him or were not fully aware of what had occurred in the subterranean room. In any case, he made short work of them with his clawed hands. He didn't often partake in manual combat, but his reserves were low, and he didn't want to waste what he had on these insects. His egress of the building found him in the space outside what appeared to be a ware-house, with large metal doors, and a large vehicle with giant rubber wheels parked in the space outside. The courtyard was otherwise empty. With the setting sun, Mystral had guessed much of the day's work had been done, and he'd killed the only workers left behind at this point.

Looking around himself, Mystral felt something that was completely alien to him in his eons-long existence: complete and utter awe. The buildings around him were as tall as World Trees, stretching beyond all reason into a sky filled with buzzing metal boxes that seemed to be carrying denizens of this world like tiny hostages.

He needed to use magic again to unfurl his wings, seemingly erupting from his back, great and bat-like, stretching behind him. With a few great beats of them, he lifted himself to the top of the nearest tower, riding the eddies between the buildings where possible to soar higher with ease, and getting more than one startled look from the prisoners of the sky boxes. Perching on the roof like an oversized bird, he surveyed the land around him. Never had he seen civilization spread to such an extreme. The boundaries of the city stretched out to beyond the horizon in every direction, with the mega structures seeming to be mostly concentrated at its core.

Mystral knew that he was going to need help, but those that he sought to engage were hard to locate even before the world was nothing but buildings as far as the eye could see. Finding them now may prove to be nigh impossible. The Wandering Council may not even still exist, though he somehow doubted that was the case. Those immortal bastards knew how to survive, and their kin would likely thrive in this kind of environment.

Mystral needed to get his bearings. Nothing in this world was familiar, and for the first time in his life, he felt very small.

6

"What the fuck was that!" Belinda whispered while fighting back blind panic. She and Melissa were cowering behind a row of bushes to the side of the courtyard of the Calvador Williams building. A creature had just crawled out of their worst nightmares, killed everyone in the loading bay, then just flown off!

They were there to meet Kaleb after he was done with his little spy games. Kaleb had planned to sneak into the first viewing of the artefact. He'd discovered it, after all, and felt that he deserved to be there. He'd been invited to the unloading process but had been forbidden entry into the room where the artefact would be studied.

Being his best friends, they knew what he'd been planning, but had no real idea how he'd achieved getting down there. The lift was biometrically locked, and it was impossible that Kaleb's handprint had been stored on file. They didn't really care how he'd managed it, though, as they were now wondering if he was even still alive.

"It's gone, right?" Melissa said as they both tracked the creature as it disappeared off among the skyscrapers. "Right? We need to see if Kaleb's okay!"

"Mel, we need to go for help! You saw what that thing did?!" Belinda protested. If that thing had crawled out of the depths of the College, what else might be down there? This building was used for experiments, after all. Perhaps there was more going on than they could ever guess.

"Help will be on the way. There is no chance that went unnoticed, but I'll be *damned* if I could have helped Kaleb, but he dies because we stood by and did nothing while waiting for someone else to show up!" Melissa had stood and started towards the building before even finishing her sentence. Cursing under her breath, Belinda followed quickly after her.

The lift shaft leading to the artefact study room had been built into the back of the loading bay, and its doors lay burst open. They had wanted to keep that thing away from pretty much everything, and making sure there was as little travel time between unloading and getting to the secure room was key to that strategy. They had to be careful moving through the unloading bay, as the floor was slick with the blood of that monster's victims. The two closest to the shaft, though, looked more like bloodless, mummified corpses.

Looking down the shaft into darkness and holding onto each other as much as the walls for support as they did so, Belinda could feel Melissa shaking. Or was that her? She normally prided herself for having nerves of steel, but this situation had pushed her beyond anything she'd ever experienced.

"How in Cado's pits are we supposed to get down there?" Belinda asked rhetorically, not expecting an answer. But, of course, Mel had one.

"Air cushions. We just push air beneath us and control our descent. Easy."

Easy? Sure! In theory, but it's not as if they went around jumping cliffs to test the best way to survive! In fact, they had very pointedly *stopped* each other from doing something that stupid. "Listen, Mel, we really shou— MEL!"

Her brilliant, beautiful, and at that moment, *utterly insane* girlfriend had just stepped into the lift shaft and started to plummet before starting to cushion her fall with air some ten feet below. "Shit. *Shit!*" She was going to have to go after her now. There was no way in Cado that she was going to let her go through this alone. They had *no idea* what they were going to be walking into.

Taking a deep breath and ensuring that she was channelling before she took the plunge, she stepped out into nothingness. Like Melissa below, it had taken a moment for the air that she was channelling as a controlled cushion to take effect. She had to be more careful than her daredevil partner as well because her air cushion had to be contained in a moving space above Mel. If she just blindly pushed against the bottom of the cavern, she would risk disrupting Mel's spell, or suffocating her, or both.

It felt like forever, but after a few moments of heart-pounding descent, they had both landed on top of the carriage and shimmied down into it. Exiting into the hall that led to the Jin Ore-lined room, they prepared themselves for what would come next. It wasn't enough.

Greeted first by the gore that had been the guards, and then the pile of bones and ash that could have been anyone, they spent the next few moments heaving the contents of their stomach onto the floor, tears streaming down their faces.

Mel was the first to compose herself enough to stand up. "Where's Kaleb . . . whose are those bones? What *happened* here?!"

Belinda tried to respond but vomited again. After it felt like she'd emptied everything in her, she managed to slowly get to her feet. Mel was at the pedestal in the middle of the room and was staring down at the book that still lay open. "This is it . . ."

she said in a hushed voice, tears streaming down her face. "This is what took my best friend from me ..."

"You can't know that, Mel." Belinda started to cross the room to try and offer any comfort but was halted as she stubbed her boot on something they hadn't noticed before. "What the—" She reached down and picked up the amulet, and as soon as she did, she went rigid, head thrown back and eyes glazed over. The last thing she heard before darkness took her was Mel's panic-stricken voice.

"Belinda! No! I can't lose you too!"

Darkness.

All-encompassing darkness.

There was no sound, no light, no sensation at all.

Where was she?

She.

She knew her gender, but all other sense of self eluded her.

"Hayley, what are you doing in the cupboard again? Your father will be home soon. Get out!"

Light. It seemed to come from between slats in front of her, the same direction as the voice. She was suddenly aware of the small space she occupied, and the fleshy body that contained her consciousness. Fuzzy memories began to drift back . . . something about an amulet ...

Something wasn't right about the situation, though. Her body felt far too light compared to that of the memories that teased at her consciousness, and she hadn't been in a cupboard since she was a little girl.

A little girl.

"I'm scared, Mummy. Daddy is always mean and angry now . . ." The voice was her own, but from a time that she had locked away. It was weak, and it trailed off at the end as heavy footsteps came into the kitchen.

"Is that stupid girl in the cupboard again? There is something wrong with her!" It was Daddy, a large imposing man with square shoulders and a heavy-set chin. Had he always been that tall? He loomed over Mummy, who had started at his entrance, nearly dropping the mixing bowl she was holding.

"There is nothing wrong with—" SMACK! Cut short by the back of Daddy's hand crashing against her face, Mummy dropped the bowl, barely balancing herself against the counter as the crash of ceramic hitting tile resounded in the kitchen. Daddy had been to the bad house again.

"Don't you *dare* talk back to me! If I say there is something wrong with her, there is something wrong!" It looked as if Mummy was going to speak up again, but the look Daddy must have given her silenced any protest as she knelt to clean the newly created mess on the floor.

"Wizard? Pah, I doubt she has a magical bone in her. She spends all her time in books and cupboards. The child's an idiot." Daddy had a bottle in his hand. It looked like the stronger stuff, not beer. Beer was not as bad as this. He took a swing, still facing away from the cupboard that held the whimpering Hayley.

"She has more talent in her little finger than you could hope to have," Mummy said before starting and covering her mouth. She was looking terrified up at Daddy, who was seething with rage now. He swung his bottle at Mummy's head, the collision sounding like a watermelon splitting, the light from Mummy's eyes vanishing as she slumped to the floor, blood flooding down her face.

The cupboard doors blew off their hinges. "NOOOO!" Fire

whirled around Hayley as she stepped into the room. "LEAVE MUMMY ALONE!" Her fear and rage erupted in volcanic fury towards Daddy, as he finally turned to face her, his face already melted from his skull. His skin fell from his bones like water, muscle and organs following quickly. This didn't stop the skeletal form of her father from striding towards her as her screams filled the air.

Just as he was reaching out to grasp her, darkness returned.

Belinda sucked in a sharp breath, as if she'd been holding it in for hours. Mel was shaking her and sobbing against her chest, saying her name over and over. She brought up a hand, the one not still clutching the amulet, and stroked Mel's hair gently. "It's okay, plumboo, I'm okay." Belinda knew that Mel wasn't fond of the pet name that lightly mocked her purple hair, but the shuddering relief that came over Mel told her that she didn't care.

"Oh, Dafron, I was so scared I'd lost you too. What happened?" It was amazing that Melissa managed to form a sentence between the shaking and sobbing, but she was always good at forcing the words out when she needed to.

Looking at the hand that still clutched the amulet, she felt both a strange stillness and at the same time a deep-set horror. She wasn't sure where the calm had come from, but the horror she had no doubt. "I think Professor Glennon is somehow . . . in this amulet? Or perhaps just her memories? I don't really understand it."

"Wait, what? You're speaking nonsense. Where did you get that from?" Melissa tried to take the amulet from Belinda, but she moved her hand away before Mel could get it, cradling it close, almost protectively.

"Uh, babe. I think you should perhaps drop that thing . . . we have no idea what it is, but I can guess where it came from." Mel pointed to the book on the pedestal at the centre of the room. "There is a recess in the pages that looks like that thing would be right at home in. There is magic far darker than we know at play here. Please, put it down," Melissa pleaded, reaching out a hand to Belinda, who backed away slowly.

"I . . . I can't, no. I can't tell you why, but I don't sense malice from the amulet. It . . . it needs me to hold on to it."

"Listen to yourself! It *needs* you?? That's clearly something dark trying to play with your mind!"

"Mel, no, stop. It's . . . difficult to explain, but . . ." She slipped the chain of the amulet around her neck and tucked it beneath her shirt, ". . . but this is important. It has something to do with Professor Glennon, and I think it might help us to understand what happened here."

Mel looked around the room as if trying to find an answer, something to convince her friend not to do what was clearly something crazy, when they heard noise coming from the corridor. Belinda shook her head, and mouthed the word, "Please." Closing her eyes and presumably cursing ever coming down here, Mel nodded, and a sense of relief that Belinda couldn't explain washed over her.

"Who's down there? Stay where you are, we're coming down!"

It was a rescue team! Coming to rescue entirely the wrong people, but the pair were relieved for the help anyway. Getting down had been the easy part. The team had apparently thrown caution regarding the artefact to the wind, as they were deploying A-Tech rescue ladders, which magically fused themselves to the walls, along with a magical harness, which would arrest any downward momentum if someone was to slip while utilizing it.

Elsa Edwards, Professor of Runology and Deputy Dean of the College of Mages, stepped out of the opening, leading a group of Mages and guards. She surveyed the scene, and then looked the girls over critically. "I think you two have some explaining to do."

7

As the world started to flood back to him, the sounds of shocked gasps greeted him first. Then he heard muttering in a language he didn't understand, followed by an angry outcry. His eyes sprang open, and he pushed himself to his feet as his brain computed his surroundings. The voices and the speakers were Carnah'lor, and they were angry with him. To be fair, he'd be a bit on the upset side if one of their kind suddenly materialized in his room.

Seconds had passed since he had appeared, gracefully embraced the floor, and righted himself, and that was all the time that one Carnah'lor needed to make his mind up on what to do about this human intruder. Light seemed to flicker in the room as energy built at the hand of the black-furred Carnah'lor. The hatred in his crimson eyes told Kaleb that these would be his last moments. All thoughts of a counter-spell fled his mind as he barely managed to stay standing.

Kaleb closed his eyes as the bolt came flying towards him, the air crackling in its wake. All other sensation seemed to leave him as though he had stepped into a vacuum. Was this it? Was he dead? If so, he thanked Dafron that death was not the torment that he'd imagined. Slowly, as though time had been compressed, awareness came to him that his side still ached from the fall, and that there were further gasps of shock in the room.

Peering through tiny slits in his eyes, barely able to bring himself to face whatever truth awaited him, he saw now that the bolt had been stopped inches from his face. He became very aware of the heat that the magical energy was emitting but dared not take a step back. The black-furred Carnah'lor wore a look of disbelieving shock, but its scrutiny was not directed at Kaleb, but instead at the Carnah'lor that stood behind him. Turning, he saw that a tall female Carnah'lor, distinguishable from the males by having drooping ears instead of erect ones, stood with her arm outstretched, a serene look on her face as she studied the Human before her.

Never had Kaleb wondered what a piece of meat felt like, but he assumed it was something like this. She strode forward, clenching her fist, and in doing so, dissipating the bolt of energy that should have been the end of Kaleb. The owner of said spell moved to prevent the movement of the one that had foiled his assassination but thought better of it. "Galrei! We must kill this Human assassin now! Clearly, he was sent to end you!" The pink inners of his ears flushed a deep red in rage as he gestured towards Kaleb, who trembled where he stood. How was he understanding them now? He couldn't speak their language.

"I was not aware that Humans were in the habit of sending frightened children to do their killing. This boy couldn't harm a fly. Algo, you think he could kill me?" Her smile was wry, and her eyes were soft as she turned them back to Kaleb. "I sensed the energy that was pulsating through that portal. The taint of it lingers on you. I know you fled something of profound horror, and it is that we must discuss."

"Galrei, you cannot mean to—"

"I mean to do as I wish, unless you mean to challenge me for my position?" Cocking an eyebrow, she strode up to him, an imposing air of dread suddenly surrounding her. Kaleb fell to his knees under its pressure, while the one called Algo managed to stand his ground but was forced to turn his head to the side, shame etched in his eyes.

"No, Galrei, of course not." He made a gesture across his chest, two fingers starting at his left shoulder and run diagonally down. Did it mean sorry? A salute, perhaps? In any case, Algo had regained some of his courage. "But you cannot trust Humans at face value! His presence speaks only of ill tidings," Algo pleaded.

Kaleb started as recognition hit him. Algo was the only Carnah'lor to ever hold a seat on the Council of Seven, and Galrei was the Grand Chief of the Carnah'lor. The Astrilians would call her a Queen, but the Carnah'lor didn't have such a structure, and the title didn't fit.

"That, Algo, is for me to decide. Now, a bit of privacy, I think." She waved her arm in a circle, and a curtain of darkness enveloped the three of them and two others. One was the opposite of Algo, with pure white fur, and was much shorter. The other had dark orange fur, and was closer to Algo in height, but much heavier built. Though the world outside the curtain was shrouded completely, the light inside seemed as universal and omnipresent as before. All noise from beyond the veil ceased as soon as the encircling was complete.

"That's better. Now, my child," began Galrei as she turned to face Kaleb once more. "Though I consider myself an open ruler of my people, I am unaccustomed to humans appearing out of thin air. Can you please explain yourself?"

Kaleb struggled to reorganize events in his mind. Everything had happened so quickly, he hadn't had time to grieve at all. Grieve, Oh, Dafron . . . the professor! The dean! They were both dead! Tears began to stream down his face, but he had to tell someone what had happened, and so, as what felt like waterfalls streamed down his cheeks and his vision blurred, he set the rest of his features, and began to recite his terrible tale.

∼

For a long while after Kaleb had finished his story, there was silence in their private dome. Galrei had listened intently and took several long moments after to process what had been said. Algo looked to be struggling to believe what had been said with hints of panic threatening to break his resolve. The others present showed no expression, but merely kept an eye on the only Human in the room. She expected no less of her sworn guardians but had expected better of Algo.

"It would seem . . . that we have a problem on our hands," Galrei finally said, slowly and purposefully.

"The only problem is that we have a Human in our inner-most sanctum!" Algo burst out, unable to contain himself any longer. "This has to be all part of some kind of elaborate plan! The Dark Lords are just a myth!"

"A myth shared among all peoples. A myth we had stories for long before we encountered the Humans. No, this is no myth. You felt that energy, Algo. It was like nothing that I've ever known. Never have I felt such malice and murderous intent enveloped in such all-devouring nothingness. The magic at work there was not of Gensa, but of a different world. If I had to guess, I would say Cado, the Dark Lords' own realm."

Algo scowled. Galrei knew him to have a constant internal struggle. He wanted lasting peace with the Humans, but his constant made mistrust him quick to judge. "Even if that were true, it is a problem of the Humans, not the Carnah'lor. Why should we—"

"Enough, Algo! You are my most trusted advisor, but you overstep yourself! I understand where your apprehension comes from, and though it often serves you well when dealing with their politicians, it is misplaced here! Think: this boy's master understood what was at stake here, and sent their student not to safety, but to bring us this warning." She gestured at Kaleb while her eyes fixed on Algo's. "She did not send him to her government, or to some distance group of Mages, but instead to us, a people more likely to kill a Human on sight, especially a Mage, than to hear them out. Why?"

Algo's body lost some of its rigidity as he took several long breaths. His eyes started to search the air over her head, as if reading an invisible book, organizing his thoughts.

"She . . . she knew that her government wouldn't believe him. Even if they did . . . they would get caught up in bureaucracy, and not act, too fearful of causing outright panic." His eyes started to widen as comprehension started to set in. "She guessed that, with the context given, you would hear him out, that you would come to the conclusion that you have done, and she knew that you could bring this before the Astrilian government to work against the threat . . ."

His eyes stopped and slowly lowered to meet Galrei's, fear pushing on the earlier panic at the edges of his expression. "Jubo protect us . . . he's telling the truth."

Placing a hand on Algo's shoulder Galrei gazed sternly back "My friend, you see now what I have seen, and the terror that this child has been through. You also make a good assessment of what needs to be done, and I shall indeed be reaching out to their government. But I fear that it may not be enough."

Galrei tapped the air, and from it materialized an ancient book. She heard the Human boy gasp, for the magic she controlled was beyond the simple understanding of Humans, and even pushed that of most Carnah'lor. There was a reason she ruled them, after all. Opening the book, she turned to a page with a full, two-page illustration.

"This," she explained, "had been gifted to us by one of the only true Humans to truly be welcome among our kind. It was long before I was born, but its teachings have been made available to any that seek them."

She pointed to the three beings of great power that were centre framed—one cowled in shadow, rags of cloth hanging from his limbs; one in dark red and black robes, standing almost majestically beside the other; and the other, almost skeletal in appearance, with the most ghastly of grins pasted across its demonic features. All three commanded dread auras about them, auras which pressed on all those that looked upon the image. Before them stood two human males, a horned female from a race that was only known in legend to Galrei and likely not at all to the others, and lastly, a Telum.

"This is a painting depicting the last time that the Dark Lords were seen anywhere in Gensa, and those that fought against them. Many more lost their lives against them, but these here are the ones that defeated them."

She pointed to one of the humans, a Mage with short blue hair, unusual for the race. "This is the one that gave us this account of what happened during these times. His name is Zel Ceen, and he is the most powerful Mage to ever walk among the Humans. His strength is said to dwarf that of any Carnah'lor, and even then, he needed help facing the Dark Lords.

"When he came to us, he was over two hundred years old, and though not uncommon for Mages to live this long among humans, it would normally mark the tail end of their lives."

She flipped through the book. "He told us of how they defeated Mystral and the other Dark Lords that had invaded them. For his brothers, Melchia and Nezbir, were also free. Melchia was the strongest of the three and led them in their goals to take over Gensa, but something inexplicable happened."

Stopping on a full-page image of the horned woman, she heard Kaleb gasp. "This is Raylu, one of the only known Zhyri to exist in Gensa. This picture here is a magical copy of the original, painted by Melchia."

At this, they all gasped, looking at Galrei in disbelief. Even so, she continued, "Melchia fell in love with Raylu. She could take any form, but her native one is the winged, horned form you see before you here. It is believed that she inspired some religions and their image of an angel. Most are likely based on this very image. It is said she is not from Gensa, but of Ortus.

"Against all odds, she actually fell in love with him back. With their aid, these heroes were able to re-forge a sword of ancient power, imbue it with Raylu's soul, and with the power of the three realms, defeated Mystral and Nezbir."

She replaced the book into the air as if placing it on a bookshelf, and it disappeared. Allai's eyes went wide after the story, as though just processing everything that had just been said. "Zel Ceen . . . he was the Human that instigated the end to the Second Great War? But that was just over a hundred years ago. These events go back at least five hundred years!"

"More." Galrei nodded. "Zel is now closer to six hundred years old and still remains the best hope for this world. After the last war ended, he went into a self-imposed exile, tired of the conflict that he had witnessed for centuries."

Tapping the air again, Galrei pulled out what looked like a clasp for a cape. "We knew, though, that we might have need for him, and so the leaders of the Carnah'lor have passed this down since he left us. A single clasp he left behind, but with our magic, something we can use to trace and find him."

Algo creased his eyebrows. "Why then, wasn't he summoned

during the last war? He surely could have swayed things in our favour?"

Galrei smiled sadly. "Because we feared he would have destroyed everything we know. He ended the second war with a warning to both sides. If conflict broke out again, he would end both nations with use of the God Slayer."

"Impossible! No one could wield that spell! It's been forbidden to even research it for longer than recorded history!"

In a day when myths and legends were proving more than story book tales, Algo still questioned her? She supposed that she was shaking perhaps every one of his core beliefs.

"When you are six-hundred years old, Algo, I doubt there will be many that question what you know, or how you learned it. We as a people owe a lot to Zel Ceen, and regardless to the truth of his statement, it gave us peace, if only for a short while. Now, though, we must break his isolation. I will be sending you, Algo, to find him, and you will take the boy with you. Reno and Allai, you will act as their escort in the matter."

All at once, a stream of objections flooded the space, all fighting for dominance over the other.

"What? Me? I'd be of no help at all!"

"My place is here with you, Galrei! What if we are attacked?!"

"Why do we need help from a Human? What can one being do against our combined might!?"

"Galrei! I have important work here I must attend to! My duties on the council, as your aide?!"

Breathing in deeply, Galrei gestured sharply in the air. Though she had cast no magic, the instant silencing of everyone present was just as effective.

Reno looked as though he barely held onto his temper, worrying, as the guard had always proven level-headed. Did he always have such enmity towards Humans? It was something with which many of the Carnah'lor struggled—some, like her aide, a bit too openly.

Allai had a look of deep concern, and she was trying to hide it with concern for her duties. Was she afraid to leave home? She was too young to have seen any of the last conflict, and had never left Jubo, so she could do with the experience.

The others reacted predictably. The boy was scared, and Algo was ever dutiful. Well, he would have to do his duty now, for all their sakes. "Algo, Zel is going to be difficult to approach, and I know no one better suited to the task than you. If we have any chance at all, it lies with you and this boy. Kaleb, I know you didn't ask for any of this, but fate has thrust you into our hands, and having a human Mage on this mission can't hurt it. It will show Zel that we are working towards a common cause, something he always wanted. Reno and Allai, the path might be a traitorous one, and these two aren't combatants. I have no doubt Algo could hold himself in a fight, but you have both trained your whole lives for this. Go, and keep them safe."

She could tell that they were not happy, but they would listen to her words. Reno seemed to relax some, but Allai seemed agitated nonetheless. Galrei let the privacy curtain fall, and the sound from the rest of the room flooded in, stopped momentarily as everyone turned to look at them, then resumed once again.

"You will set off in the morning. The location spell will take me some time to complete. Allai, show Kaleb to some quarters. Algo, I imagine you have affairs to set in order before the dawn."

At this, Galrei left the room for her private chamber, hoping that she was placing her trust in the right hands, for if they failed, the world was at stake.

8

The day was almost at an end as Taleno began to wonder if Algo was going to return at all. Though his workload could never be truly called empty, he was getting to a point where he could retire comfortably for the day. He had been back in Jubo for hours now and had yet to see his family. They understood his work kept him away, and he was grateful for that, but he did miss them and longed to spend some much-needed time with them.

He closed his Data Link terminal, resolving to be done for the night. Unlike traditional computers devised in the Alliance, Carnah'lor technology relied heavily on magic, which made it far more versatile in a lot of ways. Secure connections could be made to any data store without the need for cables or complicated infrastructure. The Alliance were starting to work on similar technology, but their Arcaneers were some ways behind Jubo's GenTeks.

Sure, the GenTeks spent a lot of time on creating the magical links and ensuring that they were secure. But once set up, they took up no space and were not as restricted by distance or structure as the radio technology used by the Alliance. They just connected to what they needed to and worked. Their range wasn't infinite, but it meant that Taleno had been able to get an early jump on his work while in transit home on the Hopper.

It was this that Taleno wanted to have integrated with the Alliance network. It would require GenTeks and the Engineers' Guild to work together, but in theory, it should be doable. It would mark a landmark achievement in Carnah'lor-Alliance relations, and if the Alliance races understood their culture better, they might empathize and think twice about starting another war.

One could only hope, and despite Algo's constant outbursts of suspicion against the Alliance and Humans in general, Taleno knew that his boss wanted the same thing. It's why Galrei had chosen him for the position, and he was why they were making any progress at all. He just needed a steadying hand at times to steer his intentions in the right direction. Algo brought the passion, and Taleno brought the calm restraint.

Standing from his desk, he was about to leave as Algo walked into his office. "Ah, I thought you'd forgotten about your humble aide. I take it the meeting went well?" Taleno could see from the tension on Algo's face that this was less than likely. Suppressing a sigh, Taleno suggested, "Dinner?" Algo wearily nodded, and they left the room together, heading towards the closet eatery in The First Tree.

~

"I ASSUME you'd like some food before we get to your rooms. I can't imagine you want to go to bed hungry?" Allai regarded the Human with equal measures of curiosity and caution. She had never met one in person and had only seen their picture via the

Data Links, but she had heard plenty of stories from her brother, which left her naturally wary.

"Erm . . . yes . . . please. Sure. What, um, exactly do Carnah'lor eat? And how can I understand everything you've been saying?" asked Kaleb. His curiosity and ignorance did a lot to combat Allai's wariness. How could this child ever be considered a threat? Surely, he was harmless. Despite herself, she felt a smile creep across her features.

"It is said that Zel Ceen cast a spell when he was here, with the aid of our strongest casters, so that all who enter Jubo could speak and be understood by anyone else. I don't know much about how the spell works, only that I speak in our language, but I can understand you, and you clearly understand me." She gestured to a door coming up on their right. "And we eat fruit mostly, a variety of plants grown locally. Anything the forest can provide, we gladly accept."

The room they entered was one of the many eateries in the First Tree, and largely resembled that of an Alliance cafeteria, except everything was larger to accommodate the Carnah'lor stature. Most of the Carnah'lor were staring openly in their direction and muttering among themselves as they approached the food counter.

"I wouldn't worry about the others. Humans are not often seen in Jubo. The Alliance Council *never* meet here, so you're probably the only Human any of them have ever seen in person, which is certainly true of myself. I imagine it's much the same when Algo attends council in Astril City. Carnah'lor don't leave the forest often if we can help it." Kaleb nodded, though if the growl from the little Human's stomach was any indication, he was *hungry*, and his attention being largely on the food arrayed before them confirmed as much.

"Erm . . . how do I pay? I have no money . . ." A few of the nearby Carnah'lor snickered, and Allai barely contained a chuckle. "Yes, I had heard that you exchange tokens for products in the Alliance. In Jubo, you provide for the whole, and the whole provides for you. Everything is free because everyone contributes. No one fights over money and possessions if everyone is afforded the same. If you choose not to work, you are exiled. If you cannot work, you are taken care of."

The boy seemed shocked at this but filled a plate with some of the local fare with gusto and followed Allai to a table. As they sat, Allai mused, "Honestly, I'm surprised that your society can function with the way things work. But the Alliance has proven equal to the Carnah'lor continuously over the last five hundred years, so who am I to judge?"

"I must admit, Allai, you are not what I expected. Growing up, we were still told horror stories of how the Carnah'lor would come and take you away if you were bad. It's less common these days with the work to improve relations, but when we picture you, it's hard not to picture fear and death. But you have been the opposite, welcoming and kind." Kaleb started to tuck into his bounty, eyes widening with delightful surprise.

"Well, we aren't barbarians, but there are many that would see us return to war. It's taken a lot of work to change attitudes towards the Alliance races here too, and a lot of strength in the form of Galrei and her leadership. She ended the last war by defeating our last leader and forcing the matter. We respect strength, and Galrei proved herself against the last ruling council, defeating all that stood against her." Allai took a bite out of her own food, savouring her first meal in hours, and then continued. "At first, there was confusion, and many feared Galrei. Now, we have learnt that she is as wise as she is strong. We follow her more now out of respect, and though there are those that would challenge her views, there are none with the strength to bring forth their convictions."

"Galrei looks no older than you, though the war ended over

fifty years ago . . ." Kaleb looked as if he could have taken back his words right away, as the look on Allai's face could have probably killed. Realising she was probably scaring the boy, she softened her expression a little.

"I shouldn't expect a *Human* to be able to tell the differences in age between Carnah'lor, but Galrei is a *lot* older than I am. She is one hundred and seven years old; I am only forty-two!" Allai frowned as Kaleb choked and seemed like he was about to say something but thought better of it. She couldn't help but smile again as the boy blushed at whatever he was thinking. Humans—they lived such short lives, and in such ignorance. It was a wonder they caused anyone any trouble at all.

SITTING in the low light of her private chamber, Galrei studied the clasp in front of her. Such a simple object, with the most Mundane of tasks, yet one that held such significance to their race, and today, the world too. What would they have done If Zel had not left this behind? Did he do it on purpose, knowing he would be needed again one day? Only he could answer that.

It didn't bear thinking what they would do if this didn't work. She feared that the combined power of the Carnah'lor and the Alliance wouldn't trouble Mystral much at full strength. Legend passed down in all cultures spoke of the Guardians of Gensa, but they had not been seen in over a millennium, and frankly, could not be counted on to step in now, as they had failed to do so the last time these monsters were free.

Double-checking that her wards were active around the room, she placed the clasp in a metal bowl. The ritual was not a simple one to carry out and would require considerable concentration so as not to disrupt the connection the clasp held to its owner. Only a few among her people knew the ritual, for it was tightly regulated. They could not have their citizens' privacy so easily compromised, and so its use was restricted even among those that knew it.

As ruler of the Carnah'lor, though, those restrictions didn't apply to her. There was no one to seek permission from, and if any would challenge her in this, they would need to bring the strength to do so in earnest. Being their leader meant that there was trust involved in that position as well, so she *did* limit her use of the spell to extreme cases, such as this.

Opening her inner channels to the life stream of Gensa, she felt power filling her. There were few races with as pure an understanding of magic as the Carnah'lor. Their understanding of the power's primal place in all things allowed them to bend it to their will. She could see the connection the clasps formed, a strand in the air leading in the direction of Zel. Though he could be anywhere on that line, the direction it led in had Galrei wondering. Would he really be there?

Focusing her energies, she began to chant the incantation of the ritual, as an ethereal map appeared in the air in front of her. The line connecting Zel to the clasp shifted to a location on the map confirming her suspicions: the line led to the Necromancer's Citadel. Though the Carnah'lor had never encountered Raziel Fenrix, his story was well known among them. The Citadel was in an area north of Old Nekalan and had never been resettled. It was avoided during all the previous wars, and never served as a staging area for either faction. It was too dangerous.

The Alliance wouldn't even harvest the resources from the area. Nobody went there. So why would Zel Ceen be there? The Necromancer hadn't been seen in nearly seven hundred years. Was Zel after his research? She sighed and released the spell. Honestly, it didn't matter; this was the path they would have to take. She hoped they would be up to the task. No, they *had* to be up to the task. There was no other choice.

The ritual had drained her, though, and the expedition wasn't set to leave till the morning. It was time to retire for the night.

~

"Oh, my . . ." Taleno's wide-eyed shock conveyed more than if anyone else had been screaming with fear. Not that Algo could ever imagine calm and collected Taleno screaming, but all the same, the story had rattled his aide. To be fair, if this didn't shake the aide, Algo couldn't imagine anything that could. "And you leave in the morning, you say?"

"Yes, Taleno, I'm sorry. I don't know how long I'll be gone."

"I guess it's a good thing I haven't unpacked then."

"Taleno, no." His aide attempted to object, but Algo stopped him with a softly raised hand. "No, please, listen to me. You need to keep things in order here. Galrei is going to need help convincing the tribunal that mobilizing to aid the Alliance is a good idea. She could convince them with force, of course, but armies fight better from loyalty than fear."

Taleno nodded. The war may have ended some time back, but there were old attitudes that would take more than fifty years to change. "The JDL will certainly kick up a fuss over this. They have been gaining far too much support lately, which is why we need to get the OmniNet pushed forward."

"If Mystral isn't contained soon, there may not be much of a network within the Alliance for us to connect to. But yes, work on the OmniNet here is also another reason you need to stay. I don't think the Alliance Council needs much more convincing on the matter, but those here may need further persuading. You need to spread the word. The Alliance are our friends." Taleno smiled at this, and Algo felt his face flush. He ranted about his distrust a lot, but the stability of the Alliance was important.

He also didn't want his aide thinking that he didn't care about this. Another war might be the last either nation saw, and they couldn't afford to take things in that direction. Exploration outside their continent had been severely stunted by the constant fighting with their closest neighbour, and now they faced destruction at the hands of a myth.

Algo also didn't want Taleno to think he was cold-hearted; he liked his aide too much for that. He liked his aide too much entirely, but that was something he would never act on. Taleno had a family that he loved very much, and Algo would never dare interfere with that.

"Besides," he said with a smile that he didn't quite feel inside, "Kalrei would kill us both if I took you away from her and the kids again so soon! Go spend some time with them."

Nodding, Taleno gave a tired smile, dabbed his mouth with a napkin, and prepared to leave, despite half his food remaining on his plate.

"Yes, yes, she would at that. Okay, Algo, you win this time, but you better come back in one piece. I can't be dealing with your work full-time. It's hard work being as highly strung as you!" He gave a sly wink and stood, taking Algo's right wrist in his hand, Algo clasping back as they pressed foreheads together. "Stay safe, and I'll see you after you've saved the world."

9

Information. It was something that Mystral currently lacked and sorely needed. Centuries trapped in a ruin meant that he had little idea of how the world around him operated, or where he would even begin his search for the V'Udol and the Wandering Council.

The old cities used to contain something the people of this realm called libraries, and they were great repositories of information, housing many thousands of books. Fools. In his realm of Cado, the populace was not allowed to amass such knowledge, as the ignorant were far easier to control. Now, Mystral would use the foolishness of these people against them, as he was certain that they would continue with such practices even in this age of flying metal boxes and buildings that touched the sky.

Realising that the Humans would probably have begun a search for him, and his rather arrogant ascent to the top of this building clearly not going unnoticed by those in the sky boxes, he decided against descending in the same manner. His reserves were woefully low, and arrogance had led to his and his brothers' downfall on more than one occasion. Mystral could ill afford such a mistake again.

As such, he headed inside via a door on the building's roof, and it led into a stark corridor and a stairwell that headed down. He would need to blend in with those in the city while he got his bearings. He hadn't gotten a close enough look at those he'd dealt with on the way out of his cage to be able to mimic them, and he guessed that the guard's uniforms would look out of place among the general populace in any case.

Several floors down, a young, pale female in overalls and a tool belt entered the stairway and started making her way up. She looked like a common worker, and that would suit his needs fine. The well-lit stairwell left little in the way of shadows for Mystral to exploit so he decided to be a bit more direct. Clearing the railing in a single stride, he plunged several floors until he was on level with the woman, and then conjured air to stop him at eye level with the worker and took great pleasure at the sudden terror that flooded her features.

To her credit, she produced some kind of tool, and looked prepared to use it against him, but Mystral was too fast, and had a clawed hand clamped over his victim's face before she could bring it to bear. His momentum caused her head to crash into the wall behind her. Edging on the brink of consciousness, she still tried to summon the will to fight, the tool she held batting limply against the Dark Lord. The fight very quickly left her, though, as she withered beneath Mystral's gaze, physically aging, and then becoming a husk-like corpse as Mystral morphed, taking on the shape and appearance of the woman he had just slain, utilizing some of her own power to aid in his transformation.

"Janet? Hey, are you all right? I heard some banging and . . . are you naked?" The voice came from the door that the woman had exited moments before and was a floor down. From where he was, the dark-skinned man could not see the corpse that Mystral had made of Janet. He let the husk drop to his feet and turned to the man with a smile on his face. "It's about time . . . come here, big boy."

The man's jaw dropped as he stared at the naked form of his co-worker, but only for a moment, before a grin spread across his face. Humans were such weak-willed, predictable creatures. Without even a word, he practically ran up the stairs into Mystral's embrace, where they shared a kiss that would be the foolish man's last.

Mystral descended the stairwell, now in the clothes of the late Janet, whose form he now inhabited. It was fortunate that the second fool had stumbled upon him, as Janet's reserves hadn't been enough to replenish the magic that he'd just used to take this guise. Usually a simple cantrip, even such basic magic was proving to come at a cost he was loathe to pay. He would need to find a more significant pool of mana to tap fast. For now, though, he needed to find the nearest library. The stairwell led all the way to the base of the tower, which was a significant distance. These buildings were so vast that he could barely see the ground floor from where he was.

During his ascent, he had spotted glass carts moving vertically along the building and surmised that they must be similar in function to the lift he couldn't get working during his escape of the College. They were larger, though, and appeared to be for more commonly used to scale the buildings. Using the stairs for another ten or so floors to put some distance between himself and the corpses, Mystral took a door that led into the building proper.

The space before him belied the scale of the building, with low ceilings and tight corridors giving the feeling of a much smaller and cramped space. There were many doors coming off each side, leading to glass-walled spaces, often filled with desks and strange tools he couldn't comprehend. He suddenly found himself longing for his brother Nezbir. The Dark Lord of Manipulation was the closest of his siblings and was able to read the minds of the lesser beings, a skill that would have been invaluable now.

Alas, he knew not what became of his brother and would have to make do without his gifts. The people in the glass rooms seemed to pay 'Janet' no heed, and those that passed him in the corridor either seemed intent on ignoring her or leered somewhat obviously. Humanity had always fought against him with such lofty ideals, declaring themselves just and good, but what Mystral saw in the hearts of these people would not have been out of place in his home of Cado.

Fought they had, though. When faced with a force they didn't understand, the Humans would always rise against it. Tenacious flesh bags that they were, Mystral would have to ensure that this time, they were crushed properly beneath his might.

Navigating the floor, he eventually found one of the lifts and stepped inside. It was busy, and everyone inside seemed to be intently trying to ignore everyone else. The control method on the wall by the door made intuitive sense, and Mystral pressed the one indicating the ground floor.

They were on the three hundredth and seventy-second floor.

The descent through the floors took some time, and it

allowed Mystral to reflect on his hatred of this realm and these people. Why did he want to continue his attempted conquest of these people so badly that it caused a raging fire deep inside of him?

It was simple, really: because he could. Those who had power, ruled, and those that were too weak to stand against the power, served. He had ruled Cado for millennia with his siblings, and there was no challenge or pride in ruling that realm. It was why they broke through into this place, known as Gensa. The Dragon Guardians had fought with the people of Gensa to stop them, and . . . they had succeeded.

Not before he and his brothers had dealt the realm and its guardians a devastating blow, however. The Dragons were not what they once were and would not prove a problem this time. And it had been long enough that the remnants of those that had entrapped him the last time would be long dead. The hearts of those around him were weak and cast in shadow. Once he'd reclaimed his strength, they would be as nothing to him.

Still some floors till his stop, he felt a sharp squeeze on his rear, and turning to his side, saw a tall man with a grin on his face staring straight ahead. The cart was still crowded, and no one else seemed to have noticed.

A sly smile spread across Janet's features as Mystral lay a hand on the groin of the man, who had clearly not expected his assault to be reciprocated, evident by the way his eyes went wide and his body stiffened at the touch. Mystral let a trickle of his dark magic seep into the heart of the man, taking a hold of the shadow that lingered there, his features glazing over.

The lift arrived at the ground floor, and everyone exited, with the pervert following Mystral closely as they went to leave the building.

"Hey, Barry, clocking out early today?" The voice came from

a man at the door who was clearly working as some form of security guard for the building. Mystral manipulated the shadow in Barry's heart and had him nod suggestively after Janet, to which the Guard smiled, resumed his post, and called after them, "Say no more!"

The Dark Lord couldn't help but sneer as they rounded the corner and headed to an alley between the building they had left and the next one across. He would have had more respect for these lowly beings had they the nerve to take what they wanted, but their hearts were weak, and so the desires that fuelled them led to leering and petty groping. In Cado, the strongest would have taken what they wanted, and killed any that tried to defy them.

Here, though . . . pathetic creatures, one and all. Once they were deep enough into the building's shadow so that none from the street could see them, he turned to the enthralled man and released the grip he had on his heart. Barry looked around confused, for as far as he knew, he had just been in the lift.

Barry's eyes finally settled on Janet and went wide with fear. "Look, lady, I don't know how you got me out here, but I was just fooling around! I didn't mean any—"

Mystral waved a hand and cut him off mid speech. If only he could command the fool to speak while enthralled, but the mindless puppets they become lose the ability to access their memories. Useful in a lot of cases, but right now, Mystral needed information.

"You will listen to me carefully, and you might retain your life this day."

Barry went white as a sheet: the voice coming out of 'Janet' was Mystral's.

"What the fu—"

"Silence! You will tell me everything you know about this

city, and where I can find more information, or I will remove your sexual organs from your body and feed them to you before you bleed out. Do I make myself clear?"

Barry looked to the side and noticed the busy street at the end of the alley. He inhaled to scream, but Mystral quickly manipulated the air around them and removed it from the man's lungs. Barry fell to his knees, gasping like a fish removed from the rivers.

"Do. I. Make. Myself. Clear?" Mystral's eyes glowed with more intensity with each word, his façade dropping just enough to show their demonic nature.

Looking up wordlessly, Barry nodded frantically, and Mystral let the air return. Barry collapsed, gasping. With an effort of will, Mystral managed to restore the guise of Janet.

"Good, let's get started . . ."

Barry had suggested that they head to a 'coffee shop' to discuss things further. The world was a considerably larger place than it had once been when Mystral had last been free. Astril City, the name of the city they were in, formed the centre of the Astrilian Alliance, comprising the Tren'Jin, Humans, Phasmia, and tentatively, the Carnah'lor, a race of people that Mystral was unfamiliar with.

Hak'Ja still existed far to the north, and the Phasmia still lived in their ethereal city nation of Algoria, halfway between this realm and another. Astril City, though, was far larger than the rest, and acted as a hub of civilization, blending technology and magic to enrich the lives of those around them.

Blergh, poetic nonsense. However, he couldn't argue the fact that the scale of the place was impressive. There were many other smaller settlements with farming and agriculture being handled outside of the city, but constant war with the Carnah'lor had led to the city being a bastion of protection, where outlying citizens would flee during the worst of the fighting.

As such, the Astrilian Alliance had not spread much beyond this continent, and though other Human colonies existed, and natives of other lands had flourished, Astril City had found itself Isolated until recent times. As such, there seemed to be more focus on exploration than ever before now that a time of peace existed.

The Engineers' Guild and the College of Mages had together done wonderous things, and now knowledge was freely accessible to anyone, anywhere within the Alliance, except the Carnah'lor home of Jubo.

Barry demonstrated this by pulling a device that looked like a glass slab from his pocket and starting to manipulate it to show images and texts detailing various histories of the nation. Mystral could sense no magic in use here, and couldn't fathom how it worked, but after a demonstration on how to use it, he decided he didn't need to understand it so long as it worked.

Barry seemed to be relaxing after a while. Whether it was the public location that set him at ease or he'd simply forgotten the danger and threat that Mystral posed, he seemed to be getting more into explaining what he clearly felt he had some expert knowledge on. Mystral smelled the testosterone coming off the man, as a sense of superiority filled him with each passing question. Knowledge did, after all, prove to lead to power.

It came, then, as a surprise to Barry when Mystral first pocketed the device, apparently called a phone, and then proceeded to take Barry's hand hard in his own.

"Thank you, Barry, you have been *most* helpful."

Then, the screams of the other patrons filled the coffee shop as they witnessed the smartly dressed man reduced to an ancient-looking corpse at the hands of a pleasant-looking maintenance worker.

10

They were sat in the office of Professor Elsa Edwards, deputy dean of the College of Mages and had been now for some hours. Though the College security had *insisted* that they be taken to the holding cells for questioning, the professor had vetoed the idea, called them a manner of unsavoury things equating to them being a bunch of lead-brained idiots, and told them to escort Melissa and Belinda to her office. Belinda imagined that Human Resources would probably get a complaint or two, but given the circumstances, she was extremely grateful that Professor Edwards had been there.

Sipping from hot chocolates that the professor's aide had brought them, Belinda couldn't help but wonder if this marked the end of their time at the College. It was obvious that Professor Edwards didn't think they had anything to do with what had happened, but they had been reckless, and were somewhere they definitely shouldn't have been. They were still clearly in big trouble.

Melissa was sobbing next to her, and Belinda tried to comfort her as best as possible. Though they were in individual seats, they had scooted them together so they could hold hands.

She was acutely aware that she should probably be sobbing too. They had witnessed more horror than she'd ever anticipated experiencing in real life, and the vision from the amulet had made her a first-person passenger to what she suspected Professor Glennon had been party to at some point in her life.

Instead, though, she felt . . . calm wasn't the right word, but numb didn't work either. She believed that the amulet she wore beneath her shirt was giving her some form of strength beyond what she was capable of. By rights, she should have tossed the thing, as there was little doubt that there was a connection between it and what had happened down there. She should toss it, or tell a teacher about it, or something, but what she knew she was going to do was everything in her power to hold on to it.

At that moment the door opened, and an extremely bedraggled Professor Edwards entered her office.

"Girls," she started, then she took a seat behind her large desk and took a few steadying breaths. "Thank you for being patient. I imagine you have a lot of questions right now—"

"Us? I thought you were going to be grilling us?" Melinda burst out, her knuckles white around the mug of hot chocolate that she held onto like a lifeline.

"Well, yes, but we've uncovered enough via our investigation in these last hours to give us an idea of why you were down there. You witnessed that . . . thing . . . leaving the building, you knew that Kaleb was down there, and you rushed in without thought for your own safety to find out what had happened?"

The girls nodded in unison.

"Right, so though you are both recklessly brave, I can't blame you. I would have done the same thing in your position. Cado's pits, I *did* do the same thing. I grabbed what security I could, and I made a beeline to find out what was going on." She leaned forward. Her face was stoic, though it was clear now that her eyes were red from crying, and she shook just a little.

"I . . . know you were both very close to Kaleb . . ."

Melissa was openly crying, her nose running as her body wracked with the force of the emotions in anticipation of the news they both knew was coming. Even in Belinda's state of supernatural control over her emotions, it was too much. Tears were streaming down her face, and separate chairs be damned, she had abandoned her hot chocolate to hold Melissa close.

Professor Edwards continued. ". . . and I'm so, *so* sorry, but we believe . . ."

Tears were now streaming down the professor's face, though she somehow managed to maintain her composure otherwise.

". . . that Kaleb, along with Professor Glennon and Dean Turner have all been . . ." She choked on the next word. "We believe they were all killed by that . . . that monster."

Belinda couldn't hold it in any longer. She and Melissa were now embracing each other in body-shaking wails. The professor made her way around the desk and, crouching next to the girls, took them both in her arms as they all cried together at their joint loss.

SOMETIME LATER, they were sat in Belinda's dorm room. Strictly speaking, they weren't allowed in other students' rooms past curfew, but no one was checking tonight. Though most of the students weren't aware of what had happened, and Professor Edwards had asked that they keep it that way for now, the College was, in fact, in disaster recovery mode.

Mel was sat on Belinda's bed, hugging a pillow, and staring out a window, while she sat at her desk, turning the amulet over in her fingers. It was largely unremarkable, a green gem at its centre and some runes or letters in a language that she didn't recognize. They might be Akonian, but it was never Belinda's strong point. She wondered how this was connected to the monster that had caused so much pain and destruction.

"I wish you would throw that thing away . . . we should have told Edwards about it." Mel's voice was strained. They had all cried so much for longer than they really knew, and it had taken its toll on them. Belinda knew Mel was right, but she also knew that it would have been taken from her, and she knew, somehow, that would be a bad idea.

She started, "I can't really explain it—"

Mel cut her off. "Yes, I *know* you don't know why, but can't you see *that* is the reason why we shouldn't be holding onto this thing! For Nerra's sake, it could have been what killed Ka—" Mel stifled a sob, holding a hand to her mouth. Invoking Nerra, the Dragon Guardian of Earth, in such a way, was blasphemy in Mel's parents' household, and it was a sign of how upset she was. It *really* wasn't surprising, after what they had been through, and how irrational Belinda was behaving. She'd be upset with Mel if she was doing the same thing. Belinda didn't know what to say to help in this situation at this moment. Her feelings were being . . . altered somehow, and she knew that was probably bad, logically, but it didn't matter.

Mel took a deep breath and looked at Belinda with something between anger and coldness in her eyes. "So, has that . . . *thing* shed any light on the situation? Have you been able to uncover the secrets of the universe?"

Her tone was mildly mocking, and Belinda knew that she should be feeling hurt and more upset, and that she should be terrified of the amulet. Mel had never treated her like this before, but she'd never dismissed Mel over something so completely either.

"No . . . I don't know how to trigger it. I think it's holding Professor Glennon's memories somehow. I saw what I think was a vision of her childhood before. Something . . . happened to her parents. It was horrible, and then—"

"And then what? Belinda? Oh, Dafron. Not again! BELINDA!"

~

"SHE'S UNSTABLE, we can't take her in."

The voice penetrated the darkness, bringing focus to the rage and fear that was her existence.

"She's scared and needs help."

This voice was different from the first. The first was frightened-sounding but firm and harsh. This voice was kind and patient.

"She destroyed her home, roasted her parents alive! We can't have her staying here. What of the other students? We can't take that risk!"

That was a lie. Daddy had killed Mummy. Did she really kill Daddy, though? It didn't seem possible. He was so big, and strong. How could she kill him? And their home? No . . . that couldn't be possible. She felt tears sting the corner of her eyes at the memory of what Daddy had done.

"The girl is gifted, and it's our failing that we didn't take her in sooner. She's suffered massive loss and is in shock, but I think with proper care, we can mitigate the risks to the others."

Why were these people talking about her like this? She wasn't a risk to others, she just wanted to sit and read! Mummy would have let her read.

Ah, yes, read. The familiar weight of a book in her lap caused her to look down. She was sitting in a corridor that was lined with ornate wooden panels, and there were several doors leading off each side.

The book in her lap was one of her favourites. It was about a wizard from long ago that had saved the world from dark forces. A common theme, but she loved the character Zel and how he fought so hard to protect the kingdom. She wanted to be like Zel someday. She opened it and tried to lose herself in the words. Books always made things better.

"I'm sorry, Robert, but if she has another episode, we'll be responsible. We must think of the safety of our students above all else. We can't accept her!"

She wasn't sure she liked the person. The lady sounded cold and uncompromising. Hayley wasn't sure she understood what that meant, but it felt like the correct description. Urgh, she just wanted them to stop. She couldn't concentrate on the book with them constantly talking about her like this.

"Sandra, what other choice do we have? If we don't take her in, no one is going to adopt her, and the state won't allow her into any of the foster homes. With her gift, she needs to be guided how to use it. Who else can offer that if not us?"

Gift, that's what Mummy always said she had. A gift. But Mummy was gone now, and so was Daddy. She had no home, no family; what use was this *gift*? Hayley heard some tapping on a keyboard as the lady sighed heavily.

"Her father had a brother, Tom Hunt. He'll have to take her in. The system states that he lives in the Dawn Mountains. She'll be far enough from anyone else that if there is an incident, it'll at least be isolated. We can set up regular visits and attempt to train her remotely."

Uncle Tom?

No.

No, no, no, no, no.

Not Uncle Tom. Daddy was bad when he drank the bad juice, but Uncle Tom was always cruel. They used to visit him in the summers, but Mummy said that they couldn't go anymore. Uncle Tom would always give Mummy strange looks, the same looks that he gave her, and it made Hayley feel dirty. Mummy told her to never trust Uncle Tom. She didn't want to go there.

"Remote training? Are you serious? She'll be at a huge disadvantage compared to the other students. We're letting this one mistake define the rest of her life, and I'm not even convinced it was a mistake!"

"Robert! Enough! Two lives were lost, and I will not risk any more unnecessarily. Need I remind you who is the dean here? I have made my decision. You will take her to her uncle's immediately, and we'll set up a study plan for the girl once she is settled."

Hayley stood up, panic setting in. She couldn't let them take her to Uncle Tom's. Anywhere would be better! She felt heat across her skin, and her breathing started to increase rapidly.

She heard the man sigh heavily, and then the scraping of chairs.

"Fine, I see your mind is made up, but I insist on overseeing her curriculum and tuition."

"We'll discuss the finer details later. Now, we've kept this girl waiting long enough."

They were coming. She had to do something. She had to get out of here! Flames started to lick across her hands, and she tried to bottle it up. She couldn't show them that they were right. She wasn't dangerous! Try as she might, though, she couldn't control her breathing. And she looked about frantically for a way to get out of this situation.

"Hayley, dear . . . are you okay?"

Her head snapped around to see a stern-looking lady in her later years with silver hair in a braid hanging over her shoulder, and a middle-aged man with glasses and a tightly trimmed beard.

It was too late. They were here. They were going to take her away and leave her with Uncle Tom.

Fire started to fill her palms. She could feel the fear and rage building to a boiling point. She was going to burst!

"Keyot!"

Suddenly, Hayley was being forced to the ground by a torrent of water. Her flames fizzled out, and the two grown-ups rushed over.

"This is exactly what I mean, Robert! She's too unstable!"

The water was then carrying her away, away into darkness. Who was she?

MOTION.

Why was she moving?

She wasn't wet anymore at least.

She hated being wet. Hayley opened her eyes. She was in the back of an air car, and they appeared to be in the mountains.

Uncle Tom! No! They were taking her there! She had failed to get away! She needed to get out. She started clawing at her seat belt, but it wouldn't release.

"Hey! It's okay, it's okay! I'm Professor Turner. We met at the college. I'm taking you to your uncle's house. You'll be safe there. Do you understand what's happening?"

She recognised the voice as the kind-sounding man, Robert. His voice had a natural soothing quality, and Hayley wanted to trust him. It was more than that, though. She knew that, normally, she would trust this man with everything in her being. How did she know that?

This time he was wrong, though. He didn't know Uncle Tom and he didn't know how cruel he was.

"Please, Mr. Turner, don't take me to Uncle Tom, I don't want to go!" Hayley didn't know how to word her anxiety and fear over being left with her uncle. Robert didn't seem unsympathetic to her pleas. The look on his face showed regret, but his words were not what she wanted to hear.

"I know it's not what you want, Hayley. I know you'd rather be with your parents." He smiled sadly into the rear-view mirror. "But your uncle is family and will be able to take good care of you. He seemed pleased that you would be staying with him now when we spoke to him."

Pleased? He hadn't even attended the funerals. Uncle Tom only cared about himself. Maybe he cared about Daddy, but since they stopped visiting, they hadn't heard from him. Why would he be so pleased?

A memory nagged at her, but it wasn't from now. It was from after now. How was that possible? Uncle Tom's hands wandering where they shouldn't. "No, Uncle Tom! Stop it!"

Everything warped, like she was being turned inside out, being pulled into the not-memory.

She wasn't in the air car with the kind professor anymore; she was in her uncle's cabin.

"I told you to call me Daddy . . ." He slapped her hard, and she tried to get loose from his grip. She wanted to burn him. She wanted to make him pay like she did Daddy, but the people at the Mages Guild had told her she needed to control her powers.

When had they told her that? She was just with them? No, she had been here for weeks now, and the first couple of weeks had been better than she expected. The professor checked in on her daily via a direct Rune-Link, a device much like a phone, but magical with a direct secure link to a paired device elsewhere. How did she know that? In these first weeks, her uncle was actually very nice.

They had set her homework and said they would check back

in a couple of weeks. It was then that things started to change. Uncle Tom started getting more like Daddy, but he drank the bad juice constantly.

And now he held her wrist tightly, and was breathing heavily in her face, the reek of bad juice and the smoke sticks pungent. He wanted to touch her, but she didn't want that. He went to again, and she broke her promise, letting the fire come to her wrist where he held her.

"Ahh! Bitch!" He released her grip, and she fled from the house, running into the woods as fast as she could. "Yeah, you better run! If I get a hold of you . . . son of a . . ."

He trailed off, obviously still in a lot of pain from the burn, but he didn't need to finish for Hayley to understand the implications. Uncle Tom was a bad man like Daddy was a bad man. She couldn't stay with him.

She had to hide. She had to get away. It felt like forever as she sprinted through the dense trees on the mountainside. She had no idea where she was, or where she was going, but if she could find her way back to the city . . .

Not watching closely where she was going, Hayley's footing suddenly gave way as she found herself at the top of a steep incline. She began sliding and rolling, the world around her spinning, until it all abruptly stopped, the darkness taking over once more.

∾

"BELINDA! LET THE CADO CURSED THING GO! BELINDA!"

What was going on? Her eyes struggled to focus through the torrent of tears that were streaming out of them, and she felt like she was hyperventilating. She'd had another vision, but this time she wasn't feeling calm. She was shaking, and not just from

Mel, who had been trying to rouse her from the trance-like state she'd gone into.

"Oh, Mel . . ."

She locked eyes with Mel, seeing a frenzied worried panic there subsiding into relief and sadness.

"Tell me what you saw, babe, let me help you with this."

Belinda sighed. She knew that Mel hadn't given up on wanting her to discard the thing, but loved her for wanting to help her with it anyway. Mel wouldn't abandon her, not now, not with everything going on. So, she recounted what she'd seen, what their professor had been through when she was just a child, so much horror at such a young age.

When she was done, they sat embracing each other for a long time, as if it could be the last time they would ever get the chance to hold each other. The world was suddenly a much darker place, with monsters both legendary and far too ordinary walking the streets.

11

Kaleb stared at the ceiling of his assigned quarters after one of the worst nights of sleep he'd ever had. The Carnah'lor favoured hammocks for beds, and though exhaustion eventually took him, he was not used to them, and it was not a restful night. As such, he'd woken some time ago, muscles aching, but too exhausted to get up.

He had no way of knowing the time, as there were no windows leading to the outside forest in his room. Even if the room was on the outside, Allai had explained that they tried to limit how much light spilled into the surrounding area. This helped keep the harmony with their forest home and the creatures that lived in it. Yes, their presence wasn't without disruption, but, if possible, they tried to do what they could.

As such, Kaleb had no idea how long he'd been asleep. Sure, there were tools and instruments in the room, but he had no idea how to work them. The forest might magically translate the language, but without context, it was like trying to use a computer if you had never seen one before. Professor Glennon had once allowed him to sit in on a lesson with some younger students as they were introduced to technology from a few decades ago, and though he found their ignorance hilarious at the time, he deeply sympathised with them now.

Feeling rather the fool, he had never quite expected to be in their shoes. When his older brother was still alive, he'd always kept Kaleb up to date, so even as a youngster, he'd experienced both old and new tech. Something he'd tried to keep up after the accident and he was forced to move into the dorms, in honour of his brother. Now, here he was staring around at this completely alien room at a loss for what to do, and the once healed-over wound felt like it was being picked at, all while he tried to deal with the new wound that was the loss of his professors.

He wasn't left waiting long, however. A pleasant melody chimed at his door, indicating that there was someone there. He awkwardly shambled out of his hammock, glad that no one could see him. As he steadied himself, he could feel the muscles in his back knot and stiffen with the movement. He took a moment to stretch, during which the door chimed again.

"All right, I'm coming, I'm coming," he called through his stretches. Pressing the root that controlled the door, it slid into the floor, revealing Allai waiting for him on the other side with a large grin across her leporid features. "Sleep well, did we? I can't blame you. They get the *best* slings in the First Tree!"

Kaleb gave her an odd look while still trying to work out the kinks in his back. "Ah, yeah, brilliant. Is it time to set off then?"

Allai nodded enthusiastically. Though she'd protested at the initial thought of being sent on this mission, it was clear she was actually very excited. Kaleb found it hard to relate, having seen two of his mentors killed in the last day, but he didn't want to spoil her mood. After all, she had been the nicest person to him since he arrived.

"Great, let me just grab my things . . ." He looked around the room. Still wearing the clothes he arrived in, and with the rune stones that sent him all this way stowed in his pocket, he didn't have anything to grab. "Scratch that. All good to go. Shall we?"

Allai gave Kaleb a bemused look, while turning to lead the way. The route to the landing pad was fairly straightforward. The guest quarters were located close to them so that any visiting clan chiefs or dignitaries from other nations would not have far to go after unloading. It was strange to think how much their nations had in common while being so different. He guessed making a guest comfortable was important everywhere.

As they exited onto the pad, Reno was in conversation with another Carnah'lor, speaking in hushed tones. He wondered if the Royal Guard was concerned that he, 'the Human,' would overhear important internal workings or some such. Reno had already made his stance clear on Humans yesterday, which, coupled with Algo's own prejudices, was sure to make for a wonderfully unpleasant experience.

Noticing their arrival, Reno and his companion ceased talking, gripped each other's forearms, and touched heads in the traditional Carnah'lor greeting, which was also used as a farewell gesture. If he remembered his classes correctly, it stemmed from a symbol of trust. Given that Carnah'lor had retractable claws which could be used as improvised weapons, cupping the forearms showed you did not fear these claws being close to vitals in the wrist, and the touching of heads together being a choice to be as close as possible to each other. It's possible there was deeper meaning, but that wasn't taught in their classes. Reno's companion quickly pulled up a hood and made a hasty exit. Kaleb didn't think anything of it, but Allai thought otherwise. "Reno, who was that? I've not seen him around the First Tree before."

"I was just dealing with a personal matter before we set out. It might be some time before we return. It is otherwise none of your business."

Kaleb was surprised by the coldness in his voice. He'd thought that Reno and Allai worked together to protect their ruler. Surely, they had a better relationship than this. Though, thinking on it, not all his professors got on all that well. Maybe they just didn't like each other?

"You? All work and no fun, Reno, personal business? What is it? Got a secret partner that you're not telling me about?"

Allai's jovial response and gentle nudging only served to darken whatever mood Reno had already been in. "This is no time for games, Allai. The fate of Jubo hangs in the balance, and you're making jokes?"

Not waiting for a response, Reno turned and stalked off into the waiting vehicle. Allai huffed, but Kaleb had been distracted by their mode of transport. He recognized it as a Hopper 2000 Executive Transport, or H2000 XT for short. Kaleb had only read articles about the Carnah'lor Air Cars and had never seen one up close. He recognised the markings on this one as being the personal transport of the Ambassador of the Carnah'lor. This was Algo's ship.

The idea that it could sustain flight over long distances with only the use of magic fascinated him. The Alliance had only managed to replicate this in slow, lumbering air ships powered by Air Crystals, and otherwise used the much more efficient, and accessible, jet engines for most of their transport. Stepping up to the hull of the vessel, he could see that it was covered in intricate runes that he couldn't hope to understand. Running a hand over them, he could feel the power they imbued, feeling both familiar and entirely foreign at the same time.

"Please remove your hand from my ship." Kaleb jumped, shoving his hand in a pocket sheepishly. Algo had just strode onto the platform, with another grey-furred Carnah'lor in tow. Kaleb guessed he was an assistant of some sort, by the way he carried one of the Carnah'lorn GenTek Data Slates. The direction they had taken regarding technology was astounding. There was so much Astrilia could learn from these people, if only they could get along better. Kaleb knew the Slate was just that, a slate of stone, but the runes carved into it allowed it to behave in the same way as the Human tablets.

The aide seemed to busy himself fussing over some supplies that had just arrived on the platform behind them, while Algo strode up to the group. His hard features softened when he regarded Kaleb. "I'm sorry. As you can imagine, things are tense, and I understand that you've had no choice in the matter. However, as fascinating as I'm sure our Rune Ships are to you, I do not know how *Human* magic might interfere with the runes. I'd rather not find out while we're three trees high that they've stopped working." At this last part, he glanced at his aide, who seemed to know to look up at that moment and nod, before setting to work inspecting the runes.

"I'm so sorry! I meant no harm, it's just . . . I've only read about these, Rune Ships, did you call them? We call them GenTek Air Cars in our studies."

Algo visibly winced. "Of course, you do, regardless of what information we give to the council to update your materials, it seems they still choose to use the wrong terms . . ." Before Algo could go off on too much of a rant, though, his aide came and laid a hand on his shoulder with a gentle smile. Odd behaviour for an aide.

"Ambassador, the runes appear to be fully responsive on a quick scan." He then turned to Kaleb and offered a hand, which Kaleb shook in the Astrilian fashion. The aide seemed amused by this, and Kaleb realised that he probably expected the Carnah'lorn exchange instead. Before Kaleb could trip over his ignorance any further, the aide waved a hand at Kaleb, seemingly sensing what was coming next.

"I am Taleno, senior aide to Ambassador Algo. You'll have to forgive his frustrations at the incorrect teachings by your educational institutes. He has been working a very long time in bridging the cultural ignorance between our nations, in both directions." Kaleb could see some of the tension visibly draining from Algo at Taleno's words and knew that his aide was clearly more than that to him, most likely a very close friend.

If an aide had acted in such a manner with a senior official in Astrilia, they would likely be out of a job, and probably on a set of blacklists to boot. Clearly, in Titanwood—no, they had called it Jubo. Clearly, in Jubo, their working relationships were a lot different.

"Thank you, Taleno. Are the supplies in order for the trip?"

"Everything on the manifest is accounted for, and the porters are loading them onto your ship now. A second check will be performed once everything is on board."

Thorough—though with someone as important as the ambassador, it was no surprise. Kaleb had heard of the Jubo Defence League, and how they were leaning towards the radical. If they caught wind that there was a Human in Jubo, who knew what might happen? How was he performing these checks so quickly, though? Was it how the GenTek worked?

"In addition, Grand Chief Galrei will be in attendance shortly to convey your heading directly. She believed it important enough not to trust to anyone else."

"Indeed, you are correct as usual, Taleno." The voice came from the entrance to the First Tree, and as if summoned by his words, Galrei stepped out onto the platform.

"I trust I have not kept you all waiting long."

The Carnah'lor all bowed, with Kaleb hastily attempting to imitate the motion a little behind the others. Even without full knowledge of their culture, it made sense to show some respect to the leader of their entire people. Especially after his indignant intrusion into their lives yesterday.

Algo was the first to straighten from the bow, the others following suit in what appeared to be order of importance within the group, the guards, then Taleno, and hoping he was interpreting the situation correctly, Kaleb himself straightened. "Not at all, Galrei. We had not long arrived, in fact."

"Good, good, and I see you are all here. Kaleb, I trust your accommodations were satisfactory?" From the slight smile on their leader's face, Kaleb suspected that she suspected Humans did not do so well in the Carnah'lor hammocks, though he didn't sense any maliciousness from her in this, only humour. They didn't get many Human guests, after all, and this was a novel experience for her.

"That's certainly a word you could use for them . . ." He felt keeping things jovial was probably the best course of action. He didn't know if Carnah'lor had a similar sense of humour to humans, but he figured it was a safe bet. When a full smile broke out on Galrei's face, he felt relief wash over him.

"Excellent. Now, onto more important matters. I have Zel's most recent location, and you're not going to like it."

She filled them in and handed them a rune stone that would interface with their craft for navigational purposes. The Carnah'lor seemed to take it in their stride that they were now set to head for the Citadel of the Necromancer as their destination. The story was an old one, but it was one everyone in Astrilia knew.

Hundreds of years ago, a Mage that specialized in necromancy had kidnapped a princess to try and wrest power from the nation. A group of heroes were sent to rescue the young princess and were successful in besting the raised horrors pitted against them. When the Necromancer saw he was losing, he made a deal *with demons* and gained their power, but it left him a hideous abomination. These so-called demons were suspected to be agents of

Cado, Mystral's own realm. The thought made Kaleb shudder.

The stories weren't clear on how, but they all agreed that the heroes rescued the princess, and she went on to become one of the greatest queens in the history of Nasadia. Though the Necromancer's schemes were foiled, there was no detail on what became of him. All that is known, and this is recorded fact, is that the Necromancer erected a force field around his Citadel, stopping any from entering or leaving, and the lands there were plagued with darkness and death. To this day, the field still stands, and those that have braved going near it report legions of the undead pressing against the barriers.

That is why no nation has ever claimed control of the lands, and they were given a *very* wide berth. There were no settlements anywhere near the Necromancer's lands, and as he had never shown himself in the years since, all were content to leave it that way. Beyond a few history lessons on it, no one spoke of the place, and its existence was only passed down to serve as a warning. Stay away.

And that warning was exactly what they would be ignoring. They were headed to the Citadel. "Are we sure it's such a good idea to go there? There is a reason no one has stepped foot there for centuries. I mean, apart from the force field and the hordes of the undead, and the constant dread and impending doom that the whole place gives off . . . surely, we can find another way to deal with Mystral. We have much bigger weapons than we used to have and—"

Galrei gently raised a hand, and Kaleb halted his ramblings. "I understand your trepidation, child, and I cannot speak to the reason why Zel is there, but yes, you need to seek him out, and that is where he is." She placed a hand on each of Kaleb's shoulders and looked into his eyes from her considerable height. "Your master had faith in you and sent you to me. Zel Cean would not be where he is without good reason, and there is no one better equipped than he to help us in the fight ahead. I don't promise the road ahead is without peril, but without his help, I fear even our combined forces would not be enough to halt Mystral's advance."

As far as reassuring speeches went, it needed work, but Kaleb felt himself calm some, nonetheless. Galrei was right. He hated it, but she was. He'd witnessed the rebirth of Mystral first-hand. His presence still weighed down on him. Steeling himself, he nodded, unable to bring himself to talk, but setting his face in what he believed to be an expression of committed resolve. It was clearly enough for Galrei, and she moved on to address Algo further.

"Algo, you are my most trusted advisor, and that is why I chose you to be ambassador to the Astrilian Alliance. I do not send you on this mission lightly, but few others have a way with words like you do. Please, take care, and we'll await your return." She grasped his forehand in the Carnah'lor fashion, and they touched foreheads. Kaleb got the distinct impression that though this was the Carnah'lorn equivalent to a handshake, the honour was still a rare one.

At that, the other Carnah'lor exchanged some simple good-byes with their leader and Taleno and boarded the craft. Even with the aid of the Rune Ship, the journey was going to take some time.

12

"I would like to call to order this closed session of the Council of the Astrilian Alliance."

It was Council Raihanah's turn to chair the session today. Even though the session was a closed one, they still followed the traditional formalities. As annoying as they might be, they did help to bring structure to these more intimate sessions.

"We commence with the Oath of the Seven." it was strange taking the oath without a seventh representative present, but since replacing their rotating seat with the Carnah'lorn ambassador, it had become necessary during these more private meetings.

As chair of the session, it was her place to start the Oath Circle. She placed her hand within her segment of the table and began, "I, Raihanah Pearson, solemnly swear by the power of the Oath Table, that I will faithfully execute the Office of Council to the Astrilian Alliance, and will to the best of my ability, preserve, protect, and defend the laws and legislations of this Alliance.

"I take this oath freely, without any mental reservation or purpose of evasion."

The Oath stopped short of preventing them from lying and could be interpreted that certain subterfuge was necessary to fully uphold the oath. Faithfulness to the office and the laws were not the same as faithfulness to each other or the people.

The power of the Table did enforce the letter of the oath during their meetings, though, and ensured that there was at least some level of cooperation. Raihanah believed the wording could be updated but felt it unlikely the rest of the council would agree to being held to tighter reigns.

The rest of the council placed their hands and said their oaths, the runes on the table lighting up as each finished to indicate that the oath was in place.

"I, Carl Taylor . . . faithfully execute the Office of Council . . ."

"I, Natdy . . . the Office of Orator . . ."

"I, Dovulq . . . the Office of Orator . . ."

"I, Aki Tamae . . . the Office of Elder . . ."

"I, Kameko Sumi . . . the Office of Elder . . ."

Each race had their own title for the same thing, and the Council respected each equally. The Phasmia used Orator, and the feline-like Tren'jin preferred Elder, as was their custom.

The Ambassador of the Carnah'lor had recently left for his home in the Titanwood and would be absent from their sessions for some time. Minutes were, of course, kept, and he was kept up to speed, but she could feel the distrust he put into these updates.

She knew he thought they were hiding something from them, and well, he was right. There were projects vital to the advancement and security of Astrilia that they all felt sharing with the Carnah'lor would potentially jeopardize. Should they fall into conflict again, they could not allow all their secrets to be known by the enemy.

And, she supposed, that was a fundamental flaw in this truce. Everyone assumed it would fail.

"Thank you, everyone. Now that is out of the way, first item of business is the Pioneer Project." At this, the Phasmia looked bored. They had less than no interest in anything being undertaken by the Engineering Corps and felt that the art of Arcaneering was a perversion of magical use. It was a shame, because their vast knowledge and experience in the ways of magic would be invaluable to the Alliance, but they refused to work with the engineers at all, and only sometimes cooperated with the Mage's College.

Raihannah believed that they only tolerated the Alliance because their nation was squarely between the two biggest players in it, Hak'ja of the Tren'jin, and Astrilia of the Humans. "Of the Humans" was probably a bit of a stretch these days, as freedom of movement existed between other races and states that had signed up to the Serenity Accord. This meant that though Humans were the most populous race in the mega city-state, there were also large numbers of Tren'jin, Telum, Krayth, Kalek and even some Eirati. They were a cultural hub for all the races that had come together to face many threats over the years, but mainly, the Carnah'lor.

The Phasmia, though they had always kept mainly to themselves, and though they provided support in the war, believed themselves above the everyday struggles and achievements of the other races.

"The Engineers' Guild reports progress to be slow. They are having trouble above a certain altitude, where certain components simply stop working." Elder Aki was one of the Alliance's leading Arcaneers and worked closely with the Engineers' Guild. Tren'jin magic worked especially well for imbuing mundane objects, and It was something the cat-like race were able to do instinctively with Jin Ore.

And as the *only* race with the knowledge on how to use Jin

Ore, the Engineers' Guild had a healthy number of Tren'jin in their employ.

Carl frowned at this. "Simply stop working? Do they not have a better explanation than that?" It was unlike the Guild to give such flippant answers, and Carl was right to be concerned. The Alliance had invested a lot of funds into the project with the promise of results.

Elder Aki nodded. "I've been to the testing site, and well, it's the best explanation we have at the moment. Without sending someone up with the rockets, we can't tell why the runes stop working. The rockets themselves operate fine, but the runes controlling guidance and feedback just stop."

"Then send somebody up . . ." Orator Natdy said lazily, almost like it was an obvious solution. Her disregard for the probable loss of life was disturbing.

"That's not an option, Orator. For a start, the vessels at this time aren't designed with crew in mind, and secondly, the recovery process is not sufficient to safely return a crew even if a test were successful." Elder Aki shook her head slowly, "No. The Guild are looking into other options. We think that perhaps we are relying on magic too heavily."

Both Phasmia scoffed at that, as if the mere idea was ludicrous, but not wanting to be dragged too deeply into a topic that they had less than a passing interest in, they chose to say no more.

Carl nodded, as if the Phasmia had been in agreement, ignoring their unprofessional behaviour. "Very well. Speaking of The Engineers' Guild . . ." Raihanah nodded, seeing where he was going, and it was indeed the next item on the agenda.

"Indeed, Councillor Carl, that brings us to our next point. Grand Master Jenner has given his full report on the incident at the Mage's College surrounding the so-called *Fom'yelet*. There appeared to be some kind of electrical failure during the initial experiments that caused the magical dampening effects of the Jin Room to be ineffective."

Elder Kameko cast a disbelieving glance towards Raihanah at this. "An electrical failure? And then a mental failure on behalf of the dean that lead to the deaths or disappearances of all involved?" So, he had reviewed the footage then. Raihanah wasn't aware it had been made available to anyone other than Carl and herself yet, but with the Tren'jin's connections to The Guild, she shouldn't be surprised.

"We cannot hazard to guess what Robert was thinking when he broke the glass, but indeed, the turn of events is unfortunate." Four guards, two professors, the dean of the College, and a student, all dead as far as they knew. That was more than unfortunate. She had to watch her words, though. They had to look like they had these events under control.

The Phasmia perked up at this, though, and Orator Natdy said, "What exactly happened? You mean that the artefact they found was genuine? We were under the impression that the article of interest was the case and those runes that we hoped to weaponize?" It would appear they hadn't seen the footage yet.

"It'll be easier to show you." Raihanah decided it was best that they were at least on the same level at this point. There was no use in having the Tren'jin with knowledge that the Phasmia weren't privy to. She entered some commands into her personal tablet, and an image appeared in the centre of the table, projected into the air so that it would appear flat and perfectly visible to every occupant.

A video began to play showing the dean and one of his top professors discussing the artefact. Clearly, they didn't know that Jenner had set up recording equipment, for they spoke as if they were alone and secure, openly discussing the government funding and potential use of the runes.

The dean's next actions alone would have probably seen him

before a Tribunal of the Assembly had his life not been ended in the most horrific of ways moments later. He broke the case and opened the book to the amulet. What happened next had the Phasmia openly gasping. Raihanah didn't think anything could have fazed those arrogant bastards, but she was wrong.

The footage *was* shocking, though, and hard to watch, even for those that had already seen it. A being of great power and darkness stood where the dean once had, and they could all feel malice through the recording, which abruptly ended shortly after the figure was released.

As the light from the projector faded, Carl took the initiative. "This being then proceeded to escape the College and has been on the run since. We believe he is currently in a weakened state, but we have our top people on his trail."

"Then your top people are likely already dead, Councillor." Orator Dovulq looked completely void of colour, which was an impressive feat for a race who glowed and had translucent skin. He had never looked more human than he did now. "You have no idea who that is, do you?"

All eyes were on the Phasmia now, but it was Raihanah who spoke. "Clearly some malevolent creature was entrapped in the amulet some time ago, and through the careless actions of the dean was released. Yes, it's a concern, bu—"

She was cut short by a mirthless laugh from Dovulq. "You short-lived races, you are precious in your ignorance of what once was. Yes, that was a malevolent being, but of such a scale you can't even being to comprehend."

In a rare show of vulnerability, Dovulq clasped Natdy's hand. "We were there the last time that being walked the fields of Gensa. We were very young then, but we witnessed the horrors it unleashed on the people of Nasadia, Nekalan, and Astrilia. That is Mystral, the Dark Lord of Shadows, and we are all doomed."

13

The Necromancer's Citadel.

Zel had been putting this moment off for a long time. He had studied lands far and wide, and now his path had finally brought him to this point.

Though he still looked like a man in his fifth decade of age, or thereabouts, Zel was now well into his fifth century. Or was it his sixth? He'd stopped counting his age a long time ago, and unless he was somewhere that kept to a Nasadian calendar, he lost track of the years.

Before him stood the giant dome encompassing the lands that held his destination. It was said that no one could enter, and none could leave. The spell itself was nearly as old as he was and was one of the longest-lasting enchantments known to Gensa-kind. Zel was but a boy at the time, barely into his fourteenth year, when Raziel had kidnapped Saria, the then future queen.

Thinking back on Saria brought a pang of sadness to Zel's heart. He'd once served as her advisor, and she was truly a magnificent queen. Her reign, though, was brought to an untimely end during the Kalek invasion of Nasadia. It was all

Zel could do to survive that catastrophe himself. He never stood a chance of saving Saria as well.

That was a lifetime ago, though. *Many* lifetimes, in fairness, and Zel had seen many good friends come and go while he carried on. Since the last Carnah'lor war, Zel had been seeking to expand on his knowledge of magic. His understanding already outstripped most Humans, who focused still on what they considered to be the four elements of magic. His time spent with the Carnah'lor and the Tren'jin had shown him how outdated this belief was.

It took a long time to break those pre-conceived notions even for himself, though, and they were so ingrained in Human understanding and magical teaching, that Zel doubted things would change soon. Their recent application of magic was promising, but they were still so far from realising their true potential.

Zel hoped that through his knowledge, he could one day lead humanity in that direction, and with a better under-standing of magic and the world, perhaps they would be less inclined towards war. At least, that was his dream.

He moved forward towards the imposing wall of the undead, endlessly clawing at the field, constantly crushing those below, never ceasing their attempts to break free of the containment their master had placed them under. The land beyond looked desolate, never recovering from the devastation caused to it, a stark comparison to the lush green meadows and beautiful mountain ranges surrounding the area, untouched by the recent wars.

Something wasn't right about this scene, though. Zel was no specialist in Necromancy, and indeed, Raziel was probably the last Mage who was, but how were the enchantments on the hoard still intact? How had the bodies simply not rotted into nothingness over the last five hundred years? If they were constantly failing, where was the supply of fresh corpses coming from?

Raising a hand, Zel tentatively walked forward until his palm was mere inches from the field before him. The creatures inside seemed completely unaware of his presence, with not even one focusing on him. Opening himself up to the channels of magic in the land, he probed outwards towards the barrier, and was surprised by what he found there.

More accurately, by what he didn't find. Sure, there was a spell at work here, a very powerful one, but there was no resistance against his probing when he reached the dome. Steeling himself, certain in his conviction, Zel took several steps forward and passed through the barrier.

The sight that lay beyond caused Zel to stop in utter shock, his breath taken away in awe.

He was not met by a wall of undead creatures vying for his flesh, of which he was very grateful, or a desolate wasteland as he had been expecting. Instead, the scene beyond was positively . . . lovely.

If not a bit strange.

There was an outer wall surrounding the perimeter of the estate, though the gates lay wide open. The meadows leading up to it were just as lush and full of life as those he'd just stepped from, and running along the bottom of the wall was a perfectly curated set of hedges, flowers, and other plants.

Looking behind him, Zel could see the faint shimmer of the dome that affected the illusion, but from the inside, it was the only clue that the spell was in place at all. Moving on through the gate, there was a stone path leading up to the entrance of the Citadel, which looked in much better repair than it had from the outside of the dome. Whereas before it had a sense of imposing dread and decay, now it looked like the stately home of a powerful lord or statesman.

Along the path, there was an assortment of trees pruned into varying geometric shapes. One pairing was even shaped like a set of skulls, in what Zel could only imagine to be humour on behalf of the groundskeepers. Speaking of which, high up on a ladder leaning against one of the trees was a figure pruning the top branches. As Zel approached, he could see that the figure was, in fact, a skeleton, somehow whistling cheerily as it cut away twigs that disrupted the desired shape, in this case, an inverted pyramid.

When Zel was near the base of the tree, the skeleton seemed to sense his presence and looked down. "Oh! Oh, my! What do we have here?" The figure slid down the ladder with practiced dexterity and landed deftly on his feet in front of Zel. His (Though "his" could be wrong, the voice had a male cadence to it.) bones were very white, lacking any of the discolouring Zel would expect from ancient bones, and they were strikingly clean. The skeleton wore no clothes and stood about the same height as Zel himself.

"Well, we don't get visitors around here often. Well, I should say ever! Oh, ho ho!" the skeleton slapped its hip and its jaw wagged as it laughed at itself. Zel found himself at a loss for words, and just gaped. He hadn't known what to expect, but this was nowhere near anything he could have guessed. "Ah, a mute, are we? Just my luck that the first new company we have in centuries, and you're dumb as a doorknob!"

At this Zel shook himself out of his stupor. "I, no . . . what? I'm sorry, no, I'm not mute, I'm . . . I'm just . . . astounded. Might I ask who you are?" Though the skeleton had no expression, for it had no face, Zel almost felt it take offence at this.

"By the seven, aren't we a rude one? First, you sit there slack-jawed and buggy-eyed as a way of introduction, and now you demand to know who I am, when it is you that intrudes on our home? Do they teach you no manners where you come from, young man?"

Zel couldn't help but smile. It had been a long time since anyone had called him *young,* but the skeleton did have a point.

"My humblest apologies, but you are quite right. My name is Zel Cean. I am a Mage, and I seek knowledge in all things. Today, I'd hoped to seek knowledge from what I'd thought to be an abandoned Citadel. So you must forgive my surprised at not finding hordes of revenants attempting to kill me, nor the grounds themselves as abandoned as I'd been led to believe."

"Hordes of revenants? Whatever do you- Oh. OH! That spell is still active? Goodness, no wonder nobody ever comes to say hello. I had no idea Master was maintaining it. That said, he is one who likes his privacy." The skeleton looked over Zel's head as if noticing the shimmer of the dome for the first time, then back down at Zel. "It is a pleasure to meet you, Zel. I am the head groundskeeper, Bill. I once had a last name, but I'm afraid it's all I can do to remember my first! It's been so long, you understand?"

Zel smiled, finding himself warming to this strange undead fellow. "Of course. Believe it or not, but I have some experience in that myself. You say your master is still maintaining the spell. Does that mean he yet lives? That he is in residence?"

"Oh, yes, yes, he is quite alive, as alive as anyone in his state can be. In residence? No, he likes to take long pilgrimages, travelling the world. Sometimes, he doesn't return for decades at a time. I think he enjoys mingling with the living from time to time, you see. He's become a lot better at hiding his . . . well, yes, yes, enough of that." Bill seemed to get a bit flustered at the thought of his master's altered appearance, and Zel guessed that Raziel was not fond if it being brought up.

"That is a shame. I had hoped to speak with him. As the case is, might I be able to impose on your hospitality? I have come a very long way and could do with a solid roof over my head for a night."

"That will be for the major-domo to decide, I'm afraid. She is in charge of all affairs when the master is away." Bill gestured towards the house. "However, I can certainly introduce you, and have some refreshments brought to you as you wait. This way, please."

Zel smiled and followed Bill, this was turning out to be a much better trip than anticipated.

14

The H2000 XT was as luxurious as Carnah'lor transport got, and for Kaleb, that was more luxury than he'd experienced in his life. All the seating was oversized by human standards, which meant he had plenty of space in any he chose. It was far larger inside than he expected. With little space needed for mechanics, the designers were able to utilize a lot more of the space inside the hull.

They currently resided in the bar/commons area of the craft, with Reno in the cockpit. Apart from their conversation, the vessel moved through the skies silently at, or exceeding, the speed of Alliance rockets! Kaleb would have to try and study under the Carnah'lor at some point.

"I had heard of the ingenuity of Jubian magic. I'd seen videos, but experiencing it is something else!" Kaleb had learned that the Carnah'lor referred to themselves as such, but their practices and language were Jubian, much like most Humans in Astrilia speak Astrilian. Kalebcould see that Algo was struggling to remain polite under the enthusiasm that Kaleb was leaking everywhere, but his sister Allai was a lot more relaxed and seemed to find it all very amusing.

"Yes, Humans have always had a primitive understanding of magic. it's a wonder that you've managed to advance at all." Algo's remarks didn't do anything to stifle Kaleb's mood, though, and he had to admit it: a shared knowledge base would probably benefit Astrilia more than it would Jubo.

Allai gently hit Algo's ears and took a seat next to him. "Be nice, brother. Kaleb is experiencing *a lot* for the first time. I can't say that I don't understand the feeling. Getting to travel so far from Jubo is exciting!"

Algo sighed, looking visibly annoyed. "If you say so, but do keep in mind the reason we are on this journey. Try to not let your enthusiasm cloud your focus. You are a chief guard. You should act more like it."

His sister gave him a narrow-eyed look, but she couldn't maintain the pretence and started laughing instead.

"Haha! Yes, yes, always so serious!" Speaking in a deeper voice, Allai mocked her brother. "'You should act more like it.'" The impression was complete with finger wagging and a puffed-out chest. "I know you're putting on a show for the Human, Algo. Try to relax already? It's what, at least four hours to the Citadel in this?"

"Three."

"See, what could we possibly need guarding from in that time while we're speeding through the air?" She headed to the bar and poured herself a drink of something very red and viscous. Taking a long swig, she sat down again next to her brother. "Do they have Jub Wine in Astrilia?"

"What is Jub Wine?" Kaleb asked curiously. Students of the college were forbidden alcohol, purely as a safety precaution. Having drunk students running around with the ability to incinerate buildings was probably not the best idea. As such, he'd rarely drunk himself. Allai looked incredulous, though, and hastily handed him the cup.

"Here, you must try some! It's my *favourite* drink, but as I'm on duty most of the time—"

"As you are now."

"Hush, brother! As I'm on duty most of the time, I don't get to enjoy it as much as I'd like!"

Kaleb took a sip from the glass. He expected a very strong taste of alcohol, and it was there, but the most dominant flavour, by far, was that of some kind of very sweet, almost sickly, fruit. The consistency was almost like a watered-down yogurt, but not quite. He found his senses struggling to truly understand the drink, but he knew that he liked it! "This is so good! What is it made from?"

"The JubJub fruit! It grows high in our forests, and it's amazing!" She eagerly took her glass back and drank some more of the wine, leaning back in her chair. "Ahhh . . ."

Kaleb turned to Algo. "Can I have a glass?"

He nodded, but also said, "Take care, both of you. We don't know what to expect when we get there." He was drinking water himself and seemed perfectly content with that.

OVER THE NEXT HOUR, Allai and Kaleb exchanged stories of their very different homes, each fascinated by the other's tales of similar yet different technology and shared their views on where the future will take both their cultures.

Eventually, looking worse for wear, Algo suggested, "Okay, I think I'm going to have a . . . nap . . . I may have . . . over . . . worked . . . Allai?"

What he hadn't realised, though, was that it had been quiet for a short while, but he'd been finding it hard to concentrate. Why was he tired? It was barely mid-morning. He looked over at the others. They were slumped over in their chairs, their wine soaking his carpet.

"Allai . . . This isn't . . . like . . . " He was struggling to talk, and the room was spinning. Something was wrong here. They needed help. Reno, he would know what to do! He struggled to his feet, made it a few steps towards the cockpit, then slumped to the floor, unconscious.

THE VIEW from the cockpit was breathtaking, with a full panoramic view of the landscape before them. They were passing over a now-rare piece of unscathed forest lands. The Humans and their Alliance had taken so much from the world, and his people had been the only ones to say no, the only ones to stand in their way.

For hundreds of years, they had been the defenders of what was right, and fought against the scourge of humanity. All they knew was hate and destruction, burning all before them. All-consuming, with a self-righteous belief that they were within their rights to claim any land not currently occupied, and if it was occupied, well, they'd better get on board or get out.

Not the Carnah'lor, though. They had given everything they had to stop the advance of the technological tide. Even their use of magic was disrespectful in their ignorance.

And now they were in bed with these scum, cosying up to them and wanting to integrate with their systems? Heresy! It went against everything they had fought so hard to defend. They had to be stopped, and Galrei wasn't going to do anything about it. She actually *wanted* this peace.

The only reason the council of chiefs listened to her was because she was too strong to oppose, taking control of the joint clans by force, as was their way, and then forcing them into this ludicrous state of affairs.

The Jubo Defence League wouldn't stand for it, though. They had been growing and building their network ever since Galrei had stripped their nation of its pride. Now, Reno was in a position where he could do something about it. He'd been manoeuvring for years to be able to do something about Galrei, but now she had handed him the key to her downfall.

Enough time had now passed that the sleeping powder he had slipped into their drinks should have taken effect. Tasteless and odourless, it was the perfect choice for this mission. He left the cockpit, knowing that, once programmed, the Rune Ship didn't need him present to get to its destination.

Stepping into the main compartment, Reno smiled to himself. Algo was sprawled in front of him, and the other two were slumped uselessly in the lounge area. Drawing a knife, he knelt next to the ambassador, pulled his head up by his ears, and slid the honed blade across his neck. Blood immediately poured out onto the lavish carpet of the ship's floor. Decadent bastard had been corrupted by their ways, and probably didn't even know it.

"Traitor!" He spat on Algo as the life drained from his body. Next, he needed those rune stones the boy had. He knew they were rare, and their spy network had also uncovered how they worked, so they would prove invaluable to him. Their magic was inferior in so many ways, but he had to admit, they'd found some ingenious uses for what they had.

And for his plan to work, he would need them to make his escape. Creeping up to the Human, his face contorted with disgust. Their furless bodies were like naked compared to the majesty of the Carnah'lor. So weak and fragile, it was a wonder how these worms ever rose to such power that they could challenge the combined might of the joint clans. He searched through the child's pockets until his fingers closed around the set of stones. Excellent.

As he withdrew his hand, the boy began to stir. How was that possible? Did the drug work differently on Humans? Surely, it should last longer, if anything.

"Noooo . . ." the boy moaned weakly, starting to shift. Reno took a step back as Kaleb's eyes opened.

"What . . . Professor?" Kaleb's eyes fixed on him. ". . . Reno?"

Fury built inside him as he bared his teeth in a blood-curdling snarl. How dare this worm sully his name with that filthy human tongue!? Disgusted at his own hesitation, he swiftly brought the knife up to end the boy.

KALEB HAD BEEN REALLY ENJOYING TALKING to Allai. She was so nice, and probably the best thing about this entire messed-up situation, but she began to drift off before even finishing her glass of wine, and he felt the tugs of sleep pulling at him, too. He tried to resist, but he figured that he must be exhausted after such an awful night's sleep and let its sweet embrace take him.

And take him it did, but it was anything but sweet. He was back there, in that room, the howling wind all around him as the professor was suspended in mid-air, her eyes pleading, her hands reaching out towards him. Any second now, she would throw the stones that could have saved her at him, forcing him to the foot of Galrei's throne.

It didn't happen, though. She just hung there, a look of utter disappointment crossing her face. He had failed them all. He'd seen what was happening and taken no action. What kind of a Mage was he? He'd let the dean die, and now he was letting his professor die. He was pathetic, but in the eyes of such evil, what could he do?

Mystral stool beyond Hayley, and for a fully cowled face and such expressionless glowing orbs for eyes, he somehow conveyed utter victory and delight. Such malice-filled delight that Kaleb had never felt. He walked up to Hayley and placed a clawed hand on her skull.

Hayley's screams filled the space, and Kaleb clasped his hands to his ears to no effect. He would wish he had covered his eyes instead. Mystral began squeezing, Hayley's features distorting as her skull broke in his vice-like grip.

"NOOOOOOOO!!!" yelled Kaleb, power welling within.

Everything around him shifted, and suddenly he wasn't in the ore-lined room anymore. Everything was blurred, and he struggled to fight through the grogginess holding onto him.

"What . . . Professor?" His eyes came into focus, locking onto Reno, who was standing over him, bloody knife in hand. ". . . Reno?"

Something seemed to set off a fire in the Carnah'lor, as he was suddenly seething with rage, bringing the knife up to attack Kaleb.

Eyes going wide and sharply inhaling, Kaleb could still feel the power that had been welling inside him during his horrific dream. Clenching his fists, he let out an explosion of air from every pore of his body just as the knife touched his skin.

Reno, the knife, and everything in the room was blown away from Kaleb; his own clothes were in tatters from the uncontrolled outburst. He heard Allai stirring from the other side of the room, having also been blasted with her fellow guard. Kaleb was having trouble making sense of what was going on around him. Algo was lying on the floor against the cockpit door, blood pooled around him, Reno was getting back to his feet, searching for the knife that had gone flying.

Allai was now on her feet surveying the situation just as Reno took hold of the blood-soaked knife. He seemed to be searching around for something else as well, when Allai's eyes locked on Algo's body.

"Brother . . . Algo . . .No!" She ran over to him, clearing the space so quickly that Kaleb was unable to follow her movements.

"No . . . nonononono . . . Brother, what happened . . ." Sobbing, she found a horrible gash opened up along her brother's neck, and then she looked up to Reno, still clutching the knife while he rummaged around the cabin, picking up small items and putting them into his pocket.

Rage, blind rage. That was all that registered across Allai's features as the air around her began swirling with energy. "RENO! YOU TRAITOUROUS BASTARD!" Reno realised that Allai was awake at last, his search apparently distracting him from this fact until now.

"Me the traitor? Ha! Your scum of a bro—" He never got to finish his sentence as he was forced to duck a power blast of energy that seared the wall where his head had been. "Are you mad? You'll take this entire craft do—" Again, he had to dodge as Allai let out burst after burst of energy at her brother's murderer.

Reno sprang around the cabin on all fours, still searching desperately while avoiding Allai's wrath. As each bolt of energy hit the walls, the whole cabin shook. "Uh, Allai, I don't think it's such a good idea to do that in here . . ." Kaleb pleaded, but Allai was deaf to his words.

"AAAAHHH!!!" She charged at Reno, clearly annoyed at his agility in avoiding her spells. Her fists were glowing balls of plasmatic light as she crashed into him, pummelling a fist into his side. Reno screamed out in pain as he retaliated with a burst of magic of his own, sending Allai flying from him.

The wound in his side oozed blood from the severe burn that she'd inflicted. Allai was very quickly back on her feet, giving Reno no respite, as she began to charge him again. Bringing the knife up sharply, Reno slashed at the air where Allai was charging, cutting a deep gash across her face.

She fell back, clutching at the blood filling her eyes, as Reno grabbed hold of another small item from the floor, a look of triumph on his face. Walking over to the downed royal guard, Reno drew back to make the killing blow—when a bolt of electricity hit him in the chest.

Kaleb stood, arm outstretched, breathing so heavily he was sure he was about to hyperventilate. "Not . . . not this time!" He let loose another bolt of electricity at the murderous Carnah'lor, screaming as he did. Reno fell back from the assault, which Kaleb let up on as the lights flickered, the craft shaking under the pressure of the magical assault.

"Fine, you can die together! Filthy scum, the lot of you!" Reno pulled from his pocket the collection of small items he'd been gathering, and Kaleb realised what they were: the teleportation Runes that Hayley had used to save his life. Reno raised his hand, palm up, the runes beginning to glow.

"Yteld'guty Jubo!"

"No!"

But it was too late. Reno stepped through the portal, and it quickly closed behind him.

15

It was a good time of year for the markets in Alcanor. The fruit harvests had just come in, and the local taverns cellars were filled with ciders and wines from the region. Raziel picked up a fresh apple from one of the stands and tossed the vendor a silver coin of the local currency. It was enough to buy a crate, but Raziel only wanted the one, and the vendor bowed endlessly, calling the blessings of Nerra down upon him.

Moving through the stalls, he spied wares from as far as Tlaxia in the far south, and from Firenz to the west. Merchants travelled far and wide here, and they found buyers in both the richest and the poorest strata of Alcanorn society, though there were separate markets for each. The rich little liked spending time with the poor and vice versa.

Raziel preferred the poorer markets. The smells were more vibrant, the colours were fanciful, and it felt so much more filled with life! He glanced over at a stall with stoves heated by fire gems, lamps that required no oil, and blankets that would keep you warm in the coldest nights, inside or out, or so the stall owner claimed.

Everything was so much purer here on Nevano, where the

strife of his homeland hadn't reached. Without the interference of Sayada and its war against Nasadia spurring an unnatural leap forward in technology, the nations and peoples of Nevano had advanced at a much slower pace. He was glad that the war with the Carnah'lor had kept the Alliance from reaching out too far from their own borders.

Chewing through his apple, Raziel entered a tavern where he could sample some of the local cider. He had tried many drinks in his long years, but cider remained one of his favourites. Throwing down a gold coin on the bar, he told the barkeep to open a tab until the coin ran out, and to put in a round for the occupants on him. The 'keep shrugged, pocketed the coin, and opened a ledger to keep track of both his spending and that of those making good on his round.

His charity got a cheer from the occupants, though there were some at the back that eyed him with dangerous eyes. Probably cutpurses looking out for easy marks and drunk nobles. They would find neither in him. He took a pitcher of cider from the 'keep and proceeded to find himself a space at a KlakKlak table.

The game consisted of a stack of ceramic disks made up from each participant, the more players, the higher the stack. The disks themselves often had patterns and pictures on them, which led to a big collectors' market, where it was popular. Each player contributed one disk to the stack, and they took turns hitting the stack with the klaker, a square piece made of wood. The aim was to cause disks from the stack to separate and flip from the stack.

If you broke any of the pieces in doing so, you were out of the game, and in this region, the custom held that you would buy the table a round. Any disks you flipped, you kept, and they were added to your collection. If you ran out of disks, you were out, and bought only the remaining players a drink. The idea was that the more you won, the harder it was to continue.

Some players bet, so some versions of KlakKlak had specific values assigned to the disks, so if you lost the disk, you owed the amount of coin assigned to that disk. Others just played for fun. In all games, though, your disks were up for grabs, and that alone had started arguments among the collectors.

Raziel pulled out his KlakKlak pouch and looked around at those on the table. "What's the game, lads?"

Smelling an easy mark, and after seeing his generosity, they grinned among themselves, welcoming him to the table. "Round betting, buy-in is five silver pieces. We were just starting a new game, so you have fortuitous timing, my generous friend." It was a slim-built man, wearing well-made but not extravagant clothing. Raziel surmised that he normally performed quite well, but in low-stakes games like this, he likely spent as much on booze as he did personal gain.

"Five silver, you say? That's a bit rich for a place like this, isn't it?"

The table grumbled at the insult, but the slim man merely smiled, stroking his moustache as he responded. "Not during market days it's not, but if you can't afford it . . ." He gestured towards the door. He was lying. Even if merchants were coming in to play, five silver was a lot, and would get you several nights' stay in a place like this, with meals.

But Raziel just smiled and added five silver to the pile. The patrons of the table seemed happier at that. There was a large man straining the stall he sat on, and a blonde woman who could do well with being introduced to a comb. They each added five silver into the pile, and Raziel suspected that it represented most of their coin. They exchanged glances that all but confirmed that they were in on whatever scam they had that would part this wealthy patron from his bulging purse.

Big gamble on the first round, though, and if they didn't have a sure-fire way to win, their bluff would be made apparent. Each player placed their disk on the stack until it was four high, Raziel's on top. They decided who would go first by rolling a die, and the large gentleman came up with the highest number. He took hold of his klaker, took aim at the stack, and launched the wooden square with practiced skill.

Just before it impacted, Raziel's disk started to glow with a blue light around the perimeter, and an arrow on top with the same glow started pointing in the direction of the slim built man. As the disk flipped into the air at the lightest touch from the klaker, Raziel reached out and snatched his disk from the air. The table exploded with protests.

"What's the big idea!"

"Hey, that's mine!"

"Cheat!"

Oh, the irony in that last statement. Raziel opened his palm to reveal the fading glow and arrow. In a very loud voice so the other patrons could hear, he said, "I think you'll find I'm not the cheater here. You see, my disks have been enchanted to detect when magic is being used on them, and to indicate the direction of flow that the magic originated from. Observe."

Raziel channelled a little wind into the disk to make it float, and it glowed with an arrow pointing at him. "As you can see, if it had been me, it would have indicated thusly."

He took his own stake, plus an extra five silver. "I don't think I'll be playing here, after all. You can argue among yourselves who loses this coin. I'll be keeping them for my trouble."

He downed his drink and left the table. But he felt their eyes on him, and the energy building around the Mage of the group as he struggled to contain his rage. Raziel wondered how many they scammed with that trick, and why they didn't build up the gamble gradually, rather than the all-or-bust that just happened. Confidence had perhaps made them too greedy.

He told the 'keep that he could keep the change from the gold and left the establishment when a rune on a bracelet he wore on his left hand started to glow. Someone or something had breached his barrier at the Citadel. He'd bet money on it being a someone, though, as pretty much all animals steered clear at the sight and sound of his illusion.

Though his staff would probably handle it, he felt the urge to go check it out. The barrier had remained unpenetrated by unsolicited guests for hundreds of years, and he was curious as to who was smart enough to figure it out, or dumb enough to chance It.

With the need for privacy so he could teleport back, he ducked into an alley at the side of the tavern, and he instantly knew that someone was following him. He got about halfway down the alley when the unkempt blonde appeared at the other side, and when he turned back, sure enough, the slim built Mage and the portly man were at the entrance.

"You made us look like fools in there, and not only that, but the 'keep has barred us with the promise to circulate the scam around the area! You're going to empty your purse now to cover our lost earnings, or you'll not live long enough to regret the mistake."

As it turned out, he wasn't the only Mage among them, and all three of them began to channel magic as they awaited his answer. Sighing, Raziel released the glamour spell he'd been holding. Now, where had once stood a tall, pale man with long red hair tied back, now stood a dark blue-skinned demonoid. His hair was still red, but now showed a series of black spikes sweeping back across his head. In certain places, like his chin and under his glowing red eyes, scaled plates were in place of normal skin. The cloak that was wrapped around his shoulder unfurled slightly to reveal wings, and he let the retracted claws in his hands flex a bit.

"I can't help but wonder who is making the mistake today . . ." he mused as panic started to come across the trio's faces. Without another word, they began chanting, channelling various magics to throw fire, ice, and lightning in his direction. Raising a hand in each direction towards them, he threw up barriers that blocked the attacks, dissipating them into the surrounding walls. Luckily, they were made of stone, else there would have been a whole other host of trouble.

"How primitive," he chided as he channelled magic that first locked each of their arms to their sides and their legs together, before pulling them within arm's reach. "You should be more wary of who you pick your fights with in future." He lashed out a clawed hand at the female, removing her throat but letting her hang in the air as she bled out. "For those of you lucky enough to have a future." He plunged his other claw into the slim Mage's chest and crushed his heart in place.

Releasing the magic, he let the bodies drop to the floor, the large man catching himself against a wall before promptly expelling the contents of his stomach onto the floor. "I let you live so that you may learn, and if there are others you encounter that would lead similar lives, you might be able to set them on the right track. Greed leads to this . . ." He gestured at himself, and then at the corpses. ". . . and should not be chased. If fortune comes your way, embrace it, but do not forget to be charitable, for it could cost you more than you are willing to part with in the end."

The man had collapsed into a weeping mess, lying in a mixture of his vomit and the gore spilling out of his former comrades. Nodding vigorously, he seemed unable to find words, and that was fine. Raziel sighed heavily at the blood on his claws and stepped away from the mess he'd created into a slightly cleaner part of the alley. Raising his right arm in front of him, he began to channel magic, and a set of stones encircling that wrist spun out and forward, forming a portal in the air that he stepped through.

When he emerged on the other side, the stones came though the portal and formed back into a band around his wrist. His return platform was on a hill some ways from his Citadel so that he could survey the area and assess the situation should he need to. He was able to see through his own illusion, and everything on the grounds seemed normal. That said, Bill had left his work on one of the decorative trees, and that wasn't like him.

Spreading his wings, he took off into the sky and towards his home to investigate the disturbance.

16

"No . . ."

Allai's sobbing was mostly drowned out by the violent shaking of the craft. She knelt on the floor, cradling the limp body of her older brother.

"Come on, big brother . . . wake up . . ."

Kaleb looked on speechless, finding it difficult to process what had just happened. Reno was a traitor. He had killed Algo. He had nearly killed Kaleb, but Allai had saved them. They were now in a craft he had no idea how to operate, likely plunging to their deaths.

The lights flickered overhead, and a particularly violent shake snapped him out of his stupor. Rising to his feet, he made his way to the cockpit. It was tough going, as the floor was covered in blood, and the unstable footing caused by the tremors through the ship made it so Kaleb had to hold onto the walls the entire way there.

The door had been left open when Reno left. Entering the deceptively simple-looking space, Kaleb gasped at the scene before him. They were close to their destination, if the shimmering dome in the distance was what he thought it was. The craft was indeed losing altitude and at an increasingly alarming rate.

Now, Kaleb may not know anything about Rune Ships, but he did know a thing or two about wind magic. The theory he'd had to allow himself to fly should hold true with a craft. It was just a matter of scale. True, he'd never tested the theory properly —thanks Mel—and he'd never considered lifting anything this large. He was going to need some help. He ran back into the main chamber and crouched by Allai and her dead brother.

"Allai, I'm really sorry. I know you are suffering, but I need your help."

She shook her head wordlessly, rocking back and forth, a vice-like grip on Algo. His blood had covered her own clothing, but she didn't seem to notice or care. Kaleb laid a hand gently on her shoulder and she started but didn't look up.

"Allai, we're both going to die in moments! Please, I need you!"

She didn't seem about to move, so Kaleb did the only thing that came to mind. He channelled wind through him and forced Algo's body from Allai's grip, flinging the corpse unceremoniously against the far side of the cabin.

Allai sprang to her feet, rage and shock flooding her features. Kaleb could feel the magic she began to channel but he grabbed her by both shoulders and shouted in her face.

"ALLAI! WE'RE GOING TO DIE! HELP ME!"

Allai's fists were balled, and plasmatic flames danced around them, but the anger in her eyes softened as she met Kaleb's, and she released the magic.

"Kaleb, I'm sorry. What's happening?"

"The runes are failing. The ship is falling. But I think we can at least slow our descent if we can both channel wind around the ship and bring her down."

"Her?" she asked quizzically.

"It's a Human thi— look, never mind. We don't have time."
He grabbed her arm and dragged her into the cockpit. "Have you
ever formed a magic circle?" She shook her head, but he took
her hand and did his best to explain as clearly as he could.
"Okay, I need you to clear your mind and focus on channelling
your energy to me. I'll use our combined power to slow the
vessel and control its descent. Understand?"

She nodded, and almost immediately he felt a surge of
power going through him. He gasped, feeling physically winded
at the torrent, and struggled to bring it under control. He nearly
fell, but she caught him under the arm and held him steady,
never relenting the stream of magic she sent his way. He'd only
done this before in class, and no-one had been as powerful as
Allai. He could scarce believe the strength she wielded.

The ground was rushing at them, though, and he started to
focus, taking deep breaths and clearing all else from his mind
other than the task at hand. Torrents of wind first filled the
cabin, threatening to burst the ship at its seams, but then it
seemed to shift through the walls as Kaleb created a bubble
around the ship. At first, the ship dropped like a stone, losing its
aerodynamic qualities supplied by the runes' manipulation of
the air. But Kaleb focused on pushing the air beneath them to
create lift.

It was having the desired effect, but they were still coming in
too fast. Knowing that if they hit the ground at these speeds
while standing unprotected in a cabin, they would be liquidized,
he then did the only thing he could think of. Pulling Allai close,
he concentrated on both pushing the nose of the craft up and
creating a bubble of air pressure around the both of them that
would hopefully protect them during the crash.

Just before impact, Kaleb sent a bust of energy at the
window, blowing it out, and then directed all the energy he
could behind their bubble, sending it shooting out at the same

instance the craft smashed into the ground. They shot out like a bullet, and crashed into the ground some distance away, the bubble bursting as they hit.

The spell had served its purpose, though, and though they were now a tangled mess of limbs and thoroughly bruised by the experience, they were alive! Separating themselves from each other, they turned towards the wreckage.

"Algo . . ."

Allai ran toward it, even though there was nothing more she could do for her late brother. Kaleb turned towards their destination. It looked like a crystal ball from here. They had crashed on a high hill, and the Citadel sat in the flat plane below. Even visible as it was, he estimated that it would be at least a few hours' walk getting there. At least it was downhill.

Something caught his eye then, what must be a huge-winged creature flying through the sky directly at the dome, and before long, passing through it. If Zel Cean was indeed in there, what manner of horror was he facing? Could they help him? He turned back towards the ship and resolved to help Allai come to what peace she could before they moved on.

"Right this way, sir. You can wait in the parlour while I fetch the major-domo of the estate." Bill led him through the main entrance of the Citadel, which was positioned up a lengthy flight of stairs. The doors themselves were colossal in size. The entrance hall could have rivalled that of the Nasadian Castle back in its day, with a high, vaulted ceiling and beautifully painted wood panelling covering every inch of the walls and ceiling. There seemed to be scenes detailing the conflict and downfall of Raziel at the hands of the Knights of Nasadia, as well as architecture and buildings from nations around the world. Zel had seen some of them in his own travels, but others were new and wondrous to him.

He saw, painted in vibrant detail, a scene of everyday life in the markets of Alcanor, a place Zel had loved visiting for its nostalgic aesthetic. He still fondly kept a set of KlakKalk disks on the chance that he ever returned there.

Zel couldn't help but wonder if the Necromancer had commissioned the works or had painted them himself. Perhaps they were the work of some of the more creative staff he kept on hand. Bill certainly had an artistic flair. It was hard to imagine the private and secretive Mage bringing in outsiders to paint murals of lands they likely would have thought made up.

He was then taken through to the promised parlour, a lavishly decorated room with high windows overlooking the grounds, long crimson velvet curtains framing each one. Housed in huge pots were large plants, from local fauna to exotic and colourful man-sized flowers, shaped like tall vases, reaching into the air.

In contrast to the main hall, the parlour's walls were covered in red wallpaper accented with golden crosses, with framed paintings hung high and out of reach. These were portraits of people, each one at least the size of Zel himself, and again, they seemed to be of people from around the world. Perhaps those the Necromancer had grown close to in his own travels? For it was certain that this would-be demon of legend was at least as well travelled as Zel himself, and the evidence would imply likely more so.

At two separate locations along the longest wall, opposite the windows, were two grand fireplaces made from a black, smooth stone. Both were at least as tall as his shoulders, and wide enough to provide adequate warmth to a large audience. There were various seats and sofas arranged facing one, coloured in the same design as the walls, while the space around the other seemed bare by contrast. He wondered if these halls had ever seen a celebration or party worthy of the scale.

Bill led Zel to one of the large armchairs before the fireplace, off to one side of which he now noticed a large hutch with many glasses on display in a series of cabinets, and cupboards that he suspected were for storing drinks. This suspicion was proven correct when Bill left and another skeletal figure strode in, fully decked out in fine, freshly pressed butler apparel, and headed straight to the cupboard, opening it.

After a brief period of arranging the bottles in such a way that Zel could easily view them, the butler turned to him and said, in what was probably one of the most practiced High Nasadian accents he'd heard in hundreds of years, "A beverage while you wait, sir?"

Smiling, Zel noticed that one of the bottles was of a brandy that hadn't been made in about as long. "Please. I'll take a glass of the Clio Reserve."

The butler nodded and turned to prepare the drink.

"A good choice. A man of taste, I see." The voice came from the doorway and was the first female he'd heard so far on this strange and unexpected adventure. Turning to face the source, Zel was surprised to see that unlike Bill and the good butler, he would have had no trouble telling this without a vocal cue.

Framed by the doorway was a tall, pale woman with raven hair flowing down her shoulders, with two thin braids extending from near her temples and running down the sides of her head to meet at the back. She was dressed in a stunning gown comprised of a tied bodice upper half coloured in blacks and deep blues and purples, pushing up her ample bosom. A set of large, layered, blue and purple frills, at least a foot deep each, ran from her waist and twisted around the large flared petticoat that was decorated with varying pinks, purples, and blues to accent the ruffles.

She was also slightly translucent and hovered an inch off the ground.

"Master Cean, I presume?" the stunning apparition said as the butler paused in his perpetrations to formally introduce her.

"May I present to you, Lady Marion Bellany Pritchard, major-domo of House Fenrix." He then returned to preparing the drink, which he promptly brought to Zel in a stout, stemmed brandy glass.

Standing and straightening the creases on his green robes as best he could, Zel gave a short bow, before accepting his glass. "My Lady, it is a welcome, yet unexpected, pleasure." Thanking the butler, who took up a position a respectful position to the side, Zel resumed his seat.

The Lady Pritchard glided across the floor and took a seat herself, a slight look on her ghostly face.

"I assure you that a female head of household is not as uncommon as you might believe."

"Oh, rest assured, that is not what I was referring to, but more to the fact that I wasn't expecting such a warm welcome, or any hospitality at all, for that matter."

"Ah, Our Lord's spell, yes. That does keep the usual riffraff out, though you, sir, are not usual by any means. Zel Cean, of House Cean, son of the High Mage Xellon Cean and Grandson of High Mage Ezra Cean. Your family is known well to me, for I once walked the Nasadian courts so very long ago. Yet, here you are, in the flesh and breathing, while I am not. Peculiar."

She did not seem annoyed by their distinct differences in fortune, but more confused that someone from so long ago in her past should show up in her present. Zel vaguely remembered the Pritchard family, and a tale of a teenage daughter that had run off to be with some secret lover. He guessed he'd found what became of her.

"Through my understanding and relationship with magic,

my life has been stretched long beyond the standard years of a Human, much like the Phasmia. If I might be so bold, why is it that you are different from the rest of the staff here?"

A sad smile came across her face as she looked back far into her memories. "I was our master's first. I Joined him when we were but teens, and our love was strong. Was. We spent a happy twenty years together, despite the protests of my family. He had inherited this land and Citadel from his own family and was the last of the Fenrix line. Raziel had been a top graduate of the Astrilian Mage's guild but did not want to be confined by their rules, so we lived here off his family's wealth and were happy.

"I, however, was unable to bear children. We tried. Oh, Dafron, we tried." A playful smile crossed her lips. "We had a lot of fun trying, but I fear my womb must have been cursed. One day, despair took me, and I ran into the woods wanting to be alone. That is when I was killed."

The playfulness was now gone from her features, as a deep sadness crossed them. "I ran straight into them, a group of bandits hiding out in the woods on our land. The things they did to me . . . When Raziel found me, I was already dead, and he razed the woods in his anger, killing every living creature in it.

"In his grief, he turned to the necromantic arts, and searched for a way to restore me to life. He was able to bind my spirit to this place, but found no way to restore my body, which had been burnt down with the forest. The rest, well, is history.

"I hated him for a long, long time after he brought me back, but after a century or so, I came to terms with my lot, and despite his flaws, he loved me. Which is also why he could never bring himself to release me. So, I offered to work as his steward for the household, and I helped bring him out of the darkness that had plagued him."

Zel's eyes widened with understanding. He hadn't expected such a story on first meeting, but felt that after centuries, the lady was unloading on the first person to stumble into their home. "That would explain why I wasn't met with a decrepit castle and hordes of the undead."

Nodding, Lady Pritchard continued, "If you had come in the beginning, that is, indeed, what you would have found. He had raised an army from the dead of nearby towns, and when he'd lost Saria, who he intended to tether my soul to, he erected the barrier in despair and locked himself away in his laboratory.

"Eventually, the staff all died, and he brought them back with their minds intact, but he had not considered the fact that their bodies would rot, and before long, they became the delightful little horrors that you've seen so far. No offence, Gerald."

"None taken, ma'am," the butler, Gerald, said from behind Zel.

"You say you've calmed the darkness inside him, my lady. But it sounds as if you are all still slaves to his desires."

"You mistake my intent, Lord Cean. They are not slaves, and upon request, I will release any one of them."

They all turned to the source of the voice. Standing now in the entrance to the parlour was a man not tall in stature, but not short, with vibrant red hair tucked back, a black cloak fastened about his neck, wearing an expensive set of clothes of a similar period as the good lady.

Unlike the good lady, this man was fully flesh and blood, and by outward appearances, far less demonic than stories had led Zel to believe.

Zel stood to greet the Necromancer as Gerald introduced his lord and master.

"May I introduce High Lord Raziel of House Fenrix, Lord of Fenrix Citadel and its surrounding lands, and protector of the fallen."

"Now, now, Gerald, enough of that. Raziel is fine." He

extended a hand towards Zel, who took it and shook it in the current Astrilian fashion. "They insist on these formal titles. Protector of the fallen, indeed! They would not need protecting had I not risen them in the first place." He gestured. "Please, take a seat."

They both took a seat back at the fireplace and re-joined Lady Pritchard. "My love," he said, sitting near her.

"My Lord," she responded. The response elicited a momentary flash of sadness across the Necromancer's face, but a polite smile returned in short order. She might have forgiven him, but clearly, the love she once had was long gone.

"Now, Zel, what brings you to my home? No one has dared even attempt to come close in hundreds of years."

Zel could sense that Raziel was channelling magic, but he wasn't sure how. Whatever he was doing was subtle, and it made him suspicious. Everything else about the man's body language, though, came across as genuine and relaxed.

"I am studying magic from across the land, across all lands. The way we Humans have understood it for so long is wrong, and I believe that by studying those used by others, I can expand not only my knowledge, but hopefully, one day, the world's.

"I have spent much time in many cultures, and I believe I understand fully the magics of this world, of Gensa, but it is my belief that you were imbued with magic not of this realm, when you made your so-called pact."

Raziel nodded thoughtfully. "You would surmise correctly, and you are right to be dubious about the term pact. I came across an amulet of one of the Dark Lords, Kraeton. He sought to use me to escape, but I instead was able to channel his energy from the amulet and fused it with that of my own. At the time, I was more powerful than I could handle, and in my hubris, I was defeated."

"When the Dark Lords of Cado were later released, a large

portion of that power was torn from me, returning to its owner like iron to a magnet. Even so, the damage was done, and I was left permanently altered."

He suddenly stopped channelling, and the reason for it became clear. He had been holding onto a glamour spell, altering his appearance, and now that he had dropped it, Zel could see Raziel for who he was.

"I have no doubt that taking in the essence of a Dark Lord has its danger, and this is not what I seek. However, if you still have a connection to Cado, and can tap into its power, *that* I would very much like to learn." He was close to what he'd come here for, and he could taste it. Zel had been expecting to fight for this knowledge, to dig through archives of ancient and crumbling tomes to find the answers, but here it was, at the tip of his fingers.

"Yes, and no." Raziel's face became very serious, though his body language was still open. Combined with his appearance, it was rather unsettling. "Yes, I can still tap into the powers of Cado. No, I will not teach you. I will not have another go down the same path as I."

Zel inhaled deeply, prepared to make his case and attempt to win the old Mage over. Zel couldn't help but smile inwardly at that thought: they were only decades apart in age, and both were centuries old. What was old anymore?

Before he could get a word out, though, a light began to glow on Raziel's wrists. "Well, well, it looks as though we have some more guests."

∾

THE INSIDE of the Rune Ship was absolute chaos. Everything that wasn't fixed down had been thrown across the cabin, and a good portion of what had been fixed had been torn out to the same effect. Blood smeared many of the surfaces and made the floor sticky to walk on. For the first time, Allai wished that the Carnah'lor had invented footwear.

It was quite dark, as the runes had all failed on impact, though this didn't much hinder her search, as her race had good vision in low light conditions. She picked her way around upturned chairs that had once been bolted in place and was careful not to tread on the broken glass. Carnah'lor feet could endure a lot, but if a larger piece pierced the leathery layer on the pads of her feet, it wouldn't be good.

She eventually found her brother's corpse behind the bar. She fell to her knees, still filled with grief. It was the first time since the attack that she had acknowledged that this was, indeed, a corpse. Her brother's spirit was now one with Gensa.

"Allai! Are you okay up there?" Kaleb's voice came floating up from outside the ship. She felt a pang of guilt for having completely forgotten about him once they were safely on the ground and had not considered that he would have been unable to clear the distance to the cockpit window that had been their egress earlier. All other entrances would be inaccessible due to the failed runes and were half buried, in any case.

Getting up, she headed back to the cockpit and looked down. Kaleb was staring up at her, and he looked concerned. Then he looked upside down. Upside down? What? "Allai!" The world had started spinning, and now she was looking up at the cockpit as a cushion of air buffeted around her. Now, she was looking up at Kaleb.

". . . what?"

Kaleb was kneeling beside her, tearing off a strip of cloth from his sleeve. "The wound you took from Reno, you've been bleeding this entire time. You must have lost so much blood!"

She reached up and touched her face. There was a long gash carved diagonally from her right cheek, over the bridge of her nose, and ending above her left eye. She had been lucky that it hadn't taken out either of her eyes.

Her sobbing and rubbing at her eyes must have kept them free from the oozing of blood enough that she had forgotten about it, and she felt foolish for that fact.

"Close your eyes," Kaleb said, and he placed his hand over her face. Softly, he said, "Keyot," and water started to flow from his palm onto her face, washing the wound, as well as clearing a good amount of the blood from her face. Taking the strip of cloth, he looped it around her head and secured it tightly against the gash, stemming the flow of blood.

"That should do for now, but we'll need to get you some proper dressing. Do you know if there is food and supplies in the ship?"

"Yes, it's normally stocked for extended stays in the capital. Algo hated the food they would prepare. We need to get his body out of there. Our customs . . ."

"I think we need to get you some strength back and then we need to head to the Citadel. If Zel is there, I think he might be in some trouble. Can you sit up? It will help stem the bleeding."

She levered herself into a sitting position, though she still felt dizzy. The adrenaline that had been pumping through her since the fight was starting to wear off, and the pain from the injuries was starting to set in.

"How do you know so much about healing?" she asked.

"Well, I don't really, but all students are taken through basic first aid. When you have a lot of hot-headed and eager students playing with magical forces, it pays to have everyone aware of what needs to be done if an accident occurs."

Kaleb stood and gazed up at the craft, looking like he was contemplating trying to climb the smooth surface into the cockpit.

"You'll never make it. I only can because I can jump that

high. Let me . . ." She tried to stand, but pain racked her limbs and head, and she slumped back into a seated position. Kaleb hadn't seemed to notice as an idea had clearly popped into his head.

"I wonder." Suddenly, air started to swirl around him, and he launched into the air like a rocket. "WOOOAH!!" Arms flailing, he arched into the cockpit and landed with a thud. There was silence for a few breath-catching heartbeats, then: "I . . . I'm okay!"

Allai let herself breath again. The man was insane. A few moments passed and he appeared back at the blown-out window. He began lowering some supply pouches in pockets of air, and then what looked like panels he'd stripped off the walls, and other assorted items. What was he planning? He'd lowered one of the supply pouches within her reach, and she found some Juba cakes, small, flat, round cakes with the pureed flesh of a Jubjub layered on top and covered with chocolate. She quickly devoured a few of them.

After a short while, he lowered Algo's body. As her brother's vessel alighted on the ground a short way off, she noticed that his clothes had been straightened up, and that some effort had been made to wash off the blood, though he was not wet. Had Kaleb washed him and then used wind magic to dry him? It was a sweet gesture, but a pointless one. For the next steps in Algo's journey, the cleanliness of his vessel was unimportant.

Next, he brought himself back down. After the many items he'd lowered, he was now quite practiced on descent; it was a lot smoother than how he'd entered the craft. Apparently satisfied that Allai was getting the food she needed, as she tore into a second pouch of Juba cakes, Kaleb began arranging the items he'd taken out.

"What are you doing?" she asked, unable to fathom the purpose of the items.

He smiled but remained focused on his task. "Making us a hover car . . . sort off. More of a hover sled? I know the principles. I've studied how our air cars work. This should help us get to the Citadel a lot faster."

"You're insane. The one time I get to hang out with a Human, and he's got JubJub for brains!"

"Delicious as that sounds, trust me."

She shrugged. Having rested and consumed some sugar, she could feel some strength return to her, though she still felt very weak. Slowly, she did manage to get to her feet this time, moving over to her brother before sinking to her knees again. In barely a whisper, she began to chant the Jubian last rites.

"From Gensa came all things, and to Gensa, all things must go. Gensa gives to us Jubo, and Jubo gives us shelter, food, security. In all we do, we take, and we give, balance in everything. As the flesh of the fruit nourishes us, so our flesh nourishes Gensa.

"Gensa, take and hold dear Algo's spirit as you hold all spirits, and may it nourish your life as his body shall nourish the land, the birds, and the animals. In life and in death, he is yours."

After she had finished, she sat in silence for a few moments, and then turned to Kaleb and immediately covered her eyes as he appeared to be welding using magic, the bright light stunning her momentarily. When her vision had recovered, she peered through her fingers to confirm he had stopped. What she saw made her jaw drop. He had fused several large panels together to create the bed of the craft. There were also two chairs welded to this bed with enough space behind them to load supplies. He'd welded sides around the supply area to help prevent anything from falling out, and he'd repurposed some curtains from the sleeping quarters to use as covering for it.

It looked crude, and she had no idea how he intended to get it to go anywhere, but it was impressive. "How on Gensa did you manage to construct that so quickly? I had only looked away for moments?!"

Kaleb lit up with pride at his creation and handiwork. "I'm a wind and water specialist. I can manipulate many things at the same time. It comes in handy when working on dig sites and having to ensure that you have light, that the ceiling isn't going to fall on you while you remove rubble, and that you're not damaging anything of potential value."

"I . . . well, then, how is this going to work?"

"First, let's get everything loaded. Shall we load Algo first? Then, we can load the supplies around him?"

"That won't be necessary. I have performed last rites, and his body is now merely an empty vessel and will nourish Gensa."

"You mean you're going to just leave him for the birds? Don't you want to bury him?"

"Bury? No, this is our way. Gensa gives and Gensa takes back. Algo is with Gensa now, and his body will feed her creations."

Kaleb looked like he found this hard to follow but didn't argue. She was grateful for this, as it would be all too easy for him to try and impose his own beliefs and customs on her, but he held his tongue. This was a great sign of respect.

"Okay, I'll load the supplies. You get yourself strapped in." Before he'd even finished the sentence, he was gliding items into the back of the makeshift vessel, and once they were all in place, he covered and secured the entire area with the curtains and rope that he'd found from somewhere inside. Allai had no choice but to trust him, and she got into one of the seats, using the emergency harnesses that had deployed during their emergency landing to secure herself in place.

Kaleb joined her shortly, and strapped himself in. "I haven't had the time to enchant the vessel to fly traditionally, so I'm going to manually manipulate the air around us to carry us over the ground. It's nowhere near the size of the Hopper, so I should be able to manage this without your aid this time. Please try to relax and gain your strength during the trip."

The whole thing sounded insane to her, but she nodded. "And you're sure that this is going to work?"

He smiled sheepishly. "No, not at all." As her eyes went wide, he started to channel wind around them, and the vessel lifted into the air.

"Kaleb!"

He didn't respond, though, as the craft suddenly shot forward at an incredible rate, and they were pressed back into their seats. The route was mostly downhill and was blessedly clear of large rocks or trees that might cause them problems. Allai was having trouble keeping her eyes open in the torrent of the wind, and she hoped that Kaleb had thought about that and was countering it in some way so he could see where they were going.

"We're . . . going . . . too . . . fast!!" Allai called, but the wind was taking her words, and Kaleb seemed to not respond. Looking sideways at him, she saw he was also struggling with the wind. foolish man! He seemed intent on getting them killed somehow with his crazy use of magic.

The ground had levelled out now, but their momentum and the winds propelling them kept them going at high speeds. Using her hands to try and shield some of the torrent of wind blowing at her, she tried to look forward, and she screamed in a panic. Kaleb had seen it too.

"KALEB! THE BARRIER!!"

He let all the wind from behind them die and started focusing on blasting wind in front of them. The huge dome covering the estate rushed at them, the gnawing and clawing hordes of undead humans fighting over each other to get out. Allai could swear she saw the hunger in their eyes.

Allai started throwing her own energy in front of them, but it wasn't helping—they were going too fast! Was this how she was to die? Either crushed against a barrier or eaten by unnatural creatures of death?

She released all her magic in panic and tried to cover her head with her arms just before they impacted.

But there was no impact.

There was nothing. Was she dead? Had she blocked the memory of being torn to pieces at the end of her life, and now she was in the afterlife? No, she was still in *far* too much pain for that. Slowly, she relaxed and opened her eyes, looking around.

There were no zombies. There was no desolation. Instead, there were clear meadows and a wall with a hedge that stretched to either side, and that was about it.

"Huh . . ." said Kaleb next to her, having about gathered himself as well. "That was . . ."

"We're never doing that again!"

"But it worked! I'm sure I can improve on it next ti—"

"NO!"

"Well, what do we have here?"

That last one was not them, and they turned as one to gaze at the demonic being standing atop the wall, two massive wings folding down and around its shoulders.

"Staying for dinner?"

Kaleb and Allai looked at each other and screamed.

17

It was always so much better when they struggled. The large woman, whom he held aloft by her head in his clawed hand as he drained the life force from her, kicked and punched fiercely, but before long, as always, the struggles grew less and less until the withered husk that remained fell limp. Mystral let the corpse fall among the others.

She had been the last, and he had saved her for dessert, for she bore in her an untapped well of magical potential that she likely was never aware of. If she had been, she'd have surely fought back with more than fists and kicks.

Loud music pumped out of devices on the wall, and colourful lights flashed on and off, but the room still felt silent compared to the last few hours' fun. When he had entered the so-called club, the bodies had been heaving from wall to wall, and he had smiled, then still in the guise of Janet.

After a brief probe to determine where all the possible routes of escape might be, he channelled some magic into sealing off all the entrances, exits and windows. Then, he feasted.

Some tried to fight back, but many fled in fear as he would

take them two at a time, draining them into husks. A pleasant surprise had come when a Phasmia had been present and attempted to counteract his own magic. She had been controlling the music system, it seemed. Perhaps the music was of her creation? Either way, she did not prove much of a challenge. Phasmia never were much in the way of fighters.

She had, in truth, been the largest font of power of the evening, but he could not save her in the same way he could the ignorant ones. They had posed no threat, whereas the Phasmia might have been able to break one of the seals, and that would have been bad. So, he took *great* pleasure in draining her considerable life force early on.

After that, he was able to move faster, feeling more invigorated and complete than he had in a long time. It still took a couple of hours still to get through the few hundred souls present. This, though, was largely due to him taking his time and enjoying himself, being able to let loose, if you will.

Gazing up through the windows high on the walls of the nightclub, Mystral could see that dawn was approaching, and so released the spell on the doors and headed out the main entrance. What greeted him there made him smile. It seemed that someone had managed to get the word out about his work.

Lining the street out front were dozens of vehicles belonging to the force known as the Astrilian Metropolitan Police. They all had those quaint metal rod weapons pointed at him. Much like inside the club, lights were flashing out here, but they were all on the vehicles that surrounded him.

"GET ON THE GROUND, NOW, WITH YOUR HANDS ON YOUR HEAD! YOU ARE SURROUNDED!"

The blaring voice came from a man behind one of the central vehicles, a device held in his hand to amplify his voice pointed at Mystral. He looked about at the surrounding buildings and sure enough, he spotted more of these police in windows and on roof tops, all with weapons pointed at him.

Mystral let his wings expand around him in an attempt at intimidation, and it must have worked, for they opened fire immediately. Rather than let the projectiles hit him this time, he erected a barrier around him, and they vaporised harmlessly against it.

What wasn't so harmless was the fireballs that started crashing into the barrier. So, they had Mages among them. Clever. The fireballs were joined by a barrage of lightning strikes, and Mystral knew he needed to handle the situation quickly. His meal had gone a long way towards restoring some much-needed energy, but it was as a starving man led to a banquet: it would sate him for now, but it would take time to regain full strength.

He aimed a finger at the man with the voice amplifier and imitated the weapons by stating loudly, "BANG!" Immediately, the ten or so officers in the direct vicinity, and three of the vehicles, found themselves rushing very quickly to occupy a space the size of an atom, as he'd repeated his gravity trick.

This caused a brief respite, as the dense gravity well caused everyone to have to steady themselves or be pulled off their feet or out of their perch. Much to Mystral's glee, several snipers fell to their grisly deaths, losing their footing where precariously perched.

The flashing lights were playing to his strength, though, as where there was light, there was shadow. Mystral faded into his own shadow and began appearing directly in the darkness his victims cast each time the sirens flashed. Each time he appeared, he tore limbs off, severed heads, or disembowelled those he came up against, all the while laughing manically.

"Kill the lights! The lights!" someone shouted. Clever little bastard. A rain of lightning came down to hit all the sirens, destroying the strobing lights instantly, and Mystral suddenly found his mobility severely reduced. Especially as the Mages seemed to have figured his trick out so completely, they were now artificially bathing the area in constant light, drastically reducing the number of shadows.

"Well, if it's going to be like that—" Before he could finish his thought, ten portals opened up in a circle around him, and out stepped a cadre of Mages, all quickly linking hands, and immediately erecting a barrier around the Dark Lord. They'd formed a circle, sharing each other's strength to allow one to cast with a greater pool of magical energy.

"We have you now. Surrender, and you may yet live, Mystral." This was clearly coming from the Mage leading the circle. Mystral could feel the pressure coming from him. As should be the case when Mages sync'd like this, the strongest should be in control.

It seemed they knew his name as well. Interesting. Someone must have recognised him during his departure from the College.

"That would be a mistake." Raising his clawed hand, he pointed it at the Mage directly opposite this leader and called forth a concentrated beam of light that pummelled into the barrier. If his magic was as base as these Humans', they would consider what he was doing a combination of all the magical disciplines into one attack. But magic wasn't so basic, and that of Cado held great destructive power.

"We need to push the barrier in, cut off his flow! Give me more of your strength!" They started moving in towards him, and Mystral merely gazed into the eyes of their leader while focusing his beam opposite.

"I can't . . . hold it . . . any longer . . ."

"No, don't give up! We nearly have him!"

The barrier suddenly failed, and the beam crashed through

the Mage that Mystral had correctly guessed was their weakest link. Where he once stood, now only legs remained. He'd also taken out the arms of the Mages standing either side in the circle, who were now screaming as blood gushed out of them.

Mystral extended his wings, grabbed hold of one of the screaming Mages by the face, and powered off into the air. Seconds later, he let the lifeless husk drop among its comrades before making his escape proper.

THAT WAS TOO CLOSE. He'd gotten cocky with his success in the club and didn't consider the presence of Mages. He'd also not considered that someone inside may have tried to contact someone outside the building. He knew about those damn communication devices, phones they were called, and he still had the one he'd stolen, but the mere concept of them still went beyond his experience. In his day, you trapped a group of help-less prey and that was the end of it.

Luckily, he'd sustained no direct hits, but he'd had to funnel a lot of his power into breaking free of the barrier, and he didn't want to chance another encounter with them. They were smart, and they adapted quickly.

He would need to enact his plan soon, and now he was armed with the information to make it happen. Using the phone he had liberated from Barry, he'd studied the history surrounding the V'Udol. The Humans were indeed resourceful and had discovered that the affliction of the bloodsuckers wasn't a curse, but a parasite. As such, they had developed a vaccina-tion against it that stopped the larval stage of V'Udol from taking root in their victims.

It seemed that adult V'Udol were unaffected by the vaccine, and could still feed, but the publicity of their existence meant those that were careless were exterminated, and those that were careful were extra so.

This would make the turning of new V'Udol nearly impossible and would rely entirely upon their ability to carry children naturally, something they could only do once every decade.

By manipulating shadows, Mystral had managed to get to an alley between two of the large buildings unseen and took on the guise of one of his victims from the nightclub, an attractive young lady. He now spared some energy to materialize the clothes as well, not having a set to wear after bursting out of Janet's when he had resumed his normal form.

He needed to find the Wandering Council and convince them he could help. Scrolling through articles on the V'Udol, he came across a few very interesting ones that piqued his interested, such as:

No-Vaxers on the Rise: Anti Vaccination movement says 'Taken' Vaccines cause Paralysis.

IT HAS BEEN close to fifty years since 'The Taken' (or the self-proclaimed V'Udol [vej-OOdol], meaning The Chosen in the Old Tongue) were discovered to be parasitic organisms that prey on Humankind, and forty since the vaccine was developed and made universally available, preventing the parasites from taking hold in new hosts.

Now, though, we have a group calling themselves 'No-Vax' with the slogan, 'My Body, My Rules!' claiming that the Taken Vaccine is causing mild to full paralysis. They claim that they have irrefutable evidence supporting this, yet when pressed, only anecdotal evidence was produced.

"My doctor told me that all vaccines are harmful, and that

humans have lived for thousands of years without poisoning our bodies with these drugs!" said one man from Lower Erato.

Another claimed, "They actually inject you with the parasites! That has to be bad for you! Not in my body, they don't! Not for my children!".

There is no scientific evidence to back their claims, and in the months since their group has started, several people have gone missing, all of whom are reported to have missed their booster appointments.

MYSTRAL SCROLLED THROUGH, reading several articles in the same vein, smiling to himself. Those clever bastards had found a way to turn mass hysteria against those that sought to purge them. He'd bet his last ounce of magic that they were behind this. He was searching for any indication of where the organization might be based when someone came up the alley at one end.

"Oh, my, what's this? A lost little lamb?" A woman, appearing to be in her thirties, strutted down in Mystral's direction. She wore jeans and a loose-fitting T-shirt and carried herself with huge amounts of confidence. Mystral returned the phone to his pocket dimension and smiled at the woman, causing her demeanour to immediately shift.

"What you smiling at, bitch? You think I'm your friend?" She was in front of Mystral in a flash, moving at inhuman speeds. Excellent, he'd been correct on his suspicion, and this would save him a lot of time. "How about I bite that smile right off your face?"

She grinned, exposing a mouth filled with filed-down teeth, and licked one of them almost seductively with her tongue as she leant in closer to Mystral. In his current form, she was a few inches taller.

The grin quickly left her face, though, as Mystral grabbed her by her neck and launched her into the wall opposite.

"What the—"

She didn't have time to finish the expletive as Mystral was on top of her in a blink of an eye, illusionary boot crushing her chest.

"Greetings, *chosen one.*" Mystral increased the pressure, though his voice was honey sweet as he spoke. "It would seem our meeting is *most* serendipitous, because, you see, I need to meet with your masters."

"Fuck you!" She spat up at him, anger and pride clouding the fact that he was far stronger than she was. He wondered what her 'gift' was. Stupidity? Foul language?

Focusing energy around the wretched creature, he stood back and forced her to her feet with the flow of magic, holding her in place so he could speak to her at eye level.

"You have two options. One, you lead me to the Wandering Council, I make it so the Taken Vaccine is no longer effective, and we all get along. Or two, I kill you and find them anyway, but you don't get to take part in the brave new world that I'll be carving for your kind."

"That's bullshit! No one can do that."

Mystral let his guise drop, now towering over the V'Udol before him. "I can, and I will, and then blood will flow in the streets of this accursed city."

THE V'UDOL WAS CALLED ALLISON, and she now sat opposite Mystral on a carriage of an underground mass-transit device she called the Tube. It flitted along a set of tracks at high-speed, stopping at various destinations, picking up and dropping off passengers. She had paid.

As it happens, Allison's gift was the ability to tell if someone was lying, and Mystral's glamour had been setting off her senses regardless of what he said. To her, he was a liar. But once he'd dropped the façade, she could see his words were true. An interesting gift, and one that likely served her well surviving in the world as she did.

The entire cocky demeanour had left her now, and she sat quietly with her head bowed. Mystral was once again in his guise, and he suspected the constant blaring lie was uncomfortable for her. It probably didn't help that she knew what he was, and that he could kill everyone on this contraption with barely a second thought. Their time would come; for now, discretion was needed.

They rode until they were at a stop in Little Erato, interestingly, though unsurprisingly, the same place as a lot of the commenters in those articles. It made sense they would be near the source. They walked around a commercial area where the buildings were a lot lower to the ground than they were in the centre of this colossal city. It felt a lot more comfortable, though still quite alien at the same time.

Allison led them out into a residential area, not far from the commercial district, and up to a large house that looked out of place among a lot of smaller ones. Outside, there were a lot of banners, posters and other propaganda regarding the Anti-Taken Vaccination campaign, and a few people ran in and out. So, this was the headquarters of No-Vax.

It seemed that anyone could enter the premises, as Allison and Mystral walked in without challenge. The first floor seemed to have been converted into an open plan office with young clerks at desks taking calls and presumably working on various campaign material. There were screens around the walls indicating various progress and targets that Mystral didn't understand or care about.

Allison led him through to an office located at the back of the ground floor. Inside sat an extremely attractive man, looking to be in his late twenties, and dressed in what Mystral assumed to be a very fine suit for this day and age. Clothes looked so plain and drab compared to when he'd last been free that he was having trouble telling what fashionable was compared to what was common wear.

A plaque on the man's desk read 'A. Colthorn, Chairman of the Board.' Mystral had no idea what a chairman was. Perhaps it had something to do with sitting at this desk all day? Whatever its meaning, Mystral recognised the Clan name, and he had a fair idea that he was standing before one of the family heads.

"Allison! A delight as always. It's been a while, and you have a guest! Please, take a seat." He gestured at the two seats in front of his desk. When they didn't move, Mystral could see Mr. Colthorn drop the smile ever so slightly for the faintest of seconds before catching himself.

"Sir, I think what she has to say will need to be heard by the whole board."

Colthorn flicked his wrist, and the door behind them closed. He let his smile drop. "Sit. Now." Allison did, but Mystral remained standing. Mr. Colthorn was attempting to assert authority, and at the mention of the board, he had decided to drop all pretence of civility.

"Unless you head the council, Colthorn, I suggest you summon them from whatever hole they have crawled into this century and bring them before me."

Colthorn's eyes narrowed at Mystral's words. It seemed he'd managed to hit some chords with his words. As far as Colthorn was concerned, though, he could be some upstart Vejling trying to start trouble.

"I am not in the habit of taking demands from some street junkie. Now, sit down." Colthorn began to rise slowly, menacingly, from his seat, but without moving a muscle, Mystral forced him back into his seat, using some of his precious reserves.

"You mistake me, good sir. I am no junkie." As he spoke, Mystral made sure that the shadows crept over the windows of the office, both those to the main work floor, and the ones to the outside world behind Mr. Colthorn.

"I am the son of Loth'ar, creator of my world."

His shadows now began to strangle the light in the room. Allison scrambled out of the way as the chairs in front of Colthorn's desk flew to the sides. Mystral slowly let his glamour fade as he took a step forward.

"Eldest of the Guardians of Cado."

His guise had entirely dropped now. Colthorn's desk launched out of his way, and the V'Udol jumped to his feet, his chair flying back behind him.

"I am the Dark Lord of Shadows."

Now fully returned to his original form, he dominated the room, his wings unfurling and touching the walls on either side.

"I am Mystral, and I have a deal for you."

18

Zel had quickly left the Citadel in chase of Raziel, though he was incapable of keeping up with the Gensa-Cado hybrid. He wasn't sure if that was technically the correct term, but with only one other example in all known history that came even close to being what Raziel now was, it would have to do.

He was followed by Lady Pritchard, who he suspected could keep up with her former lover just fine but chose to keep a closer eye on their guest instead. He couldn't imagine that they perceived him as a threat but understood the need for prudence.

Zel stopped halfway along the main path to get his bearings and looked around for the Necromancer. The grounds were huge, and with Raziel's speed, he could have managed to get to any part of it in the time Zel had taken to just leave the main hall. Luckily, he was still in sight, and Zel spotted him standing on the exterior wall to the west of the Citadel and began heading over.

It was the first time Zel had seen Raziel's wings unfurled. He'd read the reports from the time surrounding the battle against him, but the sight was still something. They reminded him much of the Dark Lords he had once fought so many years ago, which was hardly surprising given the source of this man's power.

Hearing screaming coming from the direction of the Necromancer, Zel quickened his pace. Had some fools stumbled through the barrier not knowing where they were? How could they miss it? Who even lived out this way? In his travels of the surrounding area, Zel had come across no settlements, and though he could have missed a hunter's cabin, the local woods all resided inside the walls of the Citadel, not outside them.

No, it was more likely that whoever was out there intended to be there, but had not intended, or anticipated, the vision that stood before them. Anyone meeting the Necromancer in his true form was likely to have a heart attack.

As he got closer, he could hear the Necromancer laughing through the screams. What was he doing to these people? Zel had thought he'd left his darkness behind him. Could he really be taking pleasure in someone else's torture or demise? Was this the true face of Raziel Fenrix?

Summoning wind around him, Zel lifted himself up to the top of the wall to stand next to Raziel, and what he saw before him only added to the list of bizarre things he'd encountered today. There, sitting in what looked to be some hastily constructed sled, sat a Human and a Carnah'lor, strapped into a couple of Rune Ship seats.

In their panic, they seemed to be fumbling with the restraints and were unable to free themselves. Raziel seemed to be greatly amused by either their struggle or their panic. Perhaps both. At least it was true mirth, even if it was at the expense of the poor sods that had stumbled upon his domain.

They caught sight of Zel, and both stopped screaming immediately, their fear replaced by what appeared to be disbelief. Or shock? Raziel looked from the group to Zel. "Do you know these people, Zel?"

Shaking his head, confused, Zel responded, "No, can't say that I do."

The man with the caramel skin and dark hair managed to release himself from his restraints first. He stood forward, eyes locked on Zel with a sense of purpose. "Zel Cean, we have been sent by Galrei to find you. You may be our only hope."

Thoughtfully stroking his greying blue beard, Zel turned to Raziel. "Sounds interesting. Should we invite them inside for dinner?"

"Hah! I tried that, and they screamed! And I haven't even invited you yet, you presumptuous old git!"

"Well, you seemed in such a good mood, I figured I'd try my luck. Rationing on the road can get old quick at my age. And look who's talking!"

Zel wasn't quite sure what was happening, but he was suddenly finding himself bonding with this man. He'd expected to find a demonic monster gone bitter from centuries huddled away, but instead, he'd found a kindred spirit, who had travelled far and wide, as he had, and was probably one of the only living *mostly* humans from the time of his youth. He *wanted* to like this man.

The boy below seemed unsure what to say, and the white-furred Carnah'lor, now free of her own restraints, seemed equally speechless. Zel let the wind carry him down to their level to greet them.

"He does that a lot better than you do," the Carnah'lor jibed the boy.

"He's hundreds of years old. He's had more time to practice!"

"Ahem." Zel looked at them both with an amused look on his face. "As you already know who I am, I'll skip the introduction, but if I might know who I am addressing?"

They both bowed their heads slightly. "Sorry, sir. I am Kaleb Andris, a student at the Mage's College of Astrilia."

"And I am Allai of Jubo, an honour guard to Galrei."

They could understand each other, which meant that Zel's enchantment he'd set up in Jubo was still working, and that its effects lingered outside of the forest. Excellent. He'd likely have to make them a set of translation earrings, though, before the day was out, unless he wanted to serve as translator on the morrow.

"Nice to meet you both! Raziel, I take it you give them leave to enter?"

"It didn't stop you from entering! But yes, I do." He looked behind him. "Marion, dearest, can you show them to the main gate and guide them to the dining room?"

"I swear, Raziel Fenrix, you call me dearest, my love, or darling one more time, and it'll be the last you see of me." She phased through the wall and appeared in front of the young pair.

"AAAAHHH!!!" they both screamed.

"Oh, come now. You've seen his hideous face—"

"Hey!"

". . . and you still find me that alarming? Pull yourselves together and follow me."

Something about her curt tone silenced the two, and they followed the apparition around to the main gate with stunned expressions on their face.

Zel zipped back to the top of the wall, landing next to Raziel again.

"So, what's for dinner?"

～

Kaleb and Allai walked stunned, side by side, following the Lady Marion Bellany Pritchard, as she had formally introduced herself. They were being led by a ghost to dinner with a demon and a centuries-old wizard. To top it off, there was a naked skeleton tending to the estate's topiary who tipped a non-existent hat in their direction. Kaleb was more than certain that after the events of the last two days, he was going to need to seek the services of a therapist!

"Ah, Madam Pritchard, more guests, I see? An unusually busy day. Is the Master having a party?"

"One would think, wouldn't they, Bill? No, they are all uninvited hooligans, imposing themselves on our good nature."

"Um, well, we didn't mean to intrude, ma'am," Kaleb tried, but Lady Pritchard seemed to be in a foul mood, and merely scoffed. As they approached the main entrance, they were both quite winded by the time they got to the top of the stairs, barely recovered as they were by the ordeal they had recently been through.

They stopped to catch their breath, and Lady Pritchard turned to see what was keeping them. Her face then softened as she glided back over to them. "I am sorry for my snippiness, but that man infuriates me. We haven't been lovers for centuries, but he insists on his ridiculous pet names. One of these days . . ."

She trailed off, her attention seeming to wander as she imagined whatever fanciful comeuppance she might enact on the Lord Necromancer of the Citadel. As they straightened, her attention snapped back to them.

"I have no idea what it is that you've been through, but I can see you're both in a poor state." Lady Pritchard moved close to Allai and scrutinized the crude bandage wrapped around her face. "Oh . . . Oh, dear, no, this won't do. Gerald!"

"M'Lady."

A very well-dressed skeleton suddenly stepped out of the shadows, causing them all to jump, and causing Kaleb to wonder at the comparative nudity of Bill outside.

"Gerald! Don't do that! You about gave me a heart attack!"

"You're dead, M'lady," he said in the most deadpan, droll voice. Kaleb couldn't tell if he was joking or not.

"Hmph! Yes, well, enough of that. Take this young man and get him a bath and a change of clothes. I'm going to address the young lady's head wound, lest it get infected."

Lady Pritchard could apparently exert force on the living world, which came as a surprise to both Kaleb and Allai, as she started shepherding Allai toward a room somewhere off to the left.

"This way, sir," Gerald said, turning and heading up the grand staircase splitting the entrance hall. "I will show you to your rooms for the night. Please relax while I draw you a bath."

The staircase split into two directions, and they took the right, leading into a long corridor with many doors coming off either side. Given the height and scale of the Citadel, Kaleb suspected that at least some of them were further staircases, but it seemed he wouldn't find out right now, as Gerald opened a door leading into a grand suite. The first thing that struck him was how immaculate the room was; he'd expected the place to be in some level of disrepair or neglect given they appeared, so far, to have only one living resident.

That couldn't be further from the truth, though, as there wasn't a speck of dust to be seen, not a sheet, curtain or pillow out of place. On top of that, it was literally the most luxurious room he had ever seen, and he'd been invited to dinner at the dean's private suite at the College. This, however, made that look like a cheap dorm room.

The walls were lined with deep blue silk wallpaper with a

dark oak dado rail running the perimeter and striped black and blue wallpaper on the bottom half. The windows were floor to ceiling, and the curtains framing them were a deep black. There were also wall sconce lights that were powered by light crystals and could be controlled by a switch by the door, mimicking the electric designs of the city.

There were various sofas and chairs littered around the room, a tall dark oak bookcase filled with ancient-looking volumes, and a reading chair by a lit fire. How had they known to light the fire? Did they always have one going?

Various potted plants, as well as a few decorative vases on pedestals, also littered the room. He guessed that each was likely worth more than he'd hope to earn in his lifetime.

There were another two doors leading off this main chamber, one of which Gerald disappeared through, and Kaleb could hear the start of running water. He would get no prizes for guessing that was the bathroom. The other room was a bedroom and contained the most comfortable-looking four-poster bed he'd ever seen. Its wooden frame was black, and the curtains hanging from it were the same design as those on the window in the main room.

"Erm, I don't want to get anything dirty, Gerald. How's the bath coming along?" Kaleb called through to the bathroom, feeling very self-conscious about the state he was currently in. He realised that his clothes, as well as being quite dirty, were also badly torn in places from when he'd burst air out of all his pores.

"Not long now. You may strip and leave your clothes by the door. I will dispose of them. If you are uncomfortable with your body, then there is a robe in the dresser." As it happened, Kaleb was perfectly comfortable being naked around others. They shared dorms at the college, and it was just a fact of life you had to get used to. He stripped down to his boxers, throwing his trousers and shirt into a heap on the floor.

As he exited into the main chamber, Gerald was waiting by the door. "Your bath is ready." He gestured at the door while his eyeless sockets stared at him. As Kaleb moved through the room, Gerald's creepy stare followed him.

"Is there something wrong, Gerald?"

"Apologies, sir. It's just, you are so very much alive and . . . fleshy." He paused, staring a moment longer. "I miss my body at times, but we don't usually have anyone but the master to remind us of our unusual circumstances . . ."

The butler's tone was more whimsical than Kaleb had expected from their introduction, and he wondered if the skeletal man was prone to mood shifts. He couldn't imagine what it would be like to live this existence.

Gerald seemed to snap out of it sharply, though, and resumed his matter-of-fact nature. "You had better get on with your bath, unless you want the water to run cold, sir. I shall have a fresh set of clothes ready for you once you are done. You are welcome to keep the new clothes."

"Don't you need to know my size?" Kaleb wondered.

"They'll fit," Gerald assured him before turning on a heel and leaving the room.

Kaleb entered the bathroom and was again taken aback by the sheer luxury of it all. The tub was large enough for at least four people to sit comfortably, and there was a separate shower unit hooked up, should he desire. It was all very modern-looking for a place that had supposedly been cut off from society for hundreds of years. Did they actually have working plumbing and heating, or was the Necromancer employing magic to work everything?

It would be fascinating to find out, and Kaleb couldn't help but ponder the idea of remaining in a place like this for an extended period of study. Perhaps once the world had been saved . . . Kaleb stepped up to the tub, removing his boxers, and lowered himself in. Gerald had even been as kind as to add bubbles to the mixture.

Immediately, Kaleb felt the hot water having a positive effect on his muscles, loosening knots he didn't know he had, and seeping the troubles of the past two days out of him. It was amazing what good a hot bath could do, and this was exactly what he'd needed.

I wonder how Allai is doing, he mused as he let the rest of his worries melt away, if only for now.

FOR A HOUSEHOLD of walking corpses and incorporeal beings, they sure had a decent supply of first aid equipment on hand. Lady Pritchard had cleaned, salved, and re-dressed Allai's wound in short order. On top of that, they had given her a private suite, with a bath big enough for a Carnah'lor to use, though the bed seemed to be of human design, and she wasn't sure how she'd feel about that later.

Her blood-stained clothes had been taken away and replaced with a set of clothes that were both surprisingly functional and her size. They weren't Jubian in style, and they didn't quite match what Kaleb had worn, though they weren't far off. She liked the green of the jacket, though the undershirt could do with less frills, especially around the neck.

Now, she was washed, dressed, and mended, though. They were instructed to meet for dinner in the main dining hall. Where that was was anyone's guess in a place like this. As she exited her rooms, Kaleb emerged from a door farther down the hall.

"Ah, Allai! I see they've given you similar treatment!" Kaleb was in nearly identical garb, except his jacket was blue, not green. Perhaps a set of spare clothes they had laying around? She was so much larger than Kaleb, though, and the proportions were completely different, so that couldn't be it. It didn't matter; they both looked a lot better for the hospitality of Lord Fenrix.

"Do you know where this dining hall is, Kaleb? Lady Pritchard left me with no instructions on where to go."

"No, I'm afraid that I'm no better informed than you are, though I imagine it would be on the ground floor?"

"What reasoning leads you to that conclusion? Our dining halls are all hundreds of feet in the air, for example!"

"Well, yes," he conceded. "But I *am* studying archaeology at the college, and every castle we have unearthed had what we believe to be the main halls on the ground floor, and our history books would seem to back this up."

"Well, this is a Human building, so I'll defer to your knowledge on this one." They made their way back down the long hall to the grand staircase. It would seem they had nothing to worry about, and would not need to guess anything, for Lady Pritchard awaited them patiently at the top of the stairs.

"Ah, excellent, there you are. Much better, much better. Oh, I see you have white fur, Allai, not pink. Interesting."

Allai realized that Algo's blood had probably tinted a lot of her fur, and it was not an unreasonable assumption on the apparition's behalf, not knowing any better. She smiled sadly, bowing in the Astrilian fashion as Kaleb did, but not saying anything.

Lady Pritchard was sharp-eyed, though, and seemed to realize that she had said something to upset or offend Allai but chose not to pry. Instead, she changed the subject to the next logical thing, "Dinner will be served shortly. Lord Fenrix and High Mage Cean will be in attendance. I, too, will be joining you for the evening."

"Oh, I didn't realise you could eat," Kaleb said, and immediately regretted it as Lady Pritchard scowled.

"Does everyone have to keep reminding me today that I'm dead? Does nobody have any manners? No, I can't eat, child, but I can partake in the conversation. It has been hundreds of years since we have had company. I will not pass up this opportunity!"

"I did not mean to offend; I am sorry, Lady Pritchard. Of course, your company would be delightful."

Kaleb's backtracking seemed to do just the trick, as the lady's attitude immediately perked up. They continued down the long staircase, around under them, and down another corridor before being led into a grand chamber with a ceiling so high they could barely see its peaks in the twilight.

The room could easily have hosted a banquet of several hundred but was now laid out with a single long table stretching the centre. At the head of the table, Raziel and Zel sat in conversation while Gerald refilled their cups with a wine that Allai didn't recognise. It could have been Astrilian or from anywhere else; she had little experience with non-Jubian culture.

As they approached, Gerald replaced the wine in a bucket of ice to the side and showed them to their seats as Lady Pritchard took hers. She chose to navigate the table and pull the chair out in the corporeal fashion, presumably to not seem rude by walking through the furnishings.

"Ah, welcome. Zel and I have been getting better acquainted. It seems we have travelled to many of the same places over the years." He raised a glass to the Mage before taking a sip of the contents. "We have a lot in common it seems, not least our age!"

Zel laughed before taking a sip from his own glass. The liquid in both was a deep plum and far less viscous than the JubJub wine Allai preferred. Gerald came around offering them each a glass, and she graciously accepted, sniffing it cautiously.

"Apologies, we don't have any of the Jubian delicacies you

are used to, but Zel has informed me of your race's preference towards not eating meat. As such, the kitchen is preparing a meal that should suit all of our palates." Raziel gestured towards Gerald. "If there is anything not to your liking, please don't hesitate to let Gerald know, and he will see to it. We haven't had guests in a long time, so you must forgive us, we are quite unprepared."

For being unprepared, they sure knew how to throw together a dinner party on no notice. Zel looked towards them both, a curious look about him. "So, you've been sent to find me by your current leader? I've heard about this Galrei; she sounds wise. I was planning to return to these lands when I caught wind that she'd ended your last war."

"Yes, Master Zel. We have only ourselves just learned of your existence. It seems Galrei had kept us all in the dark regarding your previous involvement." Allai was a bit bitter on this point. She thought she was among Galrei's most trusted. But, then so had Reno been. Perhaps it was for the best that Galrei did not share everything.

"It's good that my story is still passed on, though I'm surprised my warning went unheeded so quickly. Politicians forget things very conveniently when they want to, including why the fighting broke out in the first place. It is a wonder that neither nation has wiped the other from the face of the planet, but it is good that your conflict has remained contained to this region. It has allowed other nations to develop more naturally."

Kaleb's eyes lit up. "You mean there aren't other nations like ours out there? We discuss it often at the College, but expeditions are discouraged, and only a few private ventures have left our shores in the last couple of centuries in search of more."

"Though there are many other nations, they have developed more slowly, though there are some on the verge of discovering steam power, and there are some that rely more heavily on magic than others, achieving the same ends. Astrilia is advanced, *very* advanced, and what the Jubians do with magic is also astounding, but they are about to be joined on the world stage by nations very quickly catching up, provided the great barrier can be overcome.

"Astrilia has squandered its resources while fighting for more. They wanted the rich, resource-heavy lands that the Jubian forest encompass, and obviously, the Carnah'lor were against their forest home being torn apart. So, they fought back, and that is how the conflict started so many hundreds of years ago. I was barely into my hundredth year when contact was first made.

"By the time the second war had broken out—again, over resources—the Alliance had painted the Carnah'lor to be these evil barbarians. I lived among them at the time and saw the destruction the Astrilian machines caused to their home. For two hundred years, I fought to give the Carnah'lor a chance, pleaded with the Alliance to cease their efforts, but they painted me a traitor. In the end, I had to force a peace, and the pain it caused me to threaten all that I knew was too much, so I left."

Zel sat for a moment staring pensively into his wine, before raising his eyebrows, and smiling at the two of them. "So, to see a Human and a Carnah'lor together, seeking me out for assistance, gives me faith that things are going better than I'd hoped among your nations."

A pang of sadness hit Allai. "Yes, it's all thanks to the efforts of my brother and Galrei. They have worked hard to bridge the gap between the cultures, and he was even accepted as a council member on the Alliance." She closed her eyes, taking a sip of the dark liquid. Holy Gensa it burned going down! She cringed but forced herself to continue. "He's gone now, killed by traitorous hands that would have seen us dead rather than reach you to deliver our message."

Zel's smile softened, and compassion lined his features. "I'm sorry for your loss. May his spirit be with Gensa, and may his flesh nourish her."

She fought to hold back a sob, almost forgetting that Zel probably knew their customs better than she, having lived among her people for four times as long as she'd been alive.

He went on, "Let us cut to the chase then. What is this message that you bring? For it must hold great importance."

Over the next hour, Kaleb and Allai recounted all that had happened. As they told their tale, skeletal kitchen staff brought out a meal of layered pasta. Between each layer were roasted vegetables and spinach, tomato sauce, some white sauce that Allai was unfamiliar with, and cheese, a product that had only recently made its way into their markets back in Jubo. It was amazing, and the comfort of a well-cooked meal helped to stave of the panic as they were once again reminded of the peril that faced the world.

Through it all, Raziel listened in interested silence, eating his meal, and the Lady Pritchard seemed unfazed by any of it. Allai wondered if they cared at all, being as isolated from everything as they were. Once they had finished their tale, and their plates were being taken away, Zel sat back in his chair for a moment, gazing up into the high rafters. It was Raziel that spoke first.

"Zel, I shall teach you what I know. Not about Necromancy, that is a craft best left dead, excuse the pun. No, I shall teach you what I know, if I can, about my connection to Cado."

Zel slowly looked over at the Necromancer, wide-eyed, as did Kaleb. Allai didn't really understand what he meant by his connection to Cado, but it clearly made more sense to them.

"You . . . you have a connection to Cado? How is that even

possible?" Kaleb asked in what Allai thought sounded like awe. "It's established fact that those from each realm have a connection that's unique to their own realm. They can channel from it even in other realms due to the connection . . . due to the connection between realms . . ." It was like Kaleb had just understood something.

Both Zel and Raziel smiled. Obviously, they knew more about this topic. "There is hope for you, young Kaleb," Zel said fondly, while Raziel nodded almost appreciatively. "Yes, you can see now that because there *is* a connection between the realms that allows natives of each to channel when outside their home realm. Then it goes without saying that, in theory, anyone can channel the magic from any realm."

He held out both hands in front of him, palms up, and flames began to dance around his fingers, licking upwards. "Through one hand, I am channelling the magic that is native to me, that of Gensa, and through the other, I channel that of Cado. Now, focus on me. See if you can detect which is which."

From Zel's knowing smile, he clearly already knew, and Kaleb had opened himself up to Gensa to channel as well. For Allai, though, she didn't need to channel to see. Magic was a part of who she was, and she could see the flows of Gensa rising through Raziel into his left hand. But to her, it was as if the right hand was merely on fire.

"Your right hand! There is nothing flowing into it!" she blurted, and Kaleb let out an "Ah!" as he noticed it, too, though he looked a little disappointed that he hadn't got there first. Raziel released his hold on the magic and let his palms drop.

"Yes, though not quite as you say. As I said, I was channelling magic of Cado through that hand, but as you have no connection, or rather more accurately, no understanding of the connection to Cado, you cannot perceive the flows that I channel. It is this that I propose teaching to you all, though I don't fully understand it myself, for the power to do so was bestowed on me."

"Does this mean you will fight with us, Raziel? I have faced Mystral in open battle before, and I barely won last time. Were it not for the combined strength of those around me, all would have been lost."

He shook his head slowly, and before he could speak, Lady Pritchard broke her silence. "Coward."

He looked at her sternly, but she continued, "Coward! After everything you've done in your lifetime, the pain you caused, not least to me! You have a chance to help right the world, and you're going to do what you always do, hide!"

Raziel's blue skin was starting to darken, and his fists bunched on the table. "You know, dear, that I- Ouch!" She'd thrown an empty plate from the table at him, hitting him squarely in the head.

"Don't you *dare* call me dear! You want to earn my respect again, you will help these people!"

"This is not my world! It is not my fight!"

"Not your fight? Do you think Mystral is going to stop at Astrilia? If he gains power, do you think he'll just be happy with a nation? This is a being that ruled a world! And not content at that, he and his brothers crossed to rule here! If he's left unchecked, he'll turn all to ash!"

She was standing now, and Allai could sense the barely held back magic bubbling in the Necromancer. Finally, as Lady Pritchard finished, he got to his feet, his chair flying backwards.

"ENOUGH!" he commanded, and silence fell—though it was interesting that he had waited for her to finish before his outburst. The Necromancer turned face and stalked from the room, leaving the table in stunned silence. Eventually, Zel turned to the rest, dabbing his mouth. The Lady Pritchard had also gone, unheard.

"I think we should all get a good night's rest. You have both had a rough time of it, and we need his knowledge if nothing else before we proceed. Hopefully, he'll have time to calm by the morning. Thank you, Gerald, but I don't think we'll be staying for dessert tonight."

19

Andrew Colthorn, to give him credit, responded to the situation calmly. He didn't try to attack; he didn't soil himself either. As it turned out, he was the youngest member of the council, which was probably why he had babysitting duty of the organization. It would seem that Allison's opinion held some weight, though, for once she'd filled Colthorn in on the details of their encounter, he was on board with taking Mystral to the greater council.

"If you could . . . return to that Human form, we have to pass through the public area before we get to the council," the V'Udol requested.

It was not an unreasonable request, though he was getting tired of having to conceal himself. It was only for a short while longer though. Soon . . . they would all bow before him.

He channelled and returned the glamour over himself. "Fascinating," Colthorn said. "I couldn't sense you channel at all."

Mystral smiled with his now-feminine features. "Indeed, people of your realm cannot sense the powers of Cado."

"Is the same true for you of our magic?" Andrew asked, as he used some magic to gently replace the items that had been thrown about, so as not to attract suspicion.

"No, we Guardians of the realms are different from you mere mortals. Though I cannot channel the powers of your realm, I can sense when any user channels." He didn't feel the need to elaborate further for this man. He needed him, but he wasn't deserving of the complete history of his kind.

"Mortals? I'm over three hundred years old!" Andrew looked truly offended to be grouped with Humans and the other races in Mystral's eyes. *The Chosen* were always an arrogant bunch. Mystral gave an amused smile, and merely turned to leave the room. Colthorn was finished with his re-arranging, and he hated wasting more time than necessary.

Colthorn chose to hold his tongue and swallow his pride. He clearly didn't want an incident among the public-facing end of their scam, and he probably thought better than to challenge a Dark Lord of Cado.

Wise man.

He led them through the main area, and to a stairwell that was off a side corridor. A set of stairs led up, with a second set leading under the building. They took the latter and descended to a dark basement area with stores and supplies. The area spanned the size of the first floor, and they headed to a door on the far side.

"We tell anyone that enquires to this area that there are a set of private offices on a lower floor for dealing with delicate matters, such as government and press liaisons. It's not entirely untrue, so no one questions it." Colthorn placed his hand against a flat display on the wall, and as it scanned, he simultaneously channelled magic into a slab on the opposite side of the door.

"Two-point authentication, the stone recognizes my unique magic signature, while the computer scans my unique hand-print. If both do not match . . . let's just say it gets messy."

"Interesting. Magical signatures are unique?" Mystral

wondered. It was not something that they had the need to explore before, so he'd never considered it could be a thing.

"Indeed, they discovered it about a hundred years back, and for those that can afford it, it's leaps and bounds ahead of traditional security measures. It all feeds into a computer that makes the match."

The set of doors slid open as the computer confirmed the match and revealed a lift on the other side. Mystral pondered this new information, and already knew how he would fool such a system. Several ways in fact, but he kept them to himself, and wondered if anyone among these creative little flesh bags had come to the same conclusion. Probably, and in keeping it to themselves likely either secured the business or exploited the information to their own gain. Greed was a powerful motivator.

The lift took them down for a long time, and for the second time in as many days, Mystral found himself in a deep, underground environment. As the doors slid open to reveal the space, he realized that this time, it would at least be in more style.

He stepped out into a hall lined with wood panelling in dark mahogany, with doors leading off either side. Higher administration, perhaps? Colthorn led them to the doors at the end of the hall, a large double set that took them through into a huge, high-ceilinged space. It was like a combination throne room slash speak easy. There was a set of four thrones at the rear of the space on a raised dais. To the left was a stage with some microphones dotted around. There was a bar on the right, and tables scattered around the space in the middle.

One of the thrones was occupied by a Tren'jin, an odd sight among the V'Uol at all, let alone among their council. Had they figured out how to infect the Tren'jin? If so, why were they not exploiting this fact? He'd have to ask about that later. Among the tables loitered a few patrons that could have been Human or

V'Udol. It wasn't uncommon among *The Chosen* to woo one's meal before eating.

"Ladies, gentlemen, clear the room, please," Colthorn said as he strode across the room and took his throne at the end of the dais. The non-council members all stood as one and began to leave, the other council members passed curious looks among each other, but chose not to question the request as the others cleared out. As they funnelled past Mystral, he channelled and picked out a V'Udol female and a Human male and had them remain. Colthorn looked at him curiously but went along with it.

Joining Colthorn and the Tren'jin on the thrones were an emaciated figure dressed in High Nasadian style of six hundred years ago. His hair was pure white, and his sunken eyes shone yellow. Mystral knew this to be Demetrius Delgado, who had once carried the amulet of Mystral's younger brother, Melchia, utilizing the Dark Lord's power as his own. That entire course of events had led to Mystral's release all those years ago and marked their near victory, had it not been for his brother's betrayal.

Melchia's return had clearly had an adverse effect on the V'Udol, though. The power would have rushed back to its master's body on his return and it was a wonder Delgado had survived at all. The V'Udol sneered at Mystral as he passed to take his throne. Could he see what he was?

The last to take their seat was a stunning silver-haired woman, wearing a snug blue dress that hugged her in all the right places, emphasising her curves and bust. For the colour of her hair, she looked not a day over thirty, and the Human that Mystral had stopped had been at her table previously.

"What have you brought us, Andrew, another snack? We already had our meals picked out, darling." She waved seductively at the male next to Mystral; the male now was shifting uneasily. Mystral suspected that their 'meals' weren't as in the know as most of the other patrons of the throne room. The man didn't make to bolt, though, so perhaps he thought she meant it sexually? The language here had always been somewhat confusing. So many not saying what they meant.

"She's an abomination," spat Delgado. "A so-called 'Dark Lord.'"

Ah, so he *could* sense what he was. Mystral dropped the pretence and returned once more to his own form, now head and shoulders above those standing next to him. To the V'Udol's credit, she took a step back, but stood her ground. The Human, however, screamed, and then fainted. No matter, he needn't be conscious for what was to come.

The non-Tren'Jin female stood in alarm, but the rest remained seated, two already knowing what he was, and the Tren'jin seemingly unbothered by this turn of events. Perhaps she thought they could take him? They might be able to at that, still weakened as he was. He doubted that Colthorn would try anything stupid now after his previous display, and Delgado had lived through his last incursion into this realm; he understood what a Dark Lord was capable of at full strength.

"Well done, Demetrius. You remember my kind well, it seems, even after all these years."

"I could hardly forget," he said gesturing vaguely at his decrepit appearance. "Much was taken from me when you and your kind returned before, and now you stand before us, hundreds of years later. Why?"

Good. He was suspicious, but he wasn't stupid. He knew that Mystral wouldn't be here without reason, and that meant they would listen.

"I have come with a proposition. I have the means to remove the blight with which humanity has cursed, and in exchange, I merely demand loyalty and service as we take control of this world."

Delgado and the non-Tren'Jin female laughed at this. The Tren'jin merely stayed silent, listening. A wise one there, for sure. Colthorn knew what he offered but chose not to speak up at this point, all but confirming Mystral's deduction that he was the runt of this litter.

"Service? To you? Has your isolation driven you mad, Mystral?" Delgado knew his name as well; he'd done his research on the Dark Lords after his fall, it would seem. "I've tasted the false promises of power and control of your kind before and look where it got me. What makes you think we'd follow you now?"

"Darling," the non-Tren'Jin female tittered. "My good comrade is right. You come in here demanding our obedience to you, but we have lived by our own rules for millennia. It's precious to think you could sway us to think otherwise, though."

"Let him speak Cynthia." This last was from the Tren'jin, and they all turned to the feline creature in her throne, and the laughter died down.

"Xia, dear, you don't mean to take him seriously, surely?" Cynthia questioned, but there was no mockery in her tone, only respect, even with the pet name. At least now he knew all their names.

"He would not be before us without reason. Do not mock what he offers before you know the extent of what it is. Let him speak."

The others turned back to Mystral. Cynthia looked on the verge of saying something then thought better of it, and merely sat back into her throne. Delgado reluctantly also stayed silent. Colthorn smiled and chose now as his time to contribute. He looked Mystral in the eye. "Speak."

Amused by the turn of events, he decided he was not above

some light mockery of his own, making a show of bowing with a willowy flourish before straightening. "My thanks, good council."

He gestured at the male Human stirring on the floor. "I have learnt of your plight, of the vaccination that these Humans have developed against your kind. Yes, though not deadly to a fully mature V'Udol, it does stop you from growing your numbers easily."

He now moved closer to the V'Udol female, not Allison, for she had moved to the bar to be as far from this as possible, but the other whom he had stopped before she could leave. Letting a clawed hand play around her throat, he circled her, feeling her tense beneath his touch. "What if I told you I could make you immune . . ."

He wasn't looking at the council, though, and instead gazed longingly at the V'Udol in his grip. He could feel the power pulsing through her, and knew she had an extremely strong connection to the magics of this world. He longed to drain her, but she was necessary for his demonstration. She shuddered beneath his gaze, but her expression was fierce. Good, she was not weak.

"Impossible," Delgado stated almost immediately. "You are wasting our time. Get out!"

"It's not impossible." This was Colthorn.

"What?" Delgado looked incredulously at the younger V'Udol. "You would side with him?"

"No, I would side with her." He gestured to Allison. "She can tell he does not lie. He believes, one hundred percent, that he can do this."

"Words are meaningless," Xia spoke purposefully, though not loudly. Her words were easily heard by all in the room. "Belief, this is also meaningless. Actions, though, are meaningful." She focused her cat-like eyes on him. "Show us your truth with action."

Without further preamble or pleasantries, Mystral placed his claw-like hand flat on the V'Udol's back and began to channel. She gasped sharply as the power flowed through her, finding the components of her DNA, and that of the parasite's, which Mystral would need to fundamentally shift. The nameless female began to shriek, and the councillors sat forward in their seats, most unable to see what Mystral was doing, but Delgado clearly had some sense of it.

He was giving them the same immunity that he had to all diseases or invasive genetic attacks, which this was. The Taken Vaccine basically made Human hosts hostile environments, unable to thrive under constant attack. It's why it didn't have the same effect on adult parasites in unvaccinated hosts that fed, and it's why the larval stage of the parasite just died in those conditions.

What Mystral was doing would change that. The larvae themselves would be immune to the attack of the vaccine and would be immune to any such future adaptions of the vaccine. He was creating a perfect parasite, and making the entire race stronger, forever.

He released his guinea pig, letting her fall to the floor, then he channelled and pulled the Human to him. He was awake now, and stared in horror at what was happening, his own fear paralyzing him to the spot even if Mystral hadn't held him with magic.

"This Human is vaccinated. This V'Udol is altered. Have her feed on him but not kill, turn him."

"Fool, he is unvaccinated! That is why I chose him!" Cynthia said snidely, thinking she had the upper hand in this situation.

"I assure you he's vaccinated. Having fed off enough Humans myself in the last day, I know what to look for." He could almost smell it in their blood now. It was why he'd been chosen as the rest left. Cynthia looked horrified. Mystral imagined that she only liked to feed on untainted prey. Had he lied intentionally? Did he know what was going on here? It didn't matter. He would soon be one of them.

"Nadia, if you would indulge our guest . . ." Xia practically purred, motioning towards the Human and Mystral. Nadia, now the only perfect V'Udol, stood shakily.

She gave Mystral a scathing look, but did as her council bid, walking up to the shaking Human. In a way that Mystral was sure was either mockingly mimicking him or unconsciously so, she ran a hand with long nails seductively around the man's neck. Perhaps she was attempting to reassert her own power in this situation after being at his mercy.

Her thumb found the jugular, and slit a clean cut along it, a gush of blood spraying out at Mystral, he suspected intentionally, before she clasped her mouth over the opening and drank deeply. The human shuddered in her arms, now released of Mystral's hold, but was easily held up by her enhanced strength.

When she released him, he fell to the floor, and the effects were almost immediate. Another change Mystral had made, one which he considered prudent, was to increase the speed of their gestation. Normally, it could take several days, or up to a week, for the parasite to take hold in a new host, but they now worked more aggressively, improved and enhanced by his own hand.

A fever broke out on him, and the others seemed unimpressed. Mystral had read that a vaccinated human would get sick with an agonizing fever but would recover after a few days. This fever, though, was brought on by the rapidly aggressive nature of the new larvae and would be over within a couple of hours, or so he estimated. This was essentially the first of his kind.

"Mystral, it appears you have failed. The fever of the vaccine has taken him, and he will clearly recover," Delgado said lazily, seeming to rapidly lose interest in the situation. It was Nadia who spoke next, though.

"I feel fine."

It was a simple statement, but Mystral knew its meaning, and the weight of it was clearly not missed by the council as their eyes shifted as one to her. Nadia had been looking down at the fevered man, but now looked up, almost uncertainly examining herself.

"I feel fine," she repeated, this time with more confidence. Though feeding on the vaccinated was not fatal to the adult parasite, it made them feel sick, and it wasn't a pleasant experience, which was the main reason that Cynthia would have been so annoyed at the lie of the Human.

"You will need to give this man a couple of hours. The new, aggressive nature of the larvae will take its toll on the body, but as the parasite takes hold and grows stronger, so will the body recover. Far more rapidly than you are used to. Perhaps you would like to make him more comfortable in the meantime?" Mystral's tone was half mocking, half pride at his handiwork. He had them in the palm of his hands now.

Cynthia nodded to Allison at the bar, and she left, returning with two others shortly after.

"See this man to one of the suites. Make him comfortable." Cynthia was now clearly on board, but Delgado still looked unconvinced. No matter, the plan was in motion, and in a couple of hours, they would see the results. V'Udol knew their own, and there would be no doubt once the Vejling had converted.

MYSTRAL WAS INVITED to wait in one of the suites while the parasite took hold of its new host. He cared not where they stuck him and imagined that they were uncomfortable in his presence. In truth, he was thankful for the chance to gather himself. The process had taken *a lot* out of him, and he would soon be expected to perform it on many.

He would need to restore his energy soon, for he felt vulnerable among a group of beings that had no great love for him. His task was done, though. He doubted that they would need further convincing. Mystral didn't need their love; he needed their loyalty. What he hadn't disclosed when making the changes to the DNA of the larvae was that each newly hosted parasite would be born with a strong desire to serve Mystral.

It was an insurance policy, for once they had an army, the council would likely be tempted to turn on Mystral, thinking that they would have no need for him. Especially if they realised that he was weak enough that they might stand half a chance. But now they would never get the opportunity, and should they try to turn on him, they would find they held little sway over the new Vejlings.

Eventually, a knock came at his door, and a very young-looking V'Udol entered. "The council will see you now . . . um . . . My Lord?"

Mystral could forgive the boy's ignorance, and the fact that he was trying to show respect was a good sign. It meant that the contempt the council had felt for him had lessened by the time they had sent for him, leaving this young V'Udol unsure how to address him.

Mystral rose from his perch and followed the young one back to the room where their council sat arrayed on their thrones. With everything they had witnessed, they still tried to hold on to their sense of power over the situation.

Another door opened, and Nadia led in her new charge. The one-time Human had broken his fever, and now stood tall and proud. Mystral had always wondered how much of the personality of the host survived after the parasite took hold, not that it mattered.

"My Lieges, Marcus has successfully transitioned. He is a Vejling," Nadia stated, clearly proud of her charge, and showing a protective nature by the way she stood in front of him.

There was a sharp intake of breath by the councillors. Had they not known prior to calling Mystral? Perhaps not, but it struck him as odd. They might have been waiting on the news so they could openly denounce Mystral and send him away. Now, it looked as though a hard reality was flitting through their minds.

Eventually, Xia stood. "We have discussed our options, and what we would do in this eventuality while you were gone. Though not everyone was happy, it was unanimous in the end." She took a knee and bowed her head towards Mystral. "We swear fealty to you."

One by one, Colthorn, then Cynthia, and finally Delgado all stood, took a knee, and swore their loyalty to Mystral. He would have his army. He would take control of this world. Now, it was only a matter of time.

20

It had been nearly two weeks.

Two weeks since what they were calling "the Incident" at the College that had taken the lives of their dean, a professor, and their closest friend.

Two weeks since a further set of horrific attacks, one at a coffee shop and another at a night club, leaving the whole city reeling.

Two weeks, and no further attacks. No horrific uprising. Just two weeks of sadness, of a tense almost-panic in the air.

Two weeks to prepare the funeral.

The College had decided on a group funeral, one to honour Dean Turner, Professor Glennon and Kaleb all together. They had decided to make it an open event, inviting any who had lost loved ones in this time to come and mourn with them together, and as such, Mel and Belinda now found themselves among a sea of people while trying to say goodbye to their best friend.

They were all gathered in the Grand Hall, the oldest and largest hall in the oldest of the buildings on campus. Even with its incredible size, there were people standing in the halls outside, people crowding the main courtyard. There hadn't been an incident of this scale since the war, and the citizens of Astril City didn't know how to feel, how to grieve. They all longed for company, and so they all came together.

There would be other memorials and other funerals for those lost in the other incidents, but this would probably be the most public of them.

Belinda squeezed Mel's hand. She hated it. They just wanted to say goodbye to Kaleb in peace. She understood it, but she hated it. Mel's family was with them, as they had known Kaleb like a son, and they provided some buffer against the tides of human mourning, but not much.

Her own family lived on Rawlington Island, a still-independent state despite the Alliance's insistence that they would be better served joining them. As such, they didn't see the point in coming out to mourn the loss of a country not their own. It was her family's way of further snubbing her for choosing the Astrilian Mage's College over their own. She didn't need them, she had Mel.

Acting-Dean Edwards presided over the ceremony and spoke wonderful nonsense about those that had been lost. They started with Kaleb, and it was all generic niceties. "Good student" this, and "taken before his time" that.

They had been expecting someone to approach them for some words for a eulogy, if not to give one directly, but no one came, and they were left as faces in the crowd instead of being able to stand up in front of everyone and let them know exactly who Kaleb was. That kind, genius, bloody foolish boy that they had cared for deeply. Mel more so, sure, but Belinda had started to see why Mel had loved him for so long.

Mel was shaking with grief, tears streaming down her face, by the time they moved on to Professor Glennon. "She was a soul that inspired warmth in those around her, for she was one of the warmest—"

She didn't hear what came next, as darkness came out of nowhere to take her in its embrace.

THERE WAS A WARMTH AGAINST HER.

She was wet, but she was warm.

It had been raining. Where was she?

Opening her eyes, she saw a soft beam of light shining through an opening in the roof of wherever she was. She tried to move but found herself covered in heavy fur. As she shifted, a group of beavers moved off her and turned to inspect the small life they had been sleeping on, some sniffing at her clothes.

Hayley regretted moving almost immediately, realising that it was very cold. These little creatures had saved her life, for had she been left to the elements as she was, she would have certainly died. They moved over to the side of the space they were in and started nibbling at some bark they had gathered. One brought a piece over to her. Even at the notion of bark, her stomach growled in anticipation, desperate for food. She took the piece, biting down hard on the chewy substance.

The taste of the wooden snack almost caused Hayley to vomit. Bark might be what beavers preferred, but to her, it tasted foul! With little other choice, though, she chewed slowly until the bark was pulp, and swallowed. Finishing her unsavoury snack, Hayley investigated her surroundings. She'd only fallen about ten feet, and although she took a knock to the head when she landed, she otherwise seemed to have fallen on a pile of leaves and soft wood, breaking most of her fall. She was lucky, as apart from being very sore, she didn't seem to have any serious injury.

She seemed to be in some type of stone cabin, to which the years had not been kind. The space appeared to be nearly entirely buried, with tree roots penetrating parts of the walls, and the gaps that used to be windows were entirely dirt-filled. It was a wonder at all that the place survived in its current condition, but she was thankful that it had. Dirty and dank as it was, the only point of entry was where she fell through, and that meant the rest of the space was mostly dry.

A fire was what she needed. The rain had soaked her through as she slept beneath the beavers, and she needed a way to get warm and dry again. Firstly, she needed to clear an area of leaves and debris. Good, the floor was flagstone; that would make things a lot easier. Then came gathering wood that was dry enough to ignite, and enough of the drier leaves that she hoped would work as kindling. Heaping them together, she focused on channelling a small amount of fire into her hands.

The family of beavers bolted for the hole as she sent a fireball hurtling at the wall, luckily dissipating before it caught any of the debris alight. How did her furry friends get the purchase they needed to get out? She was sure she'd not be able to do the same. One problem at a time, though. She focused harder, concentrating on creating only a tiny flame, just big enough to fit in the palm of her hands.

Light flashed in her palm, flashing past her face and causing her to jump at her own magic. But she held onto it this time and willed it into a small flame. With a sigh of relief, she used it to set the wood pile ablaze.

Ahh, that was much better. The small space warmed quickly, with the smoke escaping out of the hole she had created. Stripping, she laid her clothes nearby to dry by the heat of the flames, while staying close enough herself to give the heat a chance to penetrate the cold that had settled deep into her bones. She'd never liked the cold, and it was likely why she was so connected to fire. She curled up as close as she dared to the dancing flames and, still exhausted, she was taken once more by sleep.

AS THE DAYS PASSED, the beavers had slowly returned, occasionally bringing her various things to eat. They were wary of the fire and the smoke, so would return during the periods of the day where Hayley would let it burn at low embers. The food consisted largely of grass, berries, and more bark. She had no idea how to identify berries but trusted the animals and their instincts not to pick poison ones. If they wanted her sick or dead, they would just abandon her to her fate here.

The berries were a bit tart, but night and day compared to the bark and grass, with the added benefit that they didn't make her sick. She wasn't sure she'd have the strength to survive even a mild poisoning. She spaced the berries out between meals of bark and grass, though. Not knowing how long she would be down here, she didn't want to run out in a hurry.

The days had been cold and wet, which at least allowed her to collect water in an iron bucket she'd found. It was filthy, but with a bit of scrubbing with some leaves and water, and then some fire to sterilize it, Hayley felt confident that it was suitable for her needs. She could go a lot longer without food than she could without water. Even though the rain was constant, she was sparing with the water, for they could let up at any time. No one knew she was here, and her uncle wouldn't care. Was she destined to die here?

After everything that had happened, that wasn't the worst fate she could suffer. She missed her mummy fiercely, and all that waited for her out in the world was Uncle Tom, and she would never go back to him. No, this was her home now. She'd managed to clear a decent amount of the floor in the drier half of the space, and even found an old chest with some blankets that were miraculously intact. She noticed some runes on the chest and wondered if they'd had a hand in the blankets' preservation.

It would be nice to be able to find a way to leave the space and get better food. She couldn't rely on the beavers forever, and she'd need more to eat if this was to be her home. But she was too weak for that today. Tomorrow, perhaps, she'd see what she could do.

She felt exhaustion taking its hold again, lit a fire before she was too tired, and then snuggled into her nest of blankets for the night.

"Hayley!"

Darkness held her, and she was struggling to shake it off. The voice brought comfort, and it was nice to imagine some company.

"Hayley! Where are you!"

I'm here, silly, Hayley thought. *What do you want? I'm sleeping . . .*

"HAYLEY!"

The voice was getting closer, and she realized it wasn't coming from inside her head. She rubbed at her eyes, and slowly pried them open. The fire had all but gone out, leaving a small pile of smouldering embers. It was still dark out and must have been the middle of the night.

She suddenly sat bolt upright, panic filling her core. Was Uncle Tom out looking for her? She couldn't let him find her; she wouldn't go back to him!

"HAYLEY!"

While trying to stamp out the embers, she realized that the voice was not the harsh, abusive voice of her uncle, but that of the nice teacher from the college. It was Robert!

For the first time in what felt like a lifetime, hope filled her chest, swelling her heart as she started running around the room.

"I'm—" She coughed hard. Her voice was coming through ragged and low. Was it from disuse? She felt around her throat, and it felt sore and tender to the touch. She must have gotten sick in her time down here; not surprising, but the panic threatened to return as she started to bang on the stone walls to try and get Robert's attention.

It was no use. Her impacts were absorbed by the heavy stone and dirt that was packed all around it. No one would hear that. She needed some way to get his attention, a desire filling her to be out of this hole, and anywhere else.

She felt magic flooding her, threatening to burst every pore. Her panic was causing her to react, but she fought it, and took deep breaths. The magic was still there, but it wasn't controlling her now. Looking up at the hole, an idea came to Hayley. She raised her hands and unleashed a torrent of fire through the opening, bursting into the night sky above her.

Putting everything she had into it, she felt her limbs shaking. She was still so weak, but she would not, could not, let Robert pass her. Hayley would get out of this hole. She would have a life, one she would live for her mummy, a better one than her mummy had. She would do it for them both.

Suddenly, the fire stopped and the room spun. She'd given it everything she had; it was all she could do. As she collapsed to the floor, her energy having left her, all she could think was, *Mummy, I'm so sorry.*

MOTION, like bobbing in a lake, but not . . .

Slowly moving up and down. A warmth pressed against her, comforting.

"It's okay. You're going to be okay."

Hayley opened her eyes, looking up to see the face of the kind teacher, Robert. He was carrying her in his arms.

"I'm not going to let anyone hurt you again. I'm going to get you help."

He kept on repeating this to the air. Though meant for Hayley, she thought that maybe he meant the words more for himself. Tears were streaming down his face, but he had a determined set to his features.

"Mr. Robert?" Hayley said softly, and he looked down at her, a relieved smile spreading across his face.

"Thank Daffron. You're going to be okay, child. Stay still, I'm getting you away from here."

And she did. Settling against his chest, she felt safe for the first time in a long while.

THE TRIP through the forest folded around them, bending like a blur, and suddenly she was in the back of his car again, speeding away from the mountain. She looked back and saw that there was smoke rising from the cabin where her uncle lived.

"What happened?" she asked quietly.

"I came to check on you, I know I said I'd be back in two weeks, but I was worried. When I got to your uncle's, he was a drunken mess, and claimed that you attacked him and ran into the forest. When I asked how long ago, he shrugged, saying a few days."

Hayley heard Robert take a deep breath and let it out slowly before continuing.

"At this, I got somewhat angry at him, to which he took exception, and attacked me. I regret that in the fight that ensued, his cabin caught fire, and well . . . you'll never have to see that man again, Hayley."

She sighed with relief. Hayley couldn't find it in herself to feel bad for Uncle Tom. He was a bad man, and Robert was a good man.

"What happens to me now?" Without a home to go to, and no relatives she knew of, she had no idea where she could go.

"You will come to live at the College. I don't care what the dean says, we are taking you in."

Hayley smiled, but it was a sleepy smile, and she began to drift off.

"Yes, sleep, child. You'll be home soon."

~

"WHAT DO YOU MEAN, this has happened before? Melissa, you need to answer me. What is going on? Belinda?"

She blinked a few times as the hall came back into focus. The dense crowd had somehow made space around them, and Acting-Dean Edwards was talking to Mel while trying to shake Belinda out of the trance she'd been in. The silence in a hall of so many people was unnerving.

"I- I'm fine. Stop, seriously." The shaking was getting to Belinda, and it honestly seemed unprofessional of their acting dean. Panic and stress will do that to a person, though. Their Runology professor had been dealing with a lot and had been expected to step up to handle it all. It was enough to cause cracks in anyone.

"Thank Dafron, I think we need to take you to the infirmary. Professor Lufton, can you please escort these two. And girls, I want a word with you both later about this." Edwards turned to address those around them. "It's okay, everyone is fine. There is nothing to worry about. We will resume the ceremony shortly." She gave them both another meaningful look before starting back towards the dais at the front of the hall.

Professor Lufton gestured wordlessly for them to follow as he set of in the direction of the infirmary. Well, one of them at least, the one located in this building. With the size of the College and the potential for injury, there were multiple infirmaries dotted around campus.

The crowd parted to make way for them as they went, confused faces on many of the people there, most of whom were unaware of what had caused the pause. There were also a few angry-looking faces and tutting, because how dare they have the audacity to cause a scene at such an event. Belinda gave them a face back that told them exactly what she thought. Fuck the lot of them. What did they know of her grief, of Mel's grief.

Doctor Professor Myles Myers greeted them at the Infirmary. Belinda always found his name somewhat amusing and thought his parents must have either been super lazy or having a joke at their child's expense. Whatever the case, he was a kind man in his late fifties who pulled the double duty of heading their medical staff and being the lead professor in the studies of Magical Remedies. His short and plump appearance and balding, wispy hair (which was more grey than brown these days), helped with the air of friendliness with which he carried himself.

"Ah, Professor Lufton, how can I help?" the doctor addressed his colleague. Professor Lufton was quite the opposite of the good doctor. Stern, tall, dark-skinned, with immaculate short-kept hair and a no-nonsense air about him. He was the professor of Alchemy, and given the danger involved with some of the substances they used in class, he couldn't afford to be aloof.

"Doctor, Belinda here seems to have suffered some kind of . . . episode. Her friend Melissa here has indicated that she has had them before, and Dean Edwards would like her kept here for observation and possible testing if you feel it's necessary." Lufton looked the pair over, and it was obvious he was not happy about the course of events and felt that they were directly to blame. In fairness, they were, but not really. It was the damned amulet again, but she knew telling them would be foolish.

"THANK YOU, Professor, you may return to the memorial ceremony. I'm sure I can handle two teenagers." Professor Lufton gave a curt nod, about turned, and left them without any further preamble. "So, Belinda, you have these episodes often?"

She could have killed Mel for mentioning them at all, but she knew Mel was worried about her. In the middle of a crowd like that, professors bearing down on her, she couldn't *really* blame her, but still.

"Not really . . . often? It's only happened a couple of times before, and only in the last two weeks."

"I see, are you able to tell me exactly when they started?"

"Well, it would be—"

"When she picked up that cursed amulet!" Mel blurted.

Cado's pits, what was she saying?

"A . . . cursed amulet? Belinda?" The doctor's usually kind face was now stern. None of the staff took the misuse of magical items lightly. There was too much that could go wrong, and they were already dealing with powerful primal forces. Unregistered magical items were strictly forbidden on College grounds.

"Well . . . fuck" Belinda reached inside her shirt and pulled out the amulet on the chain. Doctor Myers frowned at the curse, but his eyes went wide at the sight of the amulet.

"Belinda . . . where did you . . ."

She could sense him start to channel wind and water magic together and begin to probe the amulet. He stopped sharply, though, as the amulet drank greedily from his reserves in a way that it had only sipped against hers.

"Wait . . . did you find this in . . . that . . . place?"

It was no surprise their misadventure had been shared with the faculty, and they were probably better informed about what had happened there, on that day, than they were as students. Belinda didn't answer, but instinctively grasped the amulet in one hand.

"Stay here. Do not go anywhere. Melissa, do *not* leave her side." He walked over to one of the nurse's stations and gave some instructions to a young nurse there who looked over at them, nodded, and returned her attention to her screen. He then left with no indication of where he was going or when he'd come back.

"Well . . . we're fucked."

Mel at least had the good taste to look ashamed, but Belinda didn't have it in her to be mad, and she needed her right then. She pulled her close and held on to her as they awaited whatever fate the College had in store for them.

21

"You're still thinking like Guild Mages."

Raziel had decided to help them, but the training was slow. The morning after they had arrived, the Necromancer appeared in a foul mood, no less resolute in his decision to stay out of the conflict, but still willing to provide them the training Zel had asked for. Now, they stood in one of the many gardens of the Citadel, trying to connect with Cado.

It had been two weeks, and Kaleb couldn't help but feel anxious about what Mystral could be getting up to. Zel seemed less concerned, expecting the Dark Lord to take some time to recover his power, but he, too, was starting to get frustrated at the lack of progress they were showing.

"You know, we aren't a guild, we're a College. The Guild Mages belong to the Engineers' Gui—ow!"

Kaleb felt a sharp slap against the back of his head but didn't feel or sense anything before it hit. Raziel must have channelled Cadien magic to hit him. Bill the groundskeeper sat laughing off to one side. At least the entire household wasn't out this morning to watch Raziel berate them again. Still, didn't the groundskeeper have a shrub to trim or something?

"Enough! I don't care what they call you now, who taught you, or how many years you've spent studying the ways of the world." The last was directed squarely at Zel, who, though incredibly gifted, was still struggling with connecting to the other realm's source.

Allai was conspicuous in her absence, but that had been the same for any of their training sessions. She believed it would be going against the core tenants of her culture to try and tap into the magics of such a dark and violent realm. Her race was so attuned and in touch with Gensa that it may have proven impossible anyway, but she felt that attempting to do so would taint her somehow.

She also didn't approve of them attempting to learn, but she couldn't stop them. As such, she made herself scarce during the day, and returned for her evening meal, which they all took together.

"You need to visualize the connection between the realms. They are like streams flowing through you, and you must choose to take the more violent, pulsing river of Cado."

Kaleb thought about this for a moment, and something occurred to him. "If it's as easy as you say, does that mean that you've managed to master the connection to Ortus, and can control their flows also?" It stood to reason that if they could find the connection to Cado in this manner, that then they could connect to Ortus as easily.

"No, for reasons I don't understand, I cannot connect to the powers of Ortus."

"Then how can we be expected to connect to Cado with that analogy? There *has* to be something else that allows you to understand and use that connection." Kaleb was annoyed. He'd endured two weeks of this, two weeks of being pushed, beaten and shoved by a force he couldn't see or understand, and the whole time, Raziel treated them like they were idiots for not being able to grasp the concept.

A concept that it would seem he barely understood himself. Were they wasting their time? No, not entirely. In the two weeks since they had started their training with Raziel, Kaleb had also been working closely with Zel outside of their lessons on Cado. For a start, Kaleb was beginning to be able to pull on more of Gensan magic than he'd ever been able to. It seemed that magic use was like muscle use: the more you pushed yourself, the more you could handle.

With modern Mages using their magic in much more intricate ways, but ways that ultimately required smaller reserves of magic to be drawn upon, this 'muscle' was never flexed in the same way that it would have been in Zel's day. Kaleb was still nowhere near as adept as the old Mage. It would take more than two weeks to achieve that. But he was stronger now, and he intended to keep training and get stronger still.

"You asked for my help. I am trying to do the best I can. If that's not good enough, you can leave!"

It seemed that tempers were high all round, and Raziel's had been getting worse daily. Bill had informed them yesterday that Lady Pritchard was actively avoiding their master and would vanish anytime he entered the same room. Kaleb couldn't help but wonder why Raziel wouldn't release her spirit. If he loved her so much, then surely, he'd want her to be happy?

"Perhaps it's time we took a break. We've been at this most of the morning. Perhaps some food will help?" Zel stepped between the two of them, seeing that Kaleb was preparing to retort. It was probably for the best. Kaleb could feel his frustrations boiling to the surface, and a fight with a centuries-old demonic wizard would probably end poorly for him.

"Fine," Raziel said, clearly too annoyed to continue himself. Spreading his wings, he took off into the air and disappeared through a balcony somewhere high in the Citadel. Zel followed him with his eyes then looked back at Kaleb.

"I understand that it's frustrating, but we need this. If we can learn nothing else other than being able to detect Cadien magic, then we'll have spent our time well. Imagine fighting someone, but not being able to feel how and when they are casting magic?"

Kaleb nodded, understanding Zel's point, as they turned to enter the castle via the more pedestrian route. "I get what you're saying. I do, and Mystral is truly terrifying. Having any edge when we confront him may mean the difference between death and victory.

"But how are we supposed to get anywhere if he doesn't understand how he connects to Cado himself? I mean, sure, there is a connecting stream that connects all of the realms, but it's not as simple as that, is it?"

They made their way through some small corridors to a much smaller, more intimate dining area. The first night was clearly for show, and since then, they had taken their meals here. It served the dual benefits of being close to where they were training and feeling a lot less intimidating than the Great Hall.

"No, no, it's not. I feel like we're on the cusp of understanding, but there is this barrier before us that we can't break through. If only we could actually see what he sees when channelling."

Kaleb stopped in the doorway as Zel continued to his seat. Something had struck him like a bolt of lightning, and he stood wide-eyed.

"Kaleb, are you all right?" Zel asked, concerned.

"See what . . ." A broad smile crept across Kaleb's face as he stared into the space around Zel.

Zel walked back up to the young Mage, waving a hand in front of his face. "Kaleb?"

His eyes suddenly refocused on Zel, and he grasped the older Mage by the shoulders. "See what he sees! Don't you get it? See what he sees!"

"Um, no, you'll need to—"

"We can form a circle, Zel! We *can* see what he sees!"

"A circle?"

"Yes! Wait, you don't know what a circle is?"

"A geometric shape?"

Kaleb's face went from excited to shocked then back to excited again so quickly that Zel looked as though he was having issues keeping up.

"No! But of course! We only started practically using them within the last decade in school, and before that, only in the last wars! So, of course, you wouldn't know what I'm talking about! How could I have not seen this before? I've been so stupid! A circle! Hah! We need to find—"

"Whoa, there, slow down! Take a breath, sit down, and let's go over what a circle is, shall we?" Zel guided the overexcited student to the table and had him sit down. "Now, from the beginning, what is a circle?"

"Right, okay. Well, during the last war, the Alliance Cabals worked on a way to gain an edge over the Carnah'lor. They were *so* good with magic, and so naturally talented with it, if their soldiers got into hand-to-hand combat with ours, it was a given who would win.

"That's where the circles came in. The Cabals started experimenting with linking together their Mages and channelling the flow of magic through to the leader of the circle. This gave the leader a tremendous boost to what they could do, with one circle being able to effectively fight against many Carnah'lor at a time.

"The knowledge was kept within the military for a long time, but within the last ten years, the knowledge has been made available to the public, allowing the Mage's College and the Engineers' Guild to work on larger projects than ever."

As Kaleb wrapped up, the skeletal servants brought forth their lunch, which was a salad made up of vegetables grown on the grounds and a carafe of water. They had been given leave to drink any of the stores of wine and brandy should they wish, but they thought better off it during their training.

"Ah, I see. It's something I read about the ancient Mage's Guild doing when The Dark Lords first invaded Gensa, though they called it linking. The practice wasn't used during my time at the guild. Not much challenged the power we wielded individually, so it probably wasn't a concern." Zel tried to not make that sound like a brag, but it was true. Mages had a lot of power during the height of Nasadian dominance of the area, both physically through their control of magic, and politically through their ties to the crown. "Do you think it will work with Raziel?" he asked.

"It's worth a try, right? If he's able to channel Cadien magic during the circle, while one of us leads, it might give us something to grasp onto, though we should start with Raziel leading the circle."

"What difference would that make?"

"Well, you see, when you're linked in a circle, you can see what the leader of the circle is channelling. I don't know how well this will work with Cadien magic, obviously, but it would be better that we observe first, than to immediately try to take hold of something we have no understanding of. If you draw too deeply on someone else's reserve, it can result in that person being knulled."

At this, Zel's eyes widened. "It's possible to forcibly knull someone?" His face had lost some of its colour, and Kaleb could understand why. A knull was someone who had no connections to magic at all and could never have any connections to magic. Their existence outside of forcible knulling was rare, *very* rare, but they were documented as cropping up over the years.

To be forcibly knulled, however, was a harrowing experience, and had been banned by the alliance, even during war time. When the Cabals had discovered the unintentional side effects during their early tests, they had weaponised it against Carnah'lor prisoners.

The effects it had on both the Alliance Mages and the Carnah'lor was . . . well, there was a reason it was banned. The all-encompassing emptiness they were said to experience drove knulled Mages insane. During his training to take part in circles, Kaleb had seen a recording of a knulled Mage, and the screams still haunted him.

"Yes, and that's why, at first, I'll take you both through the practice with myself leading the circle. You are both capable of wielding *so* much, that my own capabilities wouldn't even register, and you'd overdraw from me before even knowing what had happened. Conversely, drawing from you both will be hard on me, but it won't be a risk to either of you. If I don't attempt to use your power, I should be safe."

Kaleb thought back to when he'd joined Allai in a circle, and even her flow had threatened to overwhelm him. He didn't much look forward to leading a circle with the two most powerful users he knew, but it was better than being burnt out by their ignorance on the matter.

Zel was very pensive for a moment as they chewed on their salad. Kaleb wondered what effect knulling would have on someone who had lived so long because of their connection to magic. Those affected during the war were all young Mages, nearly all of them Human. Even if Zel could survive the insanity caused by the knulling, would his body hold out?

No, that wouldn't be an issue. They would do this right, and nobody would be knulled. After a short while, Zel nodded.

"You're right. This is our best shot. Let's do it."

THEY RESUMED their lessons the next day, Raziel having not emerged from his private study until morning. Zel had attempted to head up to speak to him of their plan, but when he heard the frustrated shouts and the sounds of objects crashing around the room, he thought better on it.

Instead, he had spent the evening on his own private musings and thinking on the one magical knull he'd known personally. Sure, there were others he'd heard of in the Akonian Desert, but it was a place he seldom visited in his youth, for it was completely void of any connections to magic, much like the knull who called it home.

This knull, though—Ed the Scarred they called him—was raised in Nasadia, the shunned child of a noble family, left to his own devices at far too young an age. He made everyone around him uncomfortable and had earned his nickname because of the simple state of his mind, of which many at the time assumed was linked to his knull nature. Zel suspected it was more to do with the neglect he'd faced growing up, and how others treated him throughout his life.

The man had tragically died at the hands of overzealous Mages who tried to 'fix' the problem. No one involved in the procedure survived the accident, and the only report on it stated that there was a small crater left behind, and that everyone involved had been vaporised.

Even after all this time, Zel felt a pang of sadness for his old friend. He shook the memories away, having spent all last evening thinking about them. It was time to concentrate on the now. For the first time in a long time, he was about to experience something new, something that could potentially save Gensa.

Now that they were all together, they explained their plan to Raziel, who had knowledge of circles, but had also never partaken in them.

"Of course. I can't believe I didn't consider it earlier. I've never had the need to try one before, so it just didn't occur to me."

"We'll need to take it slow, though, and I must urge, don't use Cadien magic the first time we link. Even if I *could* grasp it first time, I will be struggling to contain the torrents that come from you both, and it could end *very* badly."

Kaleb had taken on the air of a professor and was very sternly pointing to Raziel. Zel wondered if he was imitating his own late professor. It must be an intoxicating feeling, being an authority on a subject that centuries-old Mages had little clue on. Zel decided he'd let the kid have his moment.

"Okay, we all need to link hands, and as this is the first time that we're doing this, we should probably be sat down for this."

Raziel looked ready to make some quip, but then thought better of it. Zel appreciated this, as the kid was probably a bag of nerves as it was, regardless of how brave a face he was putting on. Raziel probably recognised this too. They had both been around the block enough to know when someone needed encouragement over jibes. They all sat down.

"Okay, now, each give me a hand, and take each other's." They linked hands. "Good, we're going to start small. Open yourselves up to channel and take hold of the stream."

Zel did so and could feel the other two doing the same. Raziel blazed like a beacon next to Kaleb's candle and hoped that the kid wouldn't get cold feet. He'd seen what they could both do in their training, but holding the power was a completely different thing. It would be like holding a cup of water your whole life and being expected to know how to swim as a result.

"Great." The sweat was beginning to show on Kaleb's brow. "Channel your streams into me and—" Kaleb broke off, his grip on Zel's hand intensifying the moment that Zel and Raziel had begun channelling into the boy. He'd described how becoming a knull was caused by the lead drawing too heavily on a well, but what would happen should those wells be infinitely fuller than the host can hold?

"Mother . . . of . . . Dafron . . . AAAH!" Kaleb's eyes opened wide and were glowing orbs of light. Zel could feel the torrent of magic leaving his body and flowing into Kaleb's and attempted to stop it, but found he no longer had control over the stream.

"Kaleb! KALEB!" He needed to get through to the boy. He was going to burn himself out! Raziel obviously felt the same and started trying to pull himself away to break the connection, but the magic binding them was holding their hands together.

"This power! I could . . . nnnggh! Change . . . the world!" They started rising to their feet, wind swirling around them as the power Kaleb drew on became stronger and stronger. Zel began to panic. If he didn't stop Kaleb, they could all end up dead, but how? He couldn't control any of the magic flowing through him. He'd never felt so useless.

Suddenly, Allai was standing behind Kaleb, clutching his head in her hands. "AAAAH!!!" Smoke started to raise from the pads of her palm, but she bit down and bore it. She started chanting beneath her breath, and the glow faded from Kaleb's eyes before they sleepily fell shut.

As suddenly as it had all started, the gushing river that had been pouring into the boy ceased. Zel and Raziel both releasing their respective holds as soon as they had control again. Kaleb collapsed into Allai's arms. She lowered him to the ground, resting his hand in her lap.

"Foolish Humans, playing with what you don't understand."
She patted curiously at his hair, which had gone entirely white
during the circle, a stark contrast to his brown skin. She either
ignored or didn't notice the blisters that had formed over her
hands.

Zel knelt next to them, placing a hand on Kaleb's chest. He
gently probed with magic, checking his vitals, including the
boy's connection to Gensa, and all seemed intact. He suspected
that it would take Kaleb some time to recover after this.

"He's going to be okay, but we should get him into a bed," Zel
said to Allai. "And you should let me take a look at those
blisters."

Allai looked up at Zel, anger in her eyes. "He is so young. To
him, you are both as gods, and you would play with him as if he
were merely a tool. This is what happens when mortals and
gods get mixed up together!"

Zel rocked back on his haunches, taken aback by the
outburst, but he could see where she was coming from. "You're
right. I'm sorry. But we need all the help we can get for the
coming conflict, and Kaleb is a smart boy." He leaned forward to
stroke some hair out of Kaleb's face. "He has so much potential.
The only thing that separates us is experience. Mages of today
may seem weaker than those of my day, but it's only because
they use magic differently now. With practice, he could probably
surpass us both, Allai. I am old, but I am still mortal."

Her face softened, and she stood, channelling her own magic
to form a bed of cushioned air around him, lifting Kaleb gently
to float before her.

"I shall take him to his room. You get the major-domo and
send her to me." Allai then turned and left, Kaleb bobbing
gently in her wake.

22

Zel and Raziel left Kaleb to the care of Lady Pritchard and knew he would be well looked after. Zel had experienced something similar in his own youth when he had channelled and cast a spell that was far outside of his reach. His hair had also been stripped of its colour, and he'd been unable to use magic for a long time. He had no doubt Kaleb would recover and be stronger for it, but how long that took would depend on the boy.

For now, however, they needed to continue the work they had started. Kaleb had shown them how to form a circle, and they would now be able to continue the work. It was remarkably easy, in fairness. The hard part was the control, and either one of them was capable of overdrawing from the other. They would have to go slowly.

They sat cross-legged on the floor opposite each other and took hold of each other's hands. "Right, Raziel, you take lead. As with Kaleb, we'll only channel Gensan magic to start. Once we've established that we can hold a circle without killing each other, we can proceed to trying to channel Cadien magic."

Raziel nodded in agreement. He'd been taken aback by Kaleb's mistake and was clearly a bit shaken by the experience.

Six hundred years roaming the planet, and he'd probably never had to deal with anything so challenging. Heck, he'd probably never met anyone that could pose a threat to his existence, but in that moment, when Kaleb was drawing deep, they both felt vulnerable. For the first time in a long time, mortality had come knocking.

They both began to channel, torrents of energy entering them both.

"Ready?" Zel asked, and Raziel nodded again. Zel directed his stream into Raziel, the same as he had Kaleb, but instead of struggling to handle the flow, Raziel merely inhaled sharply, and held onto the magic without issue. Zel could see how forming circles would require a lot of practice before using them in practical situations, and he imagined that only the most skilled of Mages even attempted it outside of a classroom setting.

"Okay, I'm going to attempt to use our combined magic." Raziel's warning was appreciated, for as soon as he did, it felt like a massive pull from somewhere deep inside of him. They both started to rise into the air, a solid cushion of wind beneath them so they weren't forced into a standing position. Raziel took them to the height of the Citadel, a view which caught Zel's breath in his throat, and made him glad he was not the one channelling. It was incredible.

Slowly, Raziel returned them to the ground, and gently, released the streams. Zel was grateful the old Necromancer was not tempted to draw deeper and to try even more spectacular feats. Zel genuinely feared the knulling that could happen should he link with someone capable and willing to drain all his power.

"Good, that was . . . amazing, quite frankly, but excellent. That went well." Zel released his grip of Raziel's hands and stood to stretch, feeling tense after that experience but over all very positive about it.

"Right."

He jogged a little on the spot, stretched out his arms.

"Good."

"Are you well?"

"Yes, yes, perfect, this is all . . . it's well, exhilarating and alarming in equal measures. To feel like we could topple mountains, while feeling at the same time completely helpless as someone manipulates your magic. It's going to take some getting used to."

"Ah, yes. I do not look forward to relinquishing control again. However, the need is great, and we must press on."

"Quite right, quite right. Let's continue to keep it simple for a bit though, eh?"

They settled back into their small circle and started to practice again. This became routine over the next few hours as they took turns holding control of the circle. When Zel was in charge, it was the most exhilarating thing he had felt, and when he wasn't, it was terrifying, though it was becoming less so with each passing hour.

Trust was forming between the two Mages, a trust formed from granting someone complete control over you. When the lead in the circle pulled from your stream, you were helpless, and they were all powerful. That was not an easy thing to do, but as it built, Zel found that he was no longer scared to hand over control to Raziel, and he sensed the same was true back.

It was then that Raziel said, "It is time. I will channel Cado during the link."

Zel inhaled deeply, mentally steeling himself. He didn't know what to expect, only that everything he'd ever witnessed of Cadien magic told him it was destructive and hateful.

"Okay, let's do this."

As they had done before, they both began to channel Gensan magic to form the circle, and then Raziel began to tap into Cadien magic. At first, Zel couldn't see what was different, but he felt something was off. Then, slowly, it was like a veil being lifted, and he could see the streams, side by side, flowing into, then out of Raziel. For the first time in his life, his mind associated colour to magical streams. Before, they were just light, but now he could see they were different. Gensan appeared with a green tint, and Cadien with an orangey, yellow tint.

Zel reached out to the Cadien magic, and felt it flood him, a completely new source of power that had always been there, but he'd been ignorant to. The same but different. The same . . . but different. There was no *intent* in the magic; there was no malice. It just was, and he knew that it in and of itself held no taint. Only its wielders had proven lacking in morality thus far.

Raziel should have served as proof that it was not the magic that was evil, but the user. He'd done some terrible things in his despair, but it was the taint of the Dark Lords themselves, and not that of magic involved, that had added to Raziel's selfish, grief-filled desires.

"Let me take control . . ." whispered Zel. He could tell from Raziel's expression that he knew Zel had taken a hold of Cadien magic, but that he also doubted his control over it.

"No, you are not ready."

"Give . . . me . . . control," Zel urged. He could feel the power. An aching desire to control it gripped him.

"Zel, no, you need to practice with it before you can—"

"GIVE ME CONTROL!"

"NO!"

Raziel severed their connection, and Zel fell backwards as if he'd been shoved. He lay sprawled on the floor, gasping for breath, wide eyes searching the ceiling. The circle was broken, but he could see the power now. He could add it to his own.

"Zel, you need to rest, we are done for the night."

"No, I can do more, watch . . ."

Zel got to his feet and began channelling both Gensan and Cadien magic at the same time. He let it fill him. It was exhilarating! The air around him buffeted as Raziel took three long strides up to him and smacked him so hard around the face that it sent him sprawling to the ground again. He instantly let go of the magic he was channelling.

"Ow . . ." he said, sitting up and rubbing his cheek. Raziel looked down at him furiously, hand poised to slap him again, and Zel couldn't help but laugh. "Oh, I've been a prize twit! Thank you, friend!"

Raziel blinked and started laughing himself, lowering his hand to help Zel back to his feet.

23

Allai sat next to her friend's bedside as he lay still. He'd been out cold since she had induced sleep on him earlier that day, but the sleep was only supposed to last an hour. She had been forced to channel so much energy, though. It was the only way she could break through the pressure surrounding him.

What had he been thinking? The sheer amount of magic those two could channel was staggering. She didn't think that even Galrei could handle that, but he had tried anyway. She had not witnessed the horrors he had relayed. But she had been present when the portal that brought him had opened, and the feeling of pure, unbridled malice stuck with her to this day. She couldn't imagine what it would have been like being in the same room as that monster.

This must be why he tried, why he pushed on to bring them this far, and to try and keep up with these men that were relics of a time gone by, one of them heralded as a saviour by her own people. He knew the stakes, and he fought to be able to meet them head on. But what good was it all if he got himself killed? Foolish Humans.

She felt protective over the boy, though, like she had always felt over Algo. He had been the older sibling, and always the stronger with magic of them both, but she'd always felt that he needed watching out for, protecting against those that would do him harm. She felt the same way about Kaleb. He needed protecting.

She had failed Algo.

She would not fail Kaleb.

Could she in good conscience keep company with this group of Mages, though, when they tore her belief and reality apart, tapping into forces that should be left alone? Look what it had done to Raziel, and the life of misery and loneliness he had endured as a result. Who would want that?

They believed so strongly, though, that it was the only way they could fight Mystral, and she would never sway them. She wouldn't submit herself to the forces of Cado, though. No, her spirit would return to Gensa, and would not have the claim of multiple realms over it.

The door to the room swung open, and the two older Mages walked in, seeming to be in good spirits.

"How fares the young hero?" asked Zel.

Hero? Had they made a breakthrough? "He's fine, though still asleep. Have you two stopped playing at being gods for the day then?"

Zel laughed, and Raziel looked affronted. "Playing at? Pfft, we succeeded at!"

This earned them both a stern glare from Allai, but before she could admonish them, she was interrupted by a voice at her elbow.

"Nnngh . . . what on Gensa hit me? My head feels like I'd be better off without it . . ." Kaleb was stirring, and relief washed over Allai—relief followed by annoyance, as she promptly punched him in the arm.

"Fool of a Human! What do you think you were doing? I

already lost one brother; do you want me to lose another?" Her eyes widened as her musing of moments before spilled out of her mouth. Kaleb's eyes were wide too, but as he rubbed his arm, he smiled at Allai.

"Thank you, Allai. No, I don't want that." He looked around the room at them all. "What happened to me? Did the circle work?"

"You can say that again. A bit too well perhaps. You drew so deeply on our power that we thought you were going to kill us all!" Raziel did not blunt the edge to his words, and Kaleb looked horrified at each passing syllable.

"Dafron above, I am so sorry! How did you stop me?"

In lieu of an answer, however, they both turned as one to Allai with smiles. She felt her cheeks warm. "I put you into an enchanted sleep. From which you've only just woken."

"And saved the entire estate while at it. If it wasn't for Allai, we'd all be well and truly dead." Raziel again, not mincing his words.

Kaleb looked up at Allai, gratitude etched across his face. "Thank you, Allai. Looks like I owe you again." Again? If he meant the time on the airship, it was she who was in his debt. That failure was likely a debt she could never repay, but she'd never stop trying.

"How long have I been out?" Kaleb asked to the room. "What have I missed?"

"Approximately six hours, the entirety of which Raz and I have been practicing magic circle usage."

Raz? When had these two become so familiar?

"Indeed, Zel and I have been making good use of the time you napped. He can now channel Cadien magic."

Raziel dropped that bombshell like it was nothing, and both Kaleb and Allai stared agape at the older Mages. Two weeks of constant failure, and in one afternoon, they managed to unlock what had seemed insurmountable at breakfast. Kaleb tried to get up in his excitement, but immediately fell back against his pillow.

"Incredible! You have to- Ow! My head . . ."

"Take it easy, kid, you've been through a lot. We'll show you in good time, but right now, you can't use magic. No, no, you haven't been knulled!" Zel waved his hands at Kaleb to assuage his fears. "But you have overextended yourself, and that will have drained you to the point that you won't be able to hold onto a stream. I've been where you are now. You'll recover, but it could take a while."

Kaleb slumped into his pillow, hand on his head and gazing at the ceiling. "Where do we go from here then?"

"Well, for now, you're going to rest, and for this evening at least, I intend to do the same. For tomorrow, though, I'm going to need to come to grips with this newfound strength, and then we need to think about moving on. We've been here too long already, and Mystral will not have been standing idle this entire time."

"Where do you intend to go?" asked Raziel, and Allai wondered the same. Would they go to Astril City? She had always wanted to see the main hub of the Alliance.

"I don't suppose you know of anyone adept at Ortun magic, do you?" Zel asked. "I intend to continue my plan of mastering the magics of the three realms. I think it is key to stopping Mystral, for good this time."

"Actually, in my travels, I have heard of someone that might fit your description. I once spoke with some of the Draconic Order, and they spoke of an angelic being who has been living in their monastery for a very long time. I did some further digging, and it seemed this particular person had ram horns growing from their head."

"A Zhyri! You don't mean? It can't be Raylu. She's dead!"

"No, though you are right, it is a Zhyri. But it seems Raylu wasn't the only one that came through to our realm. Another named Manwe resides here too."

Disappointment crossed Zel's features, and Allai remembered where she knew the name Raylu. It was the name of that beautiful being painted by Melchia that had ultimately killed him. She had been the one to give her soul to the sword that had defeated Mystral in the story. Allai could see why Zel had gotten excited and now was crushed. They had seemed like close friends in the story.

But another of her kind existed on Gensa? That was incredible news. Zel seemed to realize this, and his mood shifted once more.

"Well, the Draconic Order kept that quiet from me on my last visit, but thank you, that is extremely useful information!"

Raziel looked almost sad for a moment. "So, you will be leaving soon then?"

"We'll need to wait for Kaleb to recover some more, but yes, probably in the next few days. You are welcome to join us though."

Raziel shook his head. "No, that matter is not up for discussion. I shall not be getting involved any more than I have in this fight. Though I shall be sorry to see you go, know that you will always have a place at my table, all of you."

Zel took Raziel's hand and clasped it tight. Allai could see that these two had indeed bonded strongly today.

"Thank you, Raz, for everything."

24

Another day, another standard. Since Rose had left the military ten years ago, she'd found a secure position for herself as head of security operations for AstraTek, the market leader in RuneTek distribution. She didn't know a great deal about the art of enchanting stones for augmentation with non-magical (or as the Mage's called it, Mundane) technology, and she was no magic user herself. What she did know was security, and how to keep people safe.

Since she'd been brought on, she'd successfully reduced loss of assets from a quite frankly staggering twenty percent to a five percent annual rate. That last five percent annoyed her, but it was one of the lowest rates in the city, and of that, she was proud.

Proud as she passed through the bag check and identification verification system she'd set in place.

Proud that her people stopped her *Every Time,* regardless of who she was, and did the same to every person that entered or exited the building.

Proud that not even the CEO was exempt from this practice.

In a world where people can change their identity with

magic, they had to be extra vigilant. The verification system implements charged Jin Ore to create an area that magic users couldn't cast, before stepping through to the next test of placing their hand against a magical signature verification unit. The first would dispel any glamor in place, while the second would check that there was no physical disguise or surgery being employed to fool the first point verification.

This alone had virtually stopped in-house front door theft overnight. There were still businesses with weak security in the City, and they suffered for it, but AstraTek was willing to spend the money to protect its stock and investments. That meant paying for the best, and Rose Garza was the best.

She completed passing through the security check point and entered the lift in the main lobby. Her office was on the forty-second floor, and with the number of people in the lift, it would take a little bit of time to reach her stop. She turned and surveyed the view that would gradually get more spectacular as the glass-walled lift ascended the building. AstraTek had built its complex near the outskirts of the central business district, and as such, the view on this side of the building was mostly unspoiled by neighbouring structures.

The lift began to rise, and the city opened before them. It was a view she would never get tired of. Sure, she loved the islands where she had come from, and returning for a holiday to enjoy the less industrialized spaces was nice. But this . . . this was where she belonged. She'd fought to protect this nation, and it was her home more than anywhere else.

Some of the people closer to the window started to press against it, and she heard gasps amongst them, pulling her out of her reverie. Something had grabbed their attention, and she shouldered her way to the window so she could see what had enthralled them so.

Fires had started to break out in distance, and as she

watched, an explosion decimated one of the buildings at the edge of their view. Was it the Carnah'lor? Had they breached the treaty? Rose pressed a finger to the Rune-Link in her ear, and it connected her with her team.

"Does anyone have eyes on what's happening out the west side of the building?"

"Yes, boss, but we can't tell what's going on from up here."

The response came from Rex, her second in command. He'd served in her unit in the last war, and she had hand picked him for the job. It's not every day you get to employ someone that you already would trust explicitly with your life.

"Is there anything on media channels? Anything being reported via the Ether Net?"

The others in the carriage had all gone silent when they heard her start communicating with her team. They all knew who she was, and they knew that by giving her the quiet she needed, she could do her job, but more so, she was currently their best primary source of information. Nothing silenced a room faster than potential gossip.

"The only reports are coming in from those close to the area. It seems that anywhere affected by the disturbances are currently cut off from communication."

This last communication came from Tricia, their technical expert. She was hired solely to monitor communications for suspicious activity. Rose knew few people that could navigate the net like Tricia could, and in truth, Rose understood less than half of what the tech wizard could do. What she knew was, she was great at her job.

"Blocking communications, how is that possible? Have they taken down the towers?"

All communication throughout the Alliance was handled via a set of communication relay towers interspersed throughout their territories. This allowed for instant transmission of data over large distances and was also what allowed the Ether Net to work. Rose doubted there was another nation on Gensa that could communicate as effectively as the Astrilian alliance could.

"Eyewitness accounts are stating that the towers are still up, but that there is a barrier surrounding the districts.

"Interesting, there have been no communications originating from Cali since around midday yesterday." Tricia said, apparently monitoring several news streams at once.

What? That's impossible, Rose thought. Entire towns didn't just go dark. "How does something like that go unnoticed for twenty hours?"

"It hasn't," said Tricia. "In fact, there are complaints on many messages boards that they haven't been able to contact family out that way, that deliveries expected from Cali haven't made it to the City. People have noticed."

Rose sighed. Of course, people had noticed, but it wasn't a story yet, so the media hadn't reported it. That would all change now. There was an invasion going on, and Astrilia was caught with its pants down.

Another explosion went off in the distance, and everyone in the lift gasped again; one lady screamed. Could it really be the Carnah'lor? Could they have successfully executed a plan of this scale under their noses with no one noticing?

"Execute evacuation order Alpha 1. Everyone on this link, meet me at Ops in ten minutes."

"Yes, ma'am" came the unanimous response of her team. Not a one of them questioned her decision to execute the most extreme of their company's emergency plans. This was why they were her team.

The lift opened at floor twenty, and Rose turned to everyone still in the lift.

"You heard me? Get OUT!"

Everyone streamed out of the lift as the sirens began to blare through the building, announcing a state of emergency. Instructions to all company employees were being fed through loudspeakers on every floor, in every room. As in a fire drill, the lifts were shut down, and the only exit points were via stairs or the evac tubes, which were limited to executive access and would funnel the most important members of the company out via a separate evacuation route.

Even if non-executive staff knew of the evac tubes, they wouldn't be able to access them without one of the unique keys that each exec carried. If anyone forgot their key at home today, well, they'd just have to take the stairs. There was no override.

There was an override for the lift, however, and as the doors shut behind the evacuating personnel, Rose placed her hand against a magical signature detector disguised as a plain panel next to the entrance of the lift. Should anyone other than the few authorized staff accidently lean on it, it would do nothing. After the scan confirmed her identity, a panel popped open beneath it, into which she entered her personal security code. She believed that everything should always have two-point authentication.

The lift began making a beeline for floor forty-two, and as the doors opened, she was already moving to pass through them, and then running. This entire floor was her floor. Everyone here had a job to do in this situation and would be evacuated last. The floor also had its own private evac tube system set up per her personal mandate. She refused to have her entire team be the last to leave without a secure and fast means to do so during an emergency.

She ran into Ops, coming to a dead stop at the command table situated in the centre of the room. Ops was Security Operations Command, and though her predecessor had called it SOC, she didn't like how that sounded and re-named it Ops as soon as she took control. The command table was a large holographic display, projecting a 3-D map of the building into the air. The map could be manipulated by controls at the head of the table, which is where the operator sat, ready to take orders from command.

Each member of staff that moved through the building was indicated by their ID badges as they passed certain checkpoints, showing a steady flow through the stairwells and out the building. Good, even the executive council had moved without question to their designated pods and were being ferried away by the evac tubes.

"Can we get eyes on what's happening?" Rose asked. The command table was designed to respond to threats in and around the building, but not in the greater city itself. She needed some real-time information on what was going on.

"News crews have been deployed, pulling up live feeds now." Tricia and the operator at the table seemed to be in sync as they each hit an array of keys, and the floating image was replaced with a live feed of the invasion site.

"*This is Yvonne West of can. We're here live above the site of the disturbances that have been rocking Astril City for the last hour.*"

The camera panned over and showed an aerial shot of the section of the city under attack. Smoke rose in pillars from buildings, and there was a domed barrier surrounding the area.

"*The dome you see is preventing all communication in and out of the area and is why emergency services are only reacting to the situation now. Social media on the Ether Net has been abuzz with videos shot from outside the barrier, and reports are stating that no one can pass through it in either direction.*"

"That's bad," Rose surmised. If they couldn't pass through the barrier, stopping whatever was advancing on them was going to prove difficult. Who on earth had the magical capabilities to even create a barrier like that? The drain must be enormous. Magic users were scary.

"Okay, people, we need to get to ground. Staff are being evacuated, and as soon as the protocol has run its course, we're getting out of here. We don't know what the invading force is capable of, and I'll be damned if we're caught in a skyscraper with nowhere to go."

"We have visual on the attackers. No, can that be right? It looks like . . . Humans, but they are moving too fast. Could it be Taken? I believe it is. There is a horde of Taken invading the city! How are there so many!" came Yvonne's voice from the news cast.

Shit. The Taken were hard to fight against at the best of times, but a horde? How had their numbers grown so fast? Was it those bastard No-Vaxers? Surely that wouldn't cause their numbers to swell so much so quickly, would it?

It didn't matter. Their responsibility after making sure everyone was out, was making sure they were in the executive bunker and providing protection against anything that tried to crack it.

"Pull up the building plan alongside the news feed. As soon as the last member of staff has cleared the exits, we move."

25

Things had moved quickly since his first meeting with the Wandering Council.

The name wasn't exactly apt anymore, but he guessed it kept an air of mystery about them. He had taken the first day after his demonstration to recover. The Council had provided him with a very skilled Mage among their kind as a snack. She had thought she'd been selected for some high honour, but it was merely to serve their mutual needs. She screamed, Mystral laughed, and the others sat there stoically.

Good times.

It had been the boost he needed to make the changes in the DNA of the council. He had worried that the Tren'jin would prove an issue, but the parasite was fundamentally the same; it had just adapted to an extremely hostile environment. Mystral suspected that her symbiont was already capable of producing offspring immune to the virus, but she'd refrained from siring for one reason or another.

After he'd recovered from this initial set of mutations, it was clear they would have to move quickly. If they didn't rapidly expand their numbers, they would lose the element of surprise and implementing their plan would be a lot harder. And so, the council and a group of their closest enforcers were now treated to the DNA therapy at the hands of the Dark Lord and could now sire at will at an alarming rate.

Alarming for the Humans anyhow. They decided to operate in a manner that would allow them to expand quickly at scale, with few noticing what was happening. They took one of the floating contraptions he'd seen employed through the city. As it turns out, they were a form of transport, and this one had enough space for all of them, providing Mystral glamoured himself into his smaller Human disguise.

Their journey took them out of the city, confirming to Mystral that it did indeed end somewhere, and in the air car, it didn't take them very long to clear its borders. They flew out to the west, where there were some smaller towns and villages.

Picking one of the villages, they landed, and Mystral returned to his standard form, enveloping the entire village within a barrier. This served to prevent anyone from escaping and to block communications. He'd learnt from his mistake at the night club and had adapted. The screaming was nearly instantaneous as the ancient beings descended on their prey. It was a bloodbath, and they all got caught up in the moment, being let off their proverbial leashes for the first time in centuries.

This meant that only a small portion of the populace survived to be turned, but that still gave them around fifty new recruits they didn't have before. They left no one else alive, and anyone that came near to village was slaughtered. Mystral claimed a portion of the populace to feed his own appetite, knowing that he would have to keep his reserves topped up.

Though the Vejlings finished turning after an hour, they

gave them a day to become better accustomed to their new bodies. Most would not manifest a gift at so young an age, but they were all powerful, fast, and hungry.

The next village they attacked went much the same way, though not for lack of control on the ancient one's behalf, but because the new Vejlings struggled to rein in their thirst. It would get better, and each Vejling that learnt to control their urges meant another ten, twenty, thirty newly turned Vejlings when they moved on.

They repeated this process for nearly two weeks. As their numbers grew, they moved on slower, having to travel on foot for the lack of available transport. This meant that in nearly two weeks, they had only hit a small number of villages.

Then yesterday, they came upon Cali.

It had been leading to this, the big one, so to speak. Cali was built on the ancient grounds of Calipi and had always been famous for its artisan carpenters. Or at least, it had when Mystral was last in the world, whereas now it seemed like an industrial hellscape. The lush forests that had once bordered the area were cleared, and there were groups of tightly packed housing next to sprawling factories. People packed on people packed on people. In the two weeks since they had set out, Mystral had regained a good amount of strength, but was far from full power. He was, however, able to enclose the entire town with a barrier, a task he would have sorely struggled with before. The panic spread more slowly, as the noise and general apathy led people to pay less attention to what was going on around them.

And their numbers swelled. Where the villages had provided them with hundreds of Vejlings, Cali gave them thousands. They overran the factories; they tore through the schools; they ripped apart the commercial district.

It was beautiful.

To Mystral's surprise, but apparently not the others', they also encountered a military base on the outskirts of the town. The Council had apparently intentionally chosen this town as a target so they could raid their supplies—a fact that would have changed nothing had Mystral known, but in keeping it from him made him ever more wary of his fair-weather allies.

It all played into his grand scheme, though, and worried Mystral not. The armed forces were caught with their pants down, and their horde tore through them, replenishing more of their number than they lost to resistance.

It took them most of the day, and the streets were now sticky with the blood of the fallen. Mystral had found a particularly juicy set of Mages stationed at the base and had claimed them for himself, and they all basked in the screams of thousands of Humans as they began their agonizing turn into V'Udol.

Those that were able took stock of their plunder and found that they now had enough in the way of transport to be able to move everybody at once. In addition, they had secured two hover tanks, hundreds of stored rifles and munitions, and something called a Mech. Mystral didn't know what any of these things were, but he was assured that they were powerful weapons of destruction, and that was all he needed to know.

He did recognise the rifles as the weapons that were used against him by the non-magical guards and the police force. They would serve them well against the thin-skinned Humans that would fall before their unstoppable tide.

That was all yesterday, though, and now he stood among the rubble of a building levelled by the destructive forces of one of the tanks at the edge of Astril City. The Mech hadn't arrived yet, as there had been some difficulty finding someone capable of piloting it, so it had been transported on the back of a hover truck.

Even so, the destructive power of the tanks was incredible.

Humans had found ways to destroy each other without the use of magic. They had previously had sword and bow, but the true destructive nature of battles had always been down to the Mages. No wonder Mages in this age were nothing on those of the age he'd left behind. There was no need for them to be!

Vejlings ran through the streets, those with rifles gunning down helpless civilians as they tried to flee for their lives, the ones without weapons using their enhanced attributes to chase them down, turning them more often than not. Astril City was too big to fully enclose in a barrier, too big by far, but that suited Mystral just fine. This allowed them to compartmentalize the assault and reduce their losses.

Suddenly, Mystral heard the whirring of giant gears, and felt regular impacts shake the very ground beneath him. He looked back and saw the Mech in motion. It stood around sixteen feet in height and moved with an agility that seemed impossible for its size. The pilot seemed to be having fun with no resistance at the moment, kicking civilians into the air and blasting them with a set of giant rifles attached to its wrists.

Mystral wondered if they were being too wasteful with their weapons. The city was huge, and they had a long way to go. Having spoken at length with the Wandering Council about the assault, they had several key locations that they planned to take. The first of these was the Astril City Defence Forces headquarters. This was where the main source of resistance was anticipated. They reportedly kept enough firepower on hand there to repel an invasion, but had they ever planned for something like this?

Next would be the Engineers' Guild. He had argued for the Mage's College. Mages were always tricky, but the Council had assured him that the Guild was more dangerous. They worked on a lot of the government contracts and would have experimental technology that could prove problematic. The College was apparently nothing more than a bunch of stuffy academics playing at being Mages.

He had conceded that he did not know enough about this new world and gave in to their advice on the matter. After the guild was taken care of, though, they would deal with the College. He didn't care how stuffy the V'Udol believed them to be, he'd faced a cabal already and been caught off guard; he wouldn't be taken by surprise so easily again.

After this, the Palace of Thalia, the seat of the Astrilian Council, and the central government for the Alliance as a whole. Topple that, and they would have control of the city.

With each passing block and each passing hour, their numbers grew, and their chances of victory grew with them. They moved forward street by street, those trapped inside screaming in terror, those trapped outside looking on in horror.

Curious how Humans could stand and watch the suffering of others, and yet not be seeking shelter themselves. They huddled against the barrier in the hundreds, phones out, trying to record what was on the inside. Did they think the barrier was there to protect them? Did they think their government had this all under control?

Ha! Now at the far end of his dome, he shifted its centre, capturing all the outside onlookers, who now found themselves within the new circumference. There was a moment of stunned silence as the crowd seemed ignorant to what had just happened, still trying to eagerly record this walking apparition of death before them.

Then one of them clicked and started screaming.

Too late.

Mystral was among them, laughing manically as he liberated spines from their bodies, claws tearing through flesh and clothing like they weren't there.

Oh, how they screamed.

Oh, how he laughed.

26

"We've had two weeks to find him! How has this happened?" Councillor Carl Taylor exclaimed in exasperation as the reports came in. The Council had gathered in the war room after being alerted to the fact that they were under assault. They had deployed a few recon drones to survey the area and had the newsfeed up on a display also. Maps showed the city displayed before them, and the areas under attack were highlighted in red.

"Now is not the time for panic, Council, we need to push back against this incursion," urged Orator Natdy, as annoyingly calm and collected as usual, despite the panic and mayhem that was the war room. Field Marshal George Campbell and Air Marshal Robert Johnson were present, as was the Chief of Staff of the Astril City Defence Force, Gen. Olivia Roberts.

The Admiral of the Fleet didn't partake in city defence meetings and was stationed at their main naval base. Astril City was mostly landlocked, so Admiral Irene Porter oversaw any threats on the eastern front. As it was, it felt like there were too many cooks in this particular kitchen already. The marshals were trying to wrest control of the situation from General Roberts, but she firmly held that city domestic defence was the jurisdiction of the City Defence Force.

"General Roberts, we need to work together! This is clearly an invasion!" Air Marshal Roberts pleaded, his face turning red, Marshal Campbell at his side, attempting to add weight to the cause. Carl could see why she hesitated to hand over control. As far as they were aware, this attack was akin to an act of domestic terrorism, which indeed would fall under her authority.

However, if the armed forces were to take over jurisdiction, their priority would be eliminating the threat as quickly as possible, using whatever force was needed. It was Olivia's job as head of the city's defences to first and foremost protect its citizens. If she could help it, she would not authorize unnecessary force that would put more lives at risk.

"We don't know the full extent of the attack, Marshal. There are civilians in the engagement zone that need to be our priority."

The Council hadn't been entirely open with any of them, though. They had kept as close a lid on the release of Mystral as possible in an attempt to contain widespread panic. They had been wrong, but they had needed to try. It was time to fill them in. It might require more force than General Roberts was willing to use to be able to stop The Dark Lord.

"We need to tell them," Carl said quietly now to his other Council members arrayed around him. They were far enough away from the others that they could speak quietly without being overheard, and the heads of the armed forces were loud enough that it hardly mattered. "They need to know who they are up against."

"Are you sure that's wise? We don't want to cause greater panic among the armed forces than there already is." Aki said in that sage way the Tren'jin seemed to have about them. Carl sometimes wondered if the expressiveness of the Humans made them seem as children to the other races, but then again, he had seen other Tren'jin get just as expressive. Those in official positions always had a much better handle on their emotions than it felt like Carl himself had.

And looking over at the marshals arguing with the general, he felt a little embarrassed by the way they acted. He took a deep breath and was about to respond in a calm manner.

Orator Natdy got in first. "Councillor Taylor is right. It won't do us any good keeping this information to ourselves any longer. They need to bring everything in their arsenal to bear down on this threat. We've failed in our efforts; we need their help."

Carl exhaled, a little disappointed that he hadn't gotten to make his show of being in control, but he appreciated the support from the Phasmia.

"Agreed. It'll do us no good keeping it from them, but with this information, they might be able to strategize against the Dark Lord," said Councillor Raihanah Pearson.

Both the Phasmia were nodding along, and the Tren'jin shrugged ever so slightly. "It is decided then," Elder Kameko said, his eyes narrowing slightly in the direction of the arguing three. "Let's call them into the briefing room before they claw each other's eyes out."

"General! We've just had word from Headquarters. It's been entirely overrun!" exclaimed one of the senior personnel working at one of the consoles in the room.

"What do you mean it's been overrun? Why weren't we alerted that they had pushed so far into the city?" General Roberts was seething, a tight grip on the table in front of her turning her knuckles white.

"The barrier they have been deploying, it's taken out all forms of communication inside of it, and we've lost the live news feeds! We've only had word from survivors now that they are moving on. They have raided all of our supplies stored there!"

The general was about to continue his attempt to take control of the situation, but before they could get far, Carl instructed an aide to gather the joint defence chiefs.

The six Council members had the general and marshals ushered into a private briefing room set up in conference style that was just off to the side of the war room. It didn't take them long to fill the joint defence chiefs in.

"You're telling me we're up against a faery tale? First, we have reports that the attackers are a horde of V'Udol, and now this?" Air Marshal Johnson was incensed as he stared around the room. "Next you'll tell me that dragons are falling from the sky!"

"Why would we lie to you? Especially at a time like this?" Carl asked defensively.

"Just show them the footage," Aki suggested.

The rest of the Council nodded in agreement and Carl connected his slate to the display in the room so he could securely show the security footage from two weeks ago.

They all watched in silence as the footage played back. Both the marshals' and general's jaws dropped as they sat stunned, staring at what they were being shown.

"Impossible," gasped General Roberts.

The video ended and they returned their attention to the room.

"The Council have decided that you will work together as one task force. Mystral needs to be stopped, by any means necessary." Carl could see the objection forming in the general's mouth and he headed her off. "I know, General. We will, of course, do everything we can to minimize civilian losses, but if we can't stop him, there may not be a city, or a nation, left to protect."

Silence fell on the room again as this news sunk in. The marshals still looked annoyed at being kept in the dark, but each one of them eventually nodded resolutely.

"We'll get this done. Permission to deploy the Cabals?" General Roberts asked, surprising the marshals.

Carl nodded, not even needing to run it past the rest of the Council. They knew what needed to be done.

"Permission granted. Take this bastard down."

27

"AAAAAAAAAAAAAAAAAHHH!!!!"

Timothy Jenner startled awake, sitting up in his bed. His clothes and sheets were soaked through with sweat, and his head was pounding. This has been how he'd woken every morning for the last two weeks.

Every. Single. Morning.

He'd overslept again too, by the looks of the light coming through the window. The nightmares were worse since the Council had made their enquiries, and he'd been forced to sit through the security footage, acting as if he had no idea how something like this could have happened.

The footage had cut off shortly after he'd finished watching but being forced to see his best friend die again and again, during the inquest, it was enough to break his soul. It was all his fault, and there was nothing he could do about it.

That's what he'd been telling himself anyway. His life had gone to shit since that day. With the broken promises of the being he'd released, and the taint it had left on him, he felt unclean, worthless. He was drifting apart from his husband, not helped by the fact he'd spent nearly all the last two weeks in his personal quarters at the guild.

Sure, work sometimes meant that he would have to spend a day or two on site; he was the Guild Master. But he'd never spent so long away. Ryan was starting to ask questions, and he had no way to answer him. How could he tell him that the promise of his dead wife and daughter being returned to him had caused him to commit atrocities? That the thought of holding them again had made Tim push Ryan out of his heart? Had made him completely forget what he now felt for his husband? Ryan asked if he was cheating on him. How could he answer that?

He loved Ryan *so* much, and he hated himself all the more for putting him through this. He didn't deserve it. Ryan had been there for him when he'd been at his lowest and had helped build him up. He had become Tim's world.

Or at least he'd thought he had.

Tim stripped off his sodden nightclothes and stepped into his bathroom, pausing a moment to examine himself in the mirror. His face was haggard: black lines round his eyes, cheeks sunken from not eating enough. He'd lost so much weight in two weeks; a liquid diet did that to you.

Stepping into the shower, he set the temperature as hot as it would go. For safety reasons, they couldn't burn you, but the water came close, as steam rose from it while it pummelled his skin. He felt constantly unclean, constantly filthy, and there was nothing he could do to change that. He tried every morning to burn the filth away.

He eventually stepped out of the shower, skin red as a lobster as he got dressed. It always recovered well enough before he saw anyone, but he'd reduced contact with others to a bare minimum anyway. His personal assistant had noticed, and had been trying to help him, but he couldn't let the rest of the guild see him like this. The fact that he hadn't been personally checking in on projects would be strange enough for some of them.

Once he was dressed, he poured himself a tall glass of brandy with several ice cubes and took a long sip. The burning sensation down his throat was like a deep cleansing. It wasn't enough, and never was. He'd lost count of the number of bottles he'd cleared from his personal collection, and he didn't much care.

Glass in hand, he exited his quarters, and took his personal lift, which would deposit him in his office. It was the only route the lift took, and he was the only one that had access to it. There were some places that needed to be private, and he was thankful that his quarters here were.

His office was less private, but still a sanctuary. His PA was allowed access without checking, and that was it. Everyone else had to be cleared via Gene before they could gain entrance.

The office itself was split into several sections. There was his personal workshop that was the only section that was entirely closed off to the rest of the office. It was a mess, and often his projects were top secret. Even those with clearance to meet him in his office were not allowed in there.

Then there was the board room, one long table with a display at one end, and clear windows lining both the exterior and interior walls. His desk sat in the middle of the central space with a couple of chairs facing it for smaller formal meetings, and there were a couple of sofas with a drinks cabinet to the side for less formal meetings.

The cabinet would need restocking soon.

Behind his desk was also a panoramic view of the city. Combined with the windows in the board room, it created a stunning display. As he had done a lot over the last two weeks, and anytime he was stuck in his head, in fact, he stood staring out over a city he had helped shape.

Something was different about it this morning, though. There was a thick, smoky haze covering the city, making it hard to see much farther than the next buildings. He downed his drink, placed the empty glass on his desk, and resolved to find out what was going on.

And in doing so, nearly ran over Gene coming through the door at the same time. Tim took a hasty step back to avoid them both ending up as a pile of limbs on the floor. "Sir! Sorry, sir! Good, you're in. We're in trouble!"

Panic had stricken the aide's face, confirming Tim's suspicion that something was wrong.

"What's going on, Gene?" Tim felt himself sobering up fast, though the headache refused to budge, even as adrenaline began to pump though his veins in response to Gene's state.

"We're under attack!" Straight to the point as always, but unusually lacking in detail. Tim guided Gene to the sofas and poured the man a drink.

"Who's under attack? The City? Is that why it's so hazy this morning?"

"Yes, the City, everyone. They are swarming everything!"

Handing Gene the drink, Tim took a seat on the other sofa as his aide took a long sip.

"Who are they? What do you mean everyone? Have the CDF not deployed against them?"

"V'Udol. Their numbers are insane! Every section of the city they take, the host swells in size! The assault is several hours in, but nobody realized what was going on before."

"How?"

"They have been erecting some kind of barrier that is preventing organic matter from crossing in either direction while also blocking transmissions from escaping. The Council have just now called through. ACDF HQ had been taken out before they even knew what was happening, and now the horde is here!"

Shit. Here? Now? And they had taken out the ACDF HQ? Shitshitshitshitshit.

Well, the Engineers' Guild took up a huge section of the city, dwarfing any other complex by a long way. They would not take it as easily as the ACDF. On top of that, they had access to prototypes and weapons that even the military were not privy to.

"The Council has also sent over an encrypted message for your eyes only. It is awaiting on your personal tablet as we speak." Gene had started to regain his composure. Good, they all needed to be on top of their game.

"I'll look at it shortly. We need to mobilize the guild, though. Has the College been contacted?"

"Communications with both the Council and the College cut off as soon as they transmitted the message to you. We're currently inside the barrier. We're on our own, sir."

Tim nodded solemnly. "Okay. Send out a Guild-wide alert. Battle stations. Restrictions on all projects lifted. If it can be mobilized against these bastards, I want it used. All hands on deck, Gene, all hands on deck. Go!"

The aide leapt from his seat and hastily left the room to start the alert. Tim returned to his desk and pulled up his personal slab. The message from the Council, as promised, was waiting for him.

PRIORITY ONE
TO: GUILD MASTER TIMOTHY JENNER
SUBJECT: THE DARK LORD
Tim,

.   .   .

THE DARK LORD is leading a force of V'Udol, we need you to mobilize everything at your disposal.

THE MILITARY HAVE BEEN GIVEN jurisdiction over all armed forces.

KNOWLEDGE on the Dark Lord is still restricted.

USE of the Cabals has been authorized.

USE of all necessary force has been authorized.

GOOD LUCK.

THE COUNCIL.

TIM'S HAND shook violently as he read the message, his heart pounding in his chest.

This was his fault.

All of it.

He had done this.

How many lives had been lost today? How many families torn apart? He looked out the window, and the smoke had started to take on an orange glow as fires started to break out close to the complex. He tried to grab his glass, but it shattered in his trembling grip as he grabbed it.

"Shit!"

The broken shards had cut into his palm, and for a moment, he just stared down at the blood oozing out of it. Pain slowly pulled him back to the urgency of the situation, and he pulled a first aid kit out of his desk. Cleaning the wound and sealing it with H-Gel, he knew what he had to do.

He could never make things right, but he could help stop the wrong.

As he left his office, sirens began to blare around the building, with instructions coming through the loudspeaker, the same instructions that would have been sent to every device around the complex.

"Gene, I'm going to project Titan. Alert the crew."

"But sir, even under a lift all restrictions order, that was to remain off-limits."

"I've been authorized to use all necessary force, Gene. We're using Titan."

Though incomplete, it would still be the most devastating tool available to them. Rated Dragon-level Top Secret, the highest level of secrecy that could be assigned a project, it was known to only a select number of personal. The engineers working on it lived in the specially built wing. All the scientists, the Arcaneers, heck, even the caterers, were assigned living quarters there during the length of the project to prevent leaks. Outside of those within the project site, only he, Gene, the specially trained crew, and the Council knew of its existence.

It took Tim all of ten minutes to leave the central command building, the tallest of all the guild buildings, and sitting central to the complex. As soon as he was in the open air, he could hear the battle waging. How much of the military had been deployed to the region before they'd been sealed off? How many of the people dying out there were currently his own people?

There was a line of hover carts parked next to the building

for personnel inter-building transport. Tim jumped in one and sped to the wall surrounding the Titan Project, or Project-T, as the area was known. He had to leave the vehicle there, go through a series of security checks, and then carry on via a new hover cart on the other side. Usually grateful for the high level of security involved, he couldn't help but be annoyed at how long it was taking today.

Finally, he was into the project site. Though the building looked massive and sprawling from the outside, he knew that was nothing compared to its true size. Virtually all the space used on the surface was the living quarters of those on the project. The full extent of the facility was underground. Once he reached the surface facility, he had to pass through another series of checks, all whilst the ground shook around them. The guards looked on nervously and had probably been outside the loop of the alert system for confidentiality reasons.

"Now you've confirmed who I am, know this: we're under attack. All hands on deck. Protect the guild, and good luck!" The guards snapped to attention, then ran into the building ahead of Tim to pass on the alert and have it distributed. He saw the Titan crew arriving at the same time he'd made it to the turbo shaft, a high-speed lift that would take them to the operations area.

"Good, I'm glad Gene was able to reach you. I'm taking command of Titan, and I need you all today. Everything we have ever built or worked for is today at risk. We must stop the tide here and now."

They all saluted their guild master and filed around him onto the lift. It sped them down, and after a few seconds, the ground that engulfed them opened into a colossal hanger housing the largest Mechanized Assault Warrior that had ever been seen. Unlike the five-meter models that dominated battle-fields of the last war, and still provided much of the military might of the nation, this construct stood at around forty meters tall, completely dwarfing its smaller cousins.

As such, it required a larger crew, which consisted today of Tim and the three others with him. They were Marguerite Day, Benedict Carr, and Elena Dawson. They had developed a link system that would connect their collective consciousnesses to the MAW-40 Titan and allow them to control all aspects of its complicated system. Primary tests had proven that individual pilots were unable to control a vehicle of such scale, the stress incurred overwhelming. Splitting the burden and having one core commander was their solution.

Tim was fully trained on the program, and though without as many hours spent in the simulator as the rest of his crew, he knew what he was doing. Some engineers looked up and saw them coming down the lift to the primary production floor located halfway up the Titan.

"Sir, what's going on? The guards have sounded the general alarm."

"We our under attack. We are taking her out."

"But the Titan isn't ready! She's never even left the hangar!"

"Spare me the dramatics. All tests show she'll move, and even if only half her weapons are online, it could prove decisive. Besides, I'm in charge."

The engineer paled at that last comment and spun on his heel, yelling a quick, "Yes, sir!" He rushed to start the pre-launch preparations. First things first: they needed to suit up. The first thing they had learnt when designing the smaller MAWs was that you gave the pilots the greatest chance possible. Each pilot suited up in ArcArmour Full body power suits, ArcArms for short. Arcane powered suits designed by the Engineers' Guild. A fully enclosed environment that augmented the user's speed, strength, and agility, while providing an array of armaments and protection.

If something happened to the MAW, the pilots could eject while safely enclosed in their ArcArm, and cover falls from heights far taller than the Titan with their slow-fall augmentations. They had managed to get suiting up down to an art by developing material that moulded itself to the shape of the user once they stepped into its open shell.

Magic was awesome.

Once fully fitted, Tim had a Heads-up Display, or HUD, showing the vitals of the others in his crew, as well as providing a communications link with them and the command centre that would be running operations back here and monitoring their progress, as well as making on-the- fly software updates if necessary.

Once they were suited, they were guided to a platform at the rear of the Titan and a lift that took them up into the centre of the colossus. The control room, by necessity, was tight. It had barely enough space to crawl into their respective stations. Each was a half-harness, half-seat contraption that interfaced directly with their suits, and then connected their minds to the central computer of the Titan.

Images flashed in each of their minds as they came into sync, and each became responsible for a core function of the machine while responding to the instant commands of their commander, Tim. He was aware that they were all there, but in the same way that he was aware his arms and legs were there, and control over them was subconscious.

Pre-flight diagnostic information flashed in their connected mind, and the operations crew sounded over the comms.

"Performing pre-flight checks, preparing loading mechanism for transport to the launch site."

The platforms and walkways that had surrounded them started to recede, and the entire operations centre slowly moved back along rails to give the beast of a machine more clearance.

Once it was clear, barring some supporting scaffolding running up behind it on either side, the scaffolding and the base it stood on started to slowly be moved sideways towards the launch area.

"Transport initiated. T-minus sixty seconds until launch."

Everything was taking so long; would they be too late by the time they reached the surface? Would they be able to turn the tide? Anxiety flooded the link, but the calm of the others pushed back on it and soothed Tim's emotions. Another advantage of the system they had built: it provided more than just support for controlling the MAW, it also gave each of them a stronger emotional base to rely on.

There was a loud, almost explosive series of bangs as the Titan came to a stop, and the locking mechanisms on the scaffolding disengaged.

"T-minus thirty seconds. Launch bay doors opening."

Sirens started flashing all around them, a gush of air flooding the space as the doors opened, breathing life into the stale compartment. The sounds of battle could be heard faintly again over the blare of the alarms. The base beneath them shuddered as they started to rise towards the surface.

"Releasing umbilical cord."

As soon as the head of the unit had cleared the bay doors, awareness of the surrounding area flooded the link. Tactical data started to flash up before them, advising them of the direction of battle based on both the sounds of fighting and information now being fed from ops. Once the command to launch had been given, a physical hard line to the rest of the complex would have been reconnected, allowing communication to flow freely again.

They had stopped moving, and another series of explosive bangs sounded.

"Feet clamps released, launch complete. Good luck, Titan."

And they were off. It was a strange sensation, and one the

simulators had only partially prepared them for. To support the massive frame, heavy amounts of arcane melding had been combined with mundane technology. It was, after all, what the Engineers' Guild specialized in, but it meant that everything felt very ... light.

He had expected to feel clumsy, but everything responded as if it were his body, the others in the link reacting automatically to him. Information fed into the collective from their whole surroundings, allowing them to make on-the-fly adjustments to avoid stepping on personnel or crashing into buildings.

It didn't take long for the Titan to clear the space to the outer wall of the compound, a great ten-meter-tall construct that surrounded the whole grounds and was mostly built with the intention of making it harder for the less scrupulous of the population to infiltrate. With a government sanctioned restricted airspace, and anti-air turrets in place around the perimeter, threat from above was also reduced.

What he saw on the other side of the wall, though, brought their entire collective brain to a halt. It was like a tide of bodies, as far as the eye could see, pressing against the wall, trying to scramble over each other in their frenzy to get into the base. Most of these Taken must be freshly turned to be so completely heedless of their safety.

And to be in *such* numbers, had the Taken managed to find a way around the vaccination? On top of which, a way to speed up the turning process? Adrenaline started to course through their systems as the fight instinct began to kick in after the shock of the sheer number before them.

A list of available weapons systems came online, and Tim selected the Plasma Beam Cannon built into the right arm. Aiming at the horde, they felt a hum build up through the Titan just before a beam of energy lanced out and swept through the crowd. Bodies instantly incinerated, leaving piles of dust in the beam's wake.

They contemplated stepping out into the horde but decided the protection of the wall was prudent. Introducing unknown numbers of threats around their foundation would be a bad idea. They could crush many, but if any of them were able to get at the workings, even through sheer luck, it would be foolishly putting themselves at risk for no reason.

As the beam continued to mow through their numbers, a message flashed up stating the swarm missile system was online. Excellent. A panel in each of the Titan's considerable shoulders opened, revealing a vast number of warheads. The auto targeting system very quickly flashed up with optimal firing solutions, and without a second thought, they unleashed hellfire on the invaders.

Flowing explosions engulfed the Taken along their lines, sending body parts and internal organs flying among their kin. The crazed hordes were not affected, though, and just filled the gaps. On any traditional enemy, the firepower being unleashed on them would cause morale to plummet.

There was another explosion, and shards of metal impacted the Titan's legs as a section of the wall was blown apart. Where had the attack come from? The scanners initially suggested some tanks or mechs that were engaged at the rear of the horde, but their range would have made an attack on the wall improbable.

Then a figure began to raise from the crowd. One that haunted Tim's nightmares. A being that only existed in this world through his folly.

"How quaint," the Dark Lord said, his voice perfectly audible over the sounds of battle and the screaming mass beneath him, even though it felt he hadn't raised his voice at all. "You Humans do love to build large toys for me to break."

Rage. White hot burning rage. It filled Tim's every pore, and it filled the link, threatening to overpower the collective calm, but they were angry too. They all likely knew someone in the mass below. Hatred for this being that mocked them so swelled in their hearts, and their hearts screamed out.

They brought the beam cannon to bear, its full destructive force ramming into the smug bastard. They fired a volley of missiles for good measure too and started to charge the fireball canon on the left hand, a favourite of the guild Mages.

"HAHAHAHAHA!"

The sound sent chills down their spine, but the fire ball was charged, and they launched it at the monster before them.

But it never hit. It stopped in midair.

And then flew back at them.

The impact knocked them back, causing them to stumble and barely maintain their footing, alarms going off throughout the link, warning them of damage to several systems. But they were still in fighting shape.

They went to bring the cannon back to bear and found that their feet had been surrounded by the Taken horde, who had started to climb the legs. They didn't matter now, though. Only Mystral mattered. They had to do everything they could to stop him here and now.

Their arm had stopped moving. It was locked in place. Had they taken more damage than systems reported? They brought their right arm around, and the same thing happened. Sirens started blaring as gears began to grind against an unseen resistance.

Mystral floated in front of them, his hands held out towards the arms of the giant Mech, as the sound of tearing metal filled the compartment. Warnings were flashing up constantly in their link, and a colossal snap coincided with Mystral's arms pulling apart sharply. Loud crashes to either side of the Titan confirmed what also flashed in their heads-up: their arms had just been torn off.

"Titan, you have taken catastrophic damage. You need to disengage!"

Tim agreed, but it wouldn't be that easy. The link was breaking apart as an unforeseen side effect was causing Marguerite and Benedict to seizure. They must have been tied more closely into the arms systems than the others, and their sudden separation had caused a massive feedback surge. They needed to abandon ship.

Initiate evacuation protocol, thought Tim through the link, and the computer took over. A set of explosions sounded behind them, and the link disengaged, returning them all to their own minds. A rush of air filled the compartment, and then they were being shot out the back of the Titan, back into the central complex.

As they landed, it was between two of the smaller buildings of the complex, and it was already swarming with the Taken. The grounds personnel and security forces were fully engaged, attempting to push back the tide, and they were holding for the time being.

Their harnesses released once they hit the ground, Marguerite and Benedict slumping to the ground unconscious.

"Sir, we need to go." Elena had engaged her suit's plasma blades, two wrist-mounted arcs of light that extended above her clenched fists to produce two deadly swords. He did the same, but he tried to hold his ground.

"I won't leave them! They need us!" Even as he said this, though, the Taken crashed into them, and they were forced to start cutting through the masses. The other two were already beneath the swarm of bodies, and there was nothing more he could do for them. "Damn it!"

"Come on!" Elena shouted and started fighting back towards

the central complex, aiming to regroup. "You need to survive this, sir, you're the greatest mind the guild has. We can't lose you!"

Tim felt tears at his eyes. If only she knew that this was all his fault.

28

They stood at the edge of the barrier, watching as the battle raged on at the Engineers' Guild. The Cabals had been given leave to act, reflecting the direness of the situation. The Cabals acting together within the confines of the city, outside of wartime, could be extremely destructive.

Elsa Edwards, acting dean of the College of Mages and head of the Cabal joint task force, oversaw the preparations to take down the barrier that had been plaguing the city's defences since the invasion began.

It was effectively separating the invasion into manageable chunks for the Taken forces, making a coordinated counter-offence all but impossible. Now, though, she had her Mages hastily setting up a rune circle around the perimeter of the barrier. They had purposefully waited for it to shift again, as timing was of the essence. If they were in the middle of their preparations when the barrier shifted, then everything would be for naught.

And with it currently enclosing the massive structure of the Engineers' Guild, they wouldn't get a better opportunity. Of anywhere that they could attack, they Guild be the best prepared. This was proving true, as they witnessed MAWs, ArcArms, and any able-bodied personnel taking up arms and forming defensive pockets along the perimeter of the wall that surrounded the complex. She prayed they would hold, as her brother Gene was in there, PA to Guild Master Jenner.

"Master Edwards!" One of her Cabal came running up to her, panic on her face. "The injured that have been left by the invading forces . . . they are turning! Every last one of them!"

"What?" That should be impossible. They were all exhibiting the symptoms of the vaccine fighting the larval invasion. Even if they weren't, it should take days, if not longer, for them to turn.

"We're fighting them off, but there are so many!"

"Burn them, all of them. Any injured that have been left behind, incinerate them," Elsa commanded. If they were turning through some dark, twisted miracle against them, then they couldn't take any chances. They were stretched thin as it was.

The Mage nodded frantically and headed off to relay the order. Elsa tapped the Rune-Link in her ear. "This is Commander Elsa Edwards of the Cabal forces. All injured left by the Taken must be purged. Repeat, ALL injured left by the Taken must be purged. High risk of infection. Use fire."

Flames and screams became the order of business as the Cabals set forth carrying out her orders. The Mages setting up the Runic circle would know better than to cease their work, but this was still a distraction they could have done without. But if they could reduce the potential for enemy reinforcements springing up among their own ranks, it was a necessary one.

She returned her attention to the battle for the Engineers' Guild, thus far contained to the exterior wall that had proved invaluable to the defence during this invasion. Without it, the Guild would have been overrun long ago, and the Cabals would not be able to formulate their plan thusly.

As she watched, Elsa could scarce believe what rose before her in the complex. Slowly rising into the sky, standing taller than most of the surrounding buildings, was a MAW of a size she was having trouble comprehending. As soon as it reached the pinnacle of its ascent, it burst forward with amazing agility, reaching the wall in only a few strides and unleashed an arsenal of hell on the Taken horde.

"Yes, Jenner!" she found herself exclaiming, unable to hold back the excitement at this colossus that was sure to turn the tide of the battle. Hers wasn't the only excitement, as she heard the joint forces surrounding the perimeter let out a resounding cheer.

What happened next silenced everyone. A section of the wall just ceased to be there, and a figure rose into the sky.

"How quaint. You Humans do love to build large toys for me to break."

The voice could be heard everywhere by everybody as if it had been spoken directly into their ears. It was terrifying and had the effect of drawing all attention to the being floating now before the Titan, which promptly switched its considerable firepower to pummelling it out of existence.

Except that didn't work.

"HAHAHAHAHA!"

The creature was able to stop an incoming fireball that could have levelled a building and redirected it at the MAW, blasting it back from the breach. It proceeded to rip the Mech's arms clean off. The entire display was humbling and made Elsa sick to her stomach.

She shook herself out of her stupor, though, and started shouting orders down the Rune-Link.

"We need to get the rune circle finished now! Move people! That breach changes everything!"

Affirmatives came through the link, and everyone got back to work. Whatever that thing was, it needed to be stopped. Elsa had never seen a single being wield that much power. If they didn't act fast, the entire Engineers' Guild would be lost.

Some time passed, and the battle seemed to be turning against the guild. Elsa was starting to worry their window might close when the same Mage from earlier came running back up.

"Master Edwards, the rune circle is complete, and the Cabals are ready. Are you sure this will work?"

"We only have one way to find out, and no time to ponder it. Form the Circle."

She stepped up to her space, and the message circulated for all Mages to join hands. The circle ran the entire perimeter of barrier and was probably the biggest circle that had ever been conceived. As their hands connected, and the circle became complete, Elsa could feel the massive surge of energy as everyone started to channel. They hadn't even started to direct their flows yet.

As soon as they did, Elsa had to grip hard onto her neighbours in the circle to stop from keeling over. She took deep breaths, and brought herself back under control, letting the flows run through her. It was incredible, the well of power now under her command. She could do anything! What she needed to do, though, and quickly, was take down that barrier.

She focused on collecting the different elemental forces into a focal point above the apex of the barrier. Clouds started to form, and lightning crashed through the sky as the extreme pressure began adversely affecting the local weather.

It was hard not to draw too deeply from a well this size, but she had to be mindful of the weakest among them, lest she accidently knull one of their number before the spell was executed.

Finally, after what felt like an eternity, it was ready, and she directed the full force of the built energy at the barrier. Blinding light filled the sky as the beam impacted against the shield that had been causing them so many issues.

Seconds after the impact, the pressure was felt by everyone in the circle as strong winds began to buffet them, making it difficult to hold their positions in the circle.

"Hold the line!" Elsa screamed through gritted teeth, trying to concentrate on maintaining the spell. She had to ensure that the instance the barrier broke, she was able to redirect the energy from the strike. She intended it all to hit that monster. It needed to be wiped off the face of Gensa.

"We're doing it!" someone in the circle screamed, and they were right, the barrier was starting to fluctuate. They had to keep it up, but she could feel that some of the circle were nearing their limit. They had to hold on, just a little more!

Yes! There it was, the pop in pressure she was looking for as the barrier failed, and Elsa focused on bringing the energy together, into a point of condensed super-charged energy. The air around the beam seared with its power as she threw it at the monster . . .

Who turned to face her, red glowing orbs in place where eyes should be, clearly visible even at this distance. It shook her to her core, but she kept the beam coming. She'd end that hateful, malice-filled gaze. She had to.

Then he vanished.

"NO!"

Where did he go?

The beam! Its momentum was too strong now, she couldn't stop or redirect it any longer, and it was now headed straight for the force fighting on the ground. She tried with everything she had to slow it, but she'd put so much into throwing it at that creature, that it just couldn't be done, and she watched in horror as it impacted the ground, instantly vaporising any that were in the immediate vicinity.

It tore into the ground, its force so powerful concussive waves sent flying anyone that hadn't been incinerated. It bore deep, finding the hidden complex below, turning the structure beneath into molten slag.

Explosions started to erupt from beneath the surface as the destructive force found gas and fuel lines that had been feeding the complex. The beam ripped segments of the battlefield to pieces, and all Elsa could do was look on in horror.

"Gene ... I'm sorry."

They had failed the Engineers' Guild more completely than she could have ever imagined, but she couldn't spare a thought for them now. They had to find that demon. Where had he gone?

"Find the creature! We need to take him down!" she screamed into her link, eyes darting around the complex.

"Looking for me?"

The voice came as barely a whisper in her ear, and she felt the breath catch in her throat, letting out a small whimper. Light started spilling forth from her chest as warmth filled her whole body, and blood filled her mouth.

Falling to the floor, eyes wide, she struggled to fill lungs that mostly didn't exist anymore. The last thing she saw before darkness took her was her Cabals being torn to pieces.

One by one.

29

They were too late.

Stood on a hill on the outskirts of the city, Allai, Kaleb and Zel watched as Astril City, centre of the Astrilian Alliance, burned. The boy had his phone out and was desperately trying to pull up news from within the city, but all that came through on all channels, feeds and forums was the Astral City Emergency Evacuation order.

Zel shook with rage. They should have acted sooner. He could sense the magic Mystral was casting, feel the destruction he was causing. Kaleb had initially received news alerts while still at the Citadel, not realising at first that the Necromancer had a repeater setup in his tallest spire.

The news that came through showed an invading force in the city, but the report was quickly cut off without reason. Raziel kept a modified Astrilian air car in among his collection of things from around the world, and they had used it to cross the vast distance as quickly as possible.

Even then, the journey had taken an agonizing number of hours. Hours that the city didn't have to spare.

Zel was here now, though, and he intended to settle an old

score, one that he should have squared a long time ago. He filled himself with flows of power from both Gensa and Cado, knowing he stood more of a chance now than he ever had.

The air beside them tore open, and Raziel stepped through a portal that had opened from his Citadel. In his incensed state, Zel turned on the Necromancer.

"You have the ability to create portals in thin air, and you allowed us to take the *scenic route?!*"

He felt an arm on his shoulder, and it was the boy. "Zel, he's using teleportation runes. They only allow for one user. No one has found a way to extend their use beyond that, and they are . . . so rare."

Zel let the boy's words sink in, then turned back to his city. "It matters not. I'm going to kill that bastard, and you can either help me or not."

"You would lose," Raziel said curtly. "I came, for I kept up on the news and knew you would do something stupid if I didn't stop you."

"Coward! Some of us are willing to risk our lives to save this world!"

Raziel looked truly hurt at the words, but his eyes remained kind as they gazed back at the old wizard. "Zel, I've felt this despair before, and it consumed me. You will need all the help you can get, and the boy is not ready. You *must* seek out the Draconic Order. Find Manwe. Learn the secrets of Ortus."

"I can't abandon them!"

"You won't be. You will be bringing them the help they need, as will I. The Carnah'lor need to be appraised of the seriousness of the situation, and you need to convince the Draconic Order to mobilize.

"The events of today are a result of our past mistakes, and we need to work, all of us, to repent for them. I can no longer hide behind my sins, and you cannot let today add to the list of yours."

Sense began to return to Zel, and he nodded, knowing that his friend was right. They had been arrogant to think that Mystral would not have been able to recover so quickly. The Dark Lord was cunning, probably the most cunning of all his brothers, and he'd clearly proven himself to be resourceful in the past. They should not have been so complacent.

"You are right. I'm sorry." He let his magic drop, realizing that he was acting like a beacon to the Dark Lord. "We need to get moving now, unless we want to force this confrontation."

"Agreed, I'll head straight to the Carnah'lor. It might take some convincing to have them listen to me, but I'll do my best. They have no love of me there."

"Be warned as well, my brother's killer, Reno, may be working to try and twist them against us with lies. You must take care," Allai said, her eyes sad but determined.

"Thank you. I'll tread carefully."

They all said their goodbyes, shaking hands in both the Human and Jubian fashion. Raziel then disappeared through the portal he summoned with the runes around his wrist, and they departed in the air car, heading to the south.

As they sped away, Zel hoped that the survivors of the city could hold on. He hoped that there were any survivors at all when they returned to liberate them.

He knew deep down that there would be. They had been through so much over the years that Zel had lived, and they had always pulled through. They always survived.

It would be harder than ever before, but he willed them to do it again.

Hold on and give Zel the chance to fix the sins of the past.

Printed in Great Britain
by Amazon

33200808R00149